DON'T TURN YOUR BACK I

James E. Stodghill, Jr.

Copyright © 2023 **StodghillWorks**

All rights reserved. No part of this publication may be reproduced, distributed, or transmitted in any form or by any means, including photocopying, recording, or other electronic or mechanical methods, without the prior written permission of the publisher, except in the case of brief quotations embodied in critical reviews and certain other noncommercial uses permitted by copyright law. For permission requests, write to the publisher, addressed "Attention: Book Rights and Permission," at the address below.

Published in the United States of America

ISBN 978-1-959173-73-1 (SC)

StodghillWorks
1443 Kings Point Way SW,
Conyers, GA 30094
stodghillworks@aol.com

Order Information and Rights Permission:

Quantity sales. Special discounts might be available on quantity purchases by corporations, associations, and others. For details, contact the publisher at the address above.

For Book Rights Adaptation and other Rights Permission. Call us at toll-free 1-678-358-3565 or send us an email at stodghillworks@aol.com.

Dedication

This book is
dedicated to my wonderful wife,
Marie Erwin Stodghill.
She is
God's precious gift to me
for this season of my life. She is
my soulmate, my lover, and my friend.
I am so grateful to
the Most-High God Almighty
for giving her to me.
I thank Jesus
for being the center of our union
and binding our hearts together
with His love.
I thank the Holy Spirit
for guiding us, and teaching us, how to
nurture each other.
She is
all mine and only mine.
I am
all hers and only hers.

Acknowledgments

I am eternally grateful to everyone who encouraged me along the journey of writing this book. They read my drafts and offered suggestions. They corrected spelling and grammar. Most importantly, they gave me loving support.

First, I give God all the glory and honor. He is worthy, He is Holy, He is Righteous.

I give special thanks and love to Angie Turnipseed, Mia Hill, Marian Perkins, Yvonne Williams, and Tamiya Shepherd, my first editors and my true friends.

Contents

Chapter 1	The Farewell	1
Chapter 2	The Pickup	5
Chapter 3	Murder at the Motel	16
Chapter 4	The Pursuit	23
Chapter 5	On the Run	42
Chapter 6	Caught in the Crossfire	54
Chapter 7	Just One Drink	63
Chapter 8	A Resting Place	70
Chapter 9	The Crystal	81
Chapter 10	The Discovery	88
Chapter 11	The Visitor	100
Chapter 12	A Game of Pool	118
Chapter 13	Back in the Woods	129
Chapter 14	The Arrest	135
Chapter 15	Burn It Down	143
Chapter 16	The Warning	154
Chapter 17	The Fight	162
Chapter 18	Get ME to the Church on Time	175
Chapter 19	The Preacher	184
Chapter 20	Saved	191
Chapter 21	The Release	200
Chapter 22	Showdown at the Church	207
Chapter 23	The Bridge	232

Chapter 1
The Farewell

Suddenly, a giant bolt of lightning surged down from the heavens, splitting the darkness in half. It struck the ground below with thunder so loud that the whole world seemed to shake. The rain, which had been moderate, instantly began to pour from the sky. The flowing waters raced down the street gutters choking the sewers with more water and debris than they could swallow.

The front door of a two-story house opened. David Parker appeared in the door. He was preparing to leave Anderson, South Carolina, in route to Knoxville, Tennessee. He had to set up for a five-day convention. It was one of the most enjoyable aspects of his job as an electronics engineer at Vi-Tech Industries. He was a slim, but fairly, well-built man of medium statue. He had dark brown hair and blue eyes and he appeared younger than his thirty years would seem to indicate. He frowned as he looked out into the soggy night.

"It's pretty bad out there", he said as he closed the door, turned around and faced his wife. "Maybe I should wait until it slacks up a little."

"David" she snapped, "that could be next week". She pressed her lips together and a frown appeared on her brow. Realizing that her anger was showing she turned and walked toward the closet. "You'll be fine as long as you drive at a safe speed. Anyway, you'll probably drive out of it in an hour or so," she explained. "Don't be such a baby," she said under her breath as she took his overcoat from the closet.

"Did you say something?" he asked even though he had heard her.

"Nothing", she said. She knew he had heard her as she had intended him to. "Have a nice trip, honey."

He watched her as she walked toward him with his coat draped across her arm. She was wearing a long housecoat that completely covered her very shapely body. Even though her hair was in curlers and there was no makeup on her face, she was still very lovely. Of course, that was why he had chosen her. That was a lie. She had chosen him, or maybe it was her father who made the choice. He didn't know anymore. Anyway, he had always wanted a beautiful wife, a nice home, a good job, and a sharp ride. He had everything he said he would have, but sometimes he wished he could start all over.

'Mrs. Caroline Parker', he thought, 'the prettiest gal in town.' He took his coat from her and swung it over his shoulder. 'She would be perfect if she were more affectionate,' he thought as he leaned over to kiss her. She turned her head and allowed him to kiss her on the cheek. 'And if she would pretend that she loved me every now and then,' he thought.

"Are you still angry about what happened today?" Dave said. He was offended that she had turned her head.

"Why would I be angry because my own husband, lets some thug insult me and do nothing about it."

"What was I supposed to do, punch him in the mouth because he said something about your buttock."

"You could have said something. You just stood there, like a scared punk."

"You have a cell phone just like I do," Dave said. "If you felt insulted, why didn't you call 911."

"Maybe I would have if Chuck hadn't come when he did."

"I thought his name was Charles," Dave looked at her angrily.

"He told me to call him Chuck. After all, he did come to my defense. He made that guy apologize to me," she said looking back into his eyes even more angrily.

"What was our insurance man doing at the grocery store, anyway?"

"Let me guess. He was buying groceries," she replied.

"It seemed odd to me that two days after he comes here to try to sell us a policy, we meet him at the grocery store just when some guy decides to insult you. What are the odds of that happening?"

"Take your calculator out. You'll probably figure it out. While you're at it, figure out the odds of you being promoted to production manager after marrying the boss' daughter."

"That was two years ago. Anyway, I earned that promotion." Dave was getting upset. His voice was getting louder.

"Yes, I'm sure you did, by marrying me."

"Maybe your father knew that I wasn't going to stay at Vi-Tech unless he gave me a promotion. I could have taken a job in Atlanta. Then your father would have to live without his precious daughter at his beck and call."

"What makes you think that I would leave here just because you get a job in Atlanta, or California, or anywhere?"

"Cause you're my wife, and that's what good wives do. They support their husbands. They encourage their husbands. They don't cut them down every chance they get."

"Yeah," she said turning her eyes toward the kitchen door. "Well, I'm encouraging you now. Maybe you need to get started on your trip."

Dave took a deep breath and blew it out slowly. 'Maybe you can kiss where the sun don't shine,' he thought, but it was a thought that he wished he hadn't thought. "I left my itinerary on my desk. I should get to the hotel about…"

"I know," she interrupted. "I've already read your itinerary. Call me in the morning sometime after ten. I want to sleep late."

"I'll see you in a week," he said as he walked through the kitchen into the garage. There was his Mercedes 240SL, a really, nice ride. He rubbed the shiny hood as he walked past it. He opened the door to his other car, a 1987 Chevy Caprice Classic. Carol would never allow him to take the Benz and leave her with the old Chevy. 'At least it's dependable. Shoot it still looks good and my little baby can fly,' he thought as he buckled himself into the blue cloth seat.

Carol watched from the window until she saw the car go over a nearby hill. Then she walked to the phone. Her eyes began to brighten, and a smile stretched across her face as she pressed the keys on the phone. A man answered.

"He's gone" she said, "come on over." There was no reply. "Hello"

"I was just thinking about how bad the weather is right now," he said finally. "Carol, maybe I should wait until tomorrow."

"What? Here I am allowing you to come to my home when my husband is gone for a week, and you're afraid of a little rain? You're acting more and more like my husband, and the last thing I need is a man who doesn't know what he wants." She hesitated. "I'll tell you what we'll do. We can just forget about the whole thing."

"Wait a minute," he pleaded. "I'll come, but I'm going to be soaking wet by the time I get to your door."

"Call me when you get here, and I'll open the garage door. You won't have to get wet at all." Carol smiled at the thought of seeing him.

"Give me about forty-five minutes, baby." He whispered.

"Baby?" she said indignantly. "Look! You said that you wanted to talk, so that's what we're going to do. Talk! That's it!"

"Please excuse me Mrs. Parker."

"Now don't get too formal on me. You're going from one extreme the other. I make it a rule not to let anybody call me baby until after I let them kiss me. Who knows? Maybe I'll let you call me baby before the night is over," she said coyly.

"That's interesting, because I've been thinking about your beautiful lips since the moment, I met you. I've been thinking about how wonderful it would feel to kiss you."

His voice seemed to so sexy to her. "Owww. You just made me wet my lips," she sighed.

"I wet mine, too," he whispered. "I'll see you in thirty minutes."

"Make it twenty-five," she said and hung up the phone.

Chapter 2
The Pickup

Dave had been driving for thirty minutes and he was making very, good time, until he saw a sea of red lights on the expressway up ahead of him. He knew it was an accident, but he had no idea how far ahead it was. He only knew that the traffic had come to a complete stop. He saw an exit sign indicating a gas station was at the next exit. He sat there for fifteen minutes not moving at all. The rain was still pouring. He looked down at the gas gauge. It was on a quarter of a tank. He had forgotten to fill up before he got on the expressway. He pulled on to the emergency ramp, drove to the exit, and into the gas station. He filled his tank and went inside to buy a map. The attendant was watching a basketball game on the TV.

"Do you have any maps," Dave said.

The attendant looked at him angrily. "Yeah, right there by the newspapers," the attendant said turning back to the game.

"Have you heard anything on the TV about what happened on the expressway."

"Yeah, there's an accident," the attendant said this time without looking away from the TV.

Dave waited for more information, however, did not get any. So, he watched the game for a few minutes and then proceeded break the seal on the map he had pick up.

"You're gonna pay for that, aren't you?"

"Yeah!" Dave said holding out a five-dollar bill. "Hey, can you get to I40 down this road."

"Hmm hmm. Go about forty miles until you get to this big stop sign then turn right. That will be highway 29. It will take you straight to I40."

"Thanks," Dave said as he turned and walked to the door. The rain was still coming down but not quite as hard. The expressway was still at a standstill. Dave turned his car away from the expressway into the rainy darkness. He set his trip meter so he would know when he reached forty miles.

The road was straight at first and he drove sixty, but then it started to curve. He had to slow down to almost forty. There was nobody on the on the road but him. That, however, was a good thing, because now he was able to keep his bright lights on. Still, with the rain coming down so hard and the windshield wipers going full speed, his eyes soon became strained and tired.

Suddenly there was a flash of lightening and a terrible crack of thunder. It had struck so close that he could see smoke up ahead where it had hit the ground.

"Woo Mama," he sighed. "What a night." He drove around the next curve and he could see something up ahead on the side of the road. It was a woman trying hitch a ride. She was wearing a coat which reached down to the middle of her thighs. The coat, totally covering whatever else she had on under it, did not have a hood, and her rain-soaked hair hung from her head like the strands of a mop. She had a small tote bag which hung over her shoulder like a sack of potatoes. He slowed the car to get a look at her. "What in the world is she doing out here in the middle of nowhere in this storm," he whispered to himself. "It must be some kind of trick. There's probably a man hiding in the bushes," he said aloud as he began to speed up.

Realizing that he was not going to stop, she ran out in front of his car to force him to stop. He swerved over to the other side of the road to avoid hitting her and as he did, he lost control of the car. He hit the brakes. The car slid halfway around, came to a stop in the middle of the road, and the engine cut off. He quickly put the car in park and turned the key. The engine started but before he could put the car back in drive, there she was knocking against his window on the passenger side.

"Hey Mister, give me a lift, please!" she pleaded. "Just take me to the next truck stop so I can get out of this rain, please!"

Dave looked at her rain-soaked face and her pleading eyes and thought how pretty she was, as he shook his head no. As he began to pull off, there was another flash of lightening and roar of thunder. This time it was even closer than before. He heard her scream. When he looked, she had grabbed the handle of the car and had begun to run alongside of it.

"Let go of that handle," Dave yelled as he began to speed up. He looked around to see if the man he had expected was visible. No one was there. Then the girl lost her balance, let go of the handle, and tumbled over the bank down into the muddy ditch. Dave hit his brakes. He backed up the car to the spot where he thought she had fallen. He got out went to the bank and looked down into the ditch. She was not there. He started walking quickly along the ditch. He looked around to see if anybody was about to sneak up on him. He realized then that she must have been alone. 'Where was she?' The lightning flashed again and lit up the whole area. He saw something. He had backed up too far. He ran down into the ditch where she laid face down and motionless. He grabbed her arm and began to pull her up. When she saw his face, she became wild. She swung her fist around and caught him with a backhand across his nose. He slipped and went down landing on his back. Before he knew what was happening, she was on top of him. He felt her fingernails digging into his neck and face. He caught both of her wrists and pushed them over his head, forcing her face and body down against his. He was stuck in the ditch and she was still fighting to free her hands. She missed when she attempted to knee him in his groins. He quickly cramped his legs around hers. There they laid, each struggling to gain control.

"Let me go, you bastard," she yelled gritting her teeth.

Fear gripped his heart as a horrible thought occurred to him. 'She's going to bite off my nose.' "Please Lady, I'm sorry. I didn't mean for this to happen."

"Well let me go then," she screamed.

He was afraid to release her but more afraid to hold her. He slowly released his leg clamp on her legs and then he released her hands. She began to get off him slowly. Looking up she saw that the car was still running, and the door was open. At that moment they both had the same thought, 'Get to the car first.' He knew that if she got to the car before him, she would be gone. She was almost off him and he began to raise his head up. Then without warning she push his head back and began to scramble up and out of the ditch toward the car. Dave got up as quickly as possible and dove for her as she reached the top of the ditch. He hit her ankle but could not hold on. But it was enough to trip her up. She fell but immediately began to crawl to her feet. Out of the ditch he came at full speed.

When she reached the open car door, she was moving at full speed. She grabbed the door handle to slow herself down, however, Dave came up fast behind her and pushed her hard on the shoulders. The force knocked her hand off the door handle and the door closed. She fell forward. As she fell, she reached out her hands and in one quick motion, she rolled over her shoulder, back to her feet, and slid to a stop. She immediately turned back toward Dave who had reopened the door and was about to get in. She moved up quickly and kicked the back of his left knee and pushed forward with her foot. He went down to his knees. She quickly caught his chin with her left hand and with her right positioned the fingernails of her two index fingers on his right eyeball and applied pressure.

"Ahhhh," Dave moaned.

She lowered her head next to his and whispered in his ear. "Get up."

"I can't. You've got your foot on my leg," Dave said as he slowly reached under his car seat and grabbed his lug wrench.

"I said, ah, I said get." Her voice got softer and it seem that she had forgotten what she had said. Her grip became weaker, and her head slowly dropped to his shoulder as if she was about to fall asleep. Before she could move her head, he swung the wrench and hit her in the top of her head. Instantly, her hands fell from his eye and chin and her body fell against him and the car door. He quickly got up ready to hit her again, but her body just crumbled to the pavement at his feet. He stood there in a trance for moment. He didn't know what to do. Had he killed her? He looked down at her twisted body, even the pouring rain had no effect on her. She looked dead. Her chest was not moving. He leaned down to see if she was still breathing. He didn't see any signs of life.

"I killed her," he said. "Nobody is going to believe it was in self-defense. I'm going to go to prison. I could even be sentenced to death." He began to pace back and forth. Then, an awful thought came to his mind. 'If I dump her body, no one will ever know what happened.' Before he realized, what he was doing, he was dragging her by her feet around the car toward the ditch. When he had pulled her to the top of the ditch, he walked around her, got on his knees, put one hand on her hip, put the other on her shoulder, and was about to push, when he heard something.

"Ohhhh," she moaned.

"Oh God!" he said. "She's not dead." Finally, he came back to his senses. "I need to get her to a hospital". He carefully picked her up her wet, muddy, and limp body up. It was a struggle, but he finally got her in the back seat. They both were covered with mud. "I'm sorry," he said as tears began to well up in his eyes. "I didn't mean to hurt you. I was just, scared. I'll take you wherever you want to go," he pleaded. She said nothing. She just laid there. He pulled the keys from the ignition. "You lie down there while I get your bag," he said. He ran back down the road a short distance and picked up her tote bag.

When he returned to the car, she was still lying on the seat with her eyes closed, but now she was shaking terribly. He hadn't notice before, but he was shaking himself. 'I've got to get us out of these wet clothes, before we die of pneumonia,' he thought. There was mud all over him, the front seat, the back seat, her, and even the steering wheel. "Ain't this a muddy mess," he said aloud. "Why me?"

As he began to drive, his attention returned to her. What would he do with her? "Are you okay, Miss," he said. She said nothing. "Do you live around here somewhere?" There was no response. He looked over the seat at her.

She was all balled up in a knot, shaking uncontrollably. "No, no, no," he moaned as he turned the heat up as high as it could go. "Maybe she's in shock," he whispered. "Maybe she has a concussion. Maybe? Dough. I hit her on the head with my lug wrench. She has a concussion, dummy."

He saw a sign, Motel 10 miles. 'I'll stop there,' he thought relieved that he had somewhere to go. He began to speed up. The pointer on the speedometer crept higher and higher. There were no other cars on the highway and the road was straight as far as he could see, so he pressed the accelerator down more.

Then it happened. The car began to hydroplane. Dave began to lose control of the car. He took his foot off the accelerator, but the car did not slow down. He fought with the steering wheel to keep control. "Oh no," he said when he saw the caution sign, "A curve." He pressed the brakes trying to slow down. It was useless. He knew he would never make it. He screamed as the car left the road. The car went up a small bank and was airborne. When it hit the ground again, he was bounced up against the roof, his head being forced to the side against his shoulder. He released his grip on the steering wheel. When he came down, he landed face down on the passenger side. He felt the car hit something and he was dumped to the floor. The car was still moving downhill. He pushed himself up from the floor and was about to slide himself back onto the seat when something caught his eye. There she was steering the car from the back seat.

"Step on the brakes," she yelled.

Dave tried to straighten his leg to press the brakes, but when he did his knee hit the accelerator.

"No, you idiot! The brakes!" she screamed. She switched off the ignition and threw the car lever into park. The car whined to a halt. "What are you trying to do, kill us?" she yelled.

Dave could say nothing. He crawled back onto the seat. "Get out of the way! I'll drive!" she ordered as she slid her body over the seat. He looked around unbelievingly. They were on a road. Somehow, she had weaved a path through the trees, and they were back on another road. She started the car and they began moving up the road. In only a few minutes they were back on the main road.

Dave, regaining his composure, cleared his throat. "There's a motel up the road. We can stop there." Dave said cautiously. "Are you all right? Are you hurt?"

"Other than freezing and having a headache, I don't know. I haven't had time to think about it," she said breathing a sigh of relief.

"My name is Dave Parker," he said, relieved that she was talking coherently.

"I'm Pam Williamson," she said wiping some of the mud from her face. "Are you okay?"

"Well, my neck hurts, and my knee, and my face doesn't feel so hot either," he said referring to the scratches she put on his face.

"I guess this is all my fault," she said. "If I hadn't run out in front of your car none of this would have happened."

'Yeah, that's absolutely right. It's your fault,' he thought. "No, I should have stopped, but I thought you were with a man and when I stopped the two of you would rob me," he explained.

"Oh, I see."

"It has been known to happen." Dave paused. "What were you doing out there in the rain and cold in the middle of the night, anyway?"

"There's the motel," she said excitedly. "You get the rooms. I'll pay you back later."

They drove up to the office and Dave got out and walked inside. There was mud all over his coat and pants. He was soaking wet and there was bloody mud on his head and face. The clerk, hearing the bell on the door looked Dave over in utter astonishment. The clerk was a slim man in his mid-fifties. He wore overalls and work boots. His hair was speckled with gray. Looking at Dave, he couldn't keep his mouth closed.

"I'd like two adjourning rooms for my sister and me," Dave said nonchalantly.

"What in God's name happened to you?" the clerk said in a heavy southern accent. "You must be one of them-there mud wrestlers," he said with a chuckle.

Dave wiped some mud from his forehead with his hand, looked at his hand, and then looked for a fairly, clean spot on his coat to wipe his hand off. He couldn't find one on the front, so he raised his arm and wiped under his armpit. "We ran off the road, but I'd rather not go into all the details right now. We need to get out of these wet clothes," Dave said calmly.

"Well, I ain't got but one room left."

"Okay, I'll take it. How much is it."

"That'll be twenty-five dollars," the clerk said turning the registration book around for Dave to sign. Dave gave him two soggy bills, a twenty and a five. "I better hang these out to dry," he chuckled again. "Room number five. Out the door and hang a left. "Dave took the key and began to walk out. "Oh yeah! The restaurant opens at 7:30," he said smiling as he pointed to a coffee pot in the corner of the room.

"Okay, thank you," Dave said without turning around. He was so cold his teeth were chattering. Once outside, he pointed for Pam to drive the car on down as he walked down the walk checking the numbers on the doors. When he reached number five, he immediately opened the door and turned up the heat as high as it would go. Pam came in with her tote bag and went immediately to the bathroom and closed the door. Dave went out to the car to get his bag. When he returned, she was standing in the bathroom door.

"They're all wet," she said as she walked out of the bathroom. She was shaking uncontrollably, and she appeared to be getting faint. He started toward her and panic struck his heart. His right foot was numb 'It's frost-bitten,' he thought. He pulled her into the bathroom, closed the shower curtains, and turned on the hot water. The steam began to rise to the ceiling. He guided her into the tub. The hot water began to flow down over their wet clothes. The warmth began to come through. He held her close to him as he turned them around and around, sharing the heat of the water. It appeared that they were waltzing in the shower. The precious heat put them both in a semiconscious daze, but he could still feel her body shaking in his arms. He began to take off her clothes. Round and round they went. First her blouse, and then her skirt fell at her feet. He kicked them out of the tub. Then his shirt and pants were kicked out. They were both down to their underwear and shoes. But the hot water was doing its work. They began to thaw out and she had stopped shaking.

"Oh, that feels so good," she moaned, her eyes still closed. Her moan had caused him to become aroused. They both could feel his passion rise. He pulled away and they both looked down at the same time. There was a distinct bulge in his short. She looked back at his face. He was still looking down with an expression the seemed to say, 'Now, how did that get there.' He covered his erection with his hands and as his eyes slowly climbed up her body. By the time they reached her lips his mouth was hanging open and he knew why his body had reacted. She was what? He couldn't think of a word to describe her sexiness. When his eyes met hers, his trance was broken. He blinked once and it was as if he had just awakened from a dream. He looked at her then at himself. 'Carol would kill me if she ever found out about this,' he thought. In an instant, he was out of the shower.

He went into the bedroom to put on his clothes while she continued to enjoy the warm flowing waters. She reached up to adjust the shower head and a sharp paralyzing pain hit her in the side. She slumped over holding her right side with anguish on her face. It hurt so much that she tried to breathe as little as possible. She tried to call to Dave but every time she tried to breathe in enough air for her to yell the pain would become unbearable. So, she would blow it out in whispers, "Dave."

Dave was in the bedroom doing side straddle hops. He stopped, looked down to see if he had gone down any. He had not. He began running back and forth across the room. "Get those knees up," he said aloud. He ran over to the bathroom door and began running in place. "Are you all right in there?" He did not hear a reply. He pushed the door open slowly and peeped his head inside. "Pam, is everything okay." He listened. There was a faint sound. Then he heard it again. He walked up to the shower curtains.

"Dave, help me." she whispered. He pulled the curtain back a little and saw her holding her side. He turned off the water and wrapped a towel around her and slowly helped her out of the tub and into the bedroom.

He dried her off with her bra and panties still on. Then he slipped one of his sweatshirts tops over her head. It reached the middle of her thigh. Then he got behind her, reached under the sweatshirt top, unsnapped her bra, pulled the straps over her shoulders, and let it drop to the floor. Then he helped her put her arms in the sleeves. She moaned when she put her right arm up. He then carefully reached under the top, grabbing her panties on both sides, and slowly, pulled them down. He positioned his pants on the floor so that she could step into them. Then, he pulled them up. Finally, after much moaning, she was lying in bed.

"Where does it hurt," Dave said pulling the shirt up exposing her right side. He knew even before she answered, because he could see a circular bruise on her rib cage. It was swollen and dark. It seemed infected even though the skin was not broken.

"Right here," she said softly, "but don't touch it, it's too sore."

"Did this happen tonight? Did I cause this? Are you hurt anywhere else?"

"No, not really, just here Dave," she said.

"Okay, you just relax, don't move, I'll try to get to swelling down." He began to put damp hot towels on her side. After about the fifteenth trip to the bathroom to reheat the towel, he could feel her ribs. By then she had been asleep for some time. The pain had evidently diminished a great deal because he could apply more and more pressure. 'It didn't feel like her ribs were broken. Maybe it was just a bruised bone,' he thought.

Dave gathered up the muddy clothes on the floor and Pam's tote bag. He took them to the laundry room. The clothes in the tote bag were just wet, so he put them in the dryer. He washed the others on the heavy cold cycle. After starting the clothes, Dave went to his car to get the first aid kit from the trunk. That's when he noticed a black pickup truck come speeding up. There was one person inside, a man. The car skidded to a stop. A large man got out and began to walk toward the office. Then he stopped and turned toward Dave. Even though he was 80 feet away, Dave could see hate and anger on the man's face. Dave quickly looked away and took the first aid kit back to his room. As he bandaged Pam's ribs, he could not get the hate in the strange man's face out of his mind. When he finished, he laid close to her with his arm of protection over her.

Chapter 3
Murder at the Motel

The strange man stood at the entrance of the motel office looking through the window. He saw no one inside. He did see a door leading to another room. He was sure the person on duty was there. He continued to scan the room. On the counter he saw what appeared to be a registration book. He walked to the door. It was locked. The door was made with a wood frame and twelve glass pains. He cracked one of the pains with his elbow. He quickly pulled out the broken pieces of glass from the wood. In less than a minute, he was inside. He walked cautiously to the counter and began to look at the registration list. 'February 4th,' he thought, 'if she's here I'll find her.' He read up the list starting with the last name. "Dave and Pam Parker," he said softly. "Yvette Smith, Mr. and Mrs. Mel Hoffman." He put his finger on the middle name. "Yvette Smith, that must be her," he said louder than he had anticipated. "Room number 6." On the board behind the counter were six keys. He reached over the counter and took key number 6 from its hook. He was about to put the key into his pocket when suddenly the door to the back room swung open.

"What are you doing with that key," the clerk said as he walked toward the strange man. The clerk had a twenty-two-caliber pistol in his hand. "Put your hands up, now, and get on over yonder up against that-there wall," the clerk said pointing toward the wall with the pistol.

"But she's my wife. All I want to do is take her back home," the strange man pleaded. "We had a fight. You know how is", he said as he walked toward the clerk holding the key out to him.

"Well you can't just come busting in here taking keys and scaring folks half to death," the clerk said. He lowered his gun and reached for the key. When the clerk touched the key, the strange man charged. He hit the clerk with a hard right that drove his head back with a terrible jolt. He had broken the clerk's nose and blood poured down over his mouth. The gun had fallen from the clerk's hand as he fell back against the registration desk. Then the strange man kicked him in the groin causing him so much pain that hardly a murmur could be heard of his silent scream. The clerk fell over on his knees and face holding his groins. Then the strange man raised his booted foot and brought it hard against the back of the clerk's head. The clerk fell over. He was lymph and motionless.

The strange man quickly got the pistol from the floor. He ran out of the door and down the walkway to room number 6. He leaned his ear against the door and heard nothing. A sinister smile appeared on his face as he slowly turned the key. He pushed the door to go in, but the chain latch caught it making a loud noise. The woman who had been asleep awakened and sat up quickly.

"Who's there," she yelled as her eyes remained glued to the door. "What do you want?"

"Sorry Miss, the clerk gave me the wrong key," he said as he closed the door.

The lady got out of bed and slowly walked toward the door. She wanted to make sure the man was going back to the office. She leaned against the door and pulled back, ever so slightly, the curtains covering the large picture window adjacent to the door. There was just enough of an opening for her to peep through with one eye. She looked out. What she saw filled her heart with fear. It was an eye; his eye, looking at her. She could see the anger and evilness in it. Quickly she closed the curtains. She froze in indecision for three seconds. That was too long because in two seconds he had turned the doorknob and rammed himself against the door. She didn't have time to get out of the way. The door slammed into the right side of her body, spinning her around as she fell back against a chair and rolled to the floor. The entire right side of her body was throbbing with pain as she lay there on her back.

She looked up at the door. The chain latch had held. 'Thank God,' she thought to herself as she gathered enough strength to raise her head.

Then once again the door surged forward hitting the bottom of her right foot. The chain still held but the force had broken one of the screws holding the chain to the metal door frame. As she sat up, he suddenly reached through the opening and crabbed around her left ankle. She screamed with every ounce of strength left in her body. He pulled and she began to slide toward to door. Her foot was almost at the door when she kicked the door as hard as she could with her free but aching foot. The door slammed into his wrist with a terrible cracking sound. He groaned as he released her foot and withdrew his hand. She crawled to her feet just as the door surge forward again. Still the latch held but the last screw was loose now.

"Somebody, help me," she screamed as she limped toward the bathroom.

The scream woke Pam, but she did not know what she had heard. She and Dave had somehow become embraced during their short nap. She was lying in his arms and it made her feel safe. She felt so much better. 'He bandaged my side,' she thought as she felt her side and looked up into his sleepy face. She smiled as she placed her arm around him and gently squeezed him.

Pam's peace was disturbed quickly. There was a loud crash against the wall. 'What was that,' she wondered. Dave was awakening. She closed her eyes and pretended to be just awakening herself.

"Did you hear something," Dave said as he noticed that they were so close.

She pulled away from him. Then from the next room came a loud scream.

"What was that," she whispered. They listened.

The loud crash they had heard was the door in the next room hit against the wall. The latch was broken completely now. The strange man had come through the door just as the lady darted into the bathroom and locked the door. She began to scream continuously.

"Help, somebody, help me please," she screamed.

The strange man began kicking against the bathroom door.

"What in the world is going on over there," Pam said.

"I don't know but I'd better take a look. It sounds like a woman is in some kind of trouble," Dave said as he got out of bed. After putting on his shoes he walked to the door. She followed closely behind. "When I go out you close the door behind me but be ready to let me back me back in when I come back." They both could hear more banging and screaming. Dave took a deep breath and opened the door.

"Wait," Pam yelled, "Why don't you just call the office and let them worry about it. It could be dangerous."

"Hey, don't worry. I'm not going to try to be a hero. I'm just going to look and see what's happening." He opened the door and slowly walked out. He heard the door close behind him. He could see that the door to room #6 was open. Dave peeped his head in the door and saw the man he had noticed earlier. He was trying to kick the bathroom door open. The woman's screams were coming from the bathroom. Dave couldn't decide whether the man was trying to help the lady or hurt her.

'Surely this man wouldn't be making this much noise if he was trying to harm the woman,' Dave rationalized. He took a deep breath, blew it out slowly, wiped his hand down across his mouth, and then stepped into the doorway. "Hey Buddy, ah what's going on over here. I was trying to," Dave stopped the middle of his sentence because the man turned toward him with hate all over his face. The man reached into his pocket and pulled out a pistol and began firing as fast as he could. When Dave saw the gun, he ducked. The first shot, hit the door. The next one hit the floor, recoiled, and then hit Dave in the leg. Another went through the window. Dave scrambled back to the door of his room holding his leg.

"Open the door," Dave yelled, "hurry up, hurry up."

Pam turned the knob and pulled the door to let Dave in, but the chain caught it. "Oh no, the chain," she said as she tried to push the door back for enough to unlatch the chain. She couldn't do it. Dave was pushing so hard against her she couldn't unlatch it. "Move back Dave, so I can take the chain off."

Dave stopped pushing, pulled the door back so that she could unlatch the chain, and then he looked back toward room #6. Terror made Dave freeze. The man was outside the door and he was aiming the gun directly at Dave's head. Dave watched as the hammer fell against the firing pin. There was an explosion from the barrel of the gun just as Pam opened the door. The woman in the bathroom opened her door at the same time. Dave fell into the doorway at Pam's feet. A siren could be heard in the distance. The man turned and saw the woman's face sticking out of the bathroom door. A look of shock came over him as if he were surprised to see her there. Then he frowned again, aimed the pistol at her and fired. The woman ducked back into the bathroom. The bullet hit the mirror at the back of the room. The strange man could see his reflection crack into a thousand pieces. The flashing lights of a police car could be seen coming down the highway. The car was only minutes away.

Pam leaned out of the door, grabbed Dave's belt, and began to pull. The strange man looked around and his eyes became giant balls of fire. "Pam," he roared.

Pam didn't have to look she knew who it was by his voice. She hurriedly pulled Dave into the room. Then started back to close the door. Before she got to the door, there he was. He aimed the gun at her. She began to back away. "Doug don't," she yelled.

"Die, you witch," the strange man said as he pulled the trigger. There was a loud hollow click that seemed to echo in the room as the hammer forced the firing pin into the empty bullet casing. Pam turned, ran into the bathroom as the pistol sailed past her head. Once inside she locked the door.

The police car pulled up to the motel office. One officer went in the front door and the other one went around the back. The strange man Pam had called Doug walked slowly down the walkway, around the building and into the woods.

Pam could hear the police siren very clearly. 'They must be out there by now,' she thought, as she pressed her ear against the door straining to hear any sound in the room. She heard someone moaning. "Dave," she yelled as she hurried to open the door.

Dave was beginning to regain consciousness. He began to feel his chest and stomach.

"Somebody call an ambulance," Pam yelled, "Hurry, Dave has been shot."

"How bad is it Pam, am I going to make it," he murmured as he continued to feel himself for blood. "Why did you lock me out Pam, why?" He began to cough as if it had taken all his remaining strength.

"I didn't mean to. I'm so sorry, please forgive me, please," she pleaded. She did not see any blood to any great extent. There was some on his leg, but it was just a spot. 'He must be hit in the back,' she thought. "Are you in very much pain," she said.

"No, I feel numb," he said as he closed his eyes.

Just at that moment a deputy sheriff rushed in. "An ambulance is on the way, where are you hit buddy," he said as he looked Dave over. "I'm going to roll you over on your stomach and check out your back." Dave moaned as the deputy turned him over. He found only a flesh wound on Dave's thigh. "You're okay buddy, it's only a flesh wound, but let the medics take a look at it."

Both Pam and Dave were both relieved and shocked. Pam began to laugh hysterically. "You fainted," she laughed. Dave looked embarrassed and sick.

"Don't feel bad Buddy, it might have saved your life. Did either of you get a good look at this guy?"

"I saw him, but I looked mostly at the gun he had in his hand. I guess I could recognize him if I saw him again," Dave said.

"What about you Miss?" the deputy asked.

"Ah, no I didn't see him that well. I ran into the bathroom when he came in the door," she said.

"Well when you two get yourselves together the sheriff would like to ask you some questions. Right now, it looks this guy is going to be charged with murder one, breaking and entering, attempted rape, assault with a deadly weapon, and anything else we can find. The lady in the next room was shaken up pretty, good, but she'll be okay. She got a good look at him, so we probably won't have to hold you too long. Come over to the office in about thirty minutes. The medics will be here in a few minutes to see about your leg, Buddy. The deputy walked out of the room closing the door behind him.

Pam and Dave watched as the door closed. Then they turned toward each other. They both smiled sympathetically at each other. "Well, at least we're okay," Pam said.

"No thanks to you," Dave snapped, his face turning cold.

"How do you think you got in here? You probably think you slide under the door, don't you? Well, you didn't. I pulled you in here and I could have been killed if there had been another bullet in his gun."

"What do you mean? What happened?" Dave questioned

"Well he pointed the gun at me and pulled the trigger, but it was empty, so I ran into the bathroom."

"You risked your life for me?" he asked.

"I guess I did, but you'd better believe it won't happen again. Blame it on temporary insanity."

"Then you did save my life," he said apologetically. "Sorry about what I said. Everything did work out. I should be happy. We're both safe and we didn't get shot to death," he said.

"Yeah, and we didn't die of pneumonia, thanks to you," she said.

"And we didn't die in an automobile accident thanks to you," he said. "Wow, we're been through a lot in our short relationship."

"Yeah, we could have died," she said. Suddenly fear and sadness flowed over her. Tears began to roll down her face. Dave put his arm around her.

"It's okay, crying will make you feel better," he said stroking her hair. She laid her head on his shoulder. They stayed that way until she stopped crying.

"I'd better go and check on the clothes before we go talk to the sheriff," he said as he walked out of the room.

Chapter 4
The Pursuit

"Come on in Mr. and Mrs. Parker," said a short man with a bald spot in his head. "Sit down over here," he said pointing to a nearby sofa. "I've got a few questions I need for you to answer, if you please."

This man wore a highly starched dark blue uniform with a patch on the sleeve which said Sheriff Jefferson County. His shoes were shining like black gold, as he stood there with one foot resting on the coffee table. He was leaning over his raised leg writing on a notepad. Dave and Pam walked forward until they saw the outline of a person on the floor. They stopped in shock and then walked around it. They knew what it meant. Someone had been killed. Dave's mouth dropped open as he looked at the outline. The head appeared to be facing the wrong way.

"P. W., let me know as soon as Sam gets here with Sally and Prince," the short man said looking over at a tall husky man dressed in the same uniform.

"Roger Chief," P. W. replied as he walked out of the room.

"I'm Sheriff Davis, sheriff of Jefferson County," he paused. A frown appeared on his brow as he looked down at the outline on the floor. "We don't have trouble like this very often in my county. One person was brutally murdered, another assaulted, and I see here that you were shot in the leg, Mr. Walker."

"Yeah," Dave said nervously, "but it's just a flesh wound, and the medics took care of it."

"Did either of you get a good look at this guy," said the sheriff starring at Dave and then at Pam. They both shook their heads, 'no.'

"Everything happened so fast. Even though I was standing right in front of him, my eyes were glued to the gun," Dave said. "I've never been shot at before."

"And you didn't get a good look at him either," the Sheriff said looking at Pam.

"No, I never saw his face," she said.

"So, neither of you could identify him if you saw him again?" "No," they both said together.

"Well, why don't you tell me just what happened, Mr. Parker," the sheriff said. "Then you can tell your version, Mrs. Walker."

Pam could feel her facial expression change when he said 'Mrs Walker' but she did not look toward the sheriff. She waited for Dave to correct him, but Dave said nothing. She could feel the sheriff's eyes on her, scanning her facial expression. She didn't want to give herself away so she crossed her legs slowly so that he could see her thighs. She began to rub her ankle as if she were in some pain. Then she looked up quickly to see if he was looking under her dress. He was and she had caught him. She expected him to look away, but he didn't. A little smile appeared on his face as he continued to look at her thighs. She quickly turned her knees away from him toward the figure on the floor. Now it seemed that the figure on the floor had broken his neck trying to look under her dress. She felt uncomfortable so she uncrossed her legs and then looked back at the sheriff. She gave him a 'How dare you look under my dress' look, and he gave her a 'Nice thighs' smile.

All this time, Dave was telling his version of the earlier events, but he felt that nobody was listening, so he stopped. The silence broke their trance. They both looked at Dave and Dave continued until he had explained everything that had happened from the time, he had seen the strange man drive up, until the present time.

"You're driving that light blue Chevy with the black vinyl top, right? Dave nodded.

"I see you've had an accident recently. It looks like you've got about fourteen or fifteen hundred dollars, worth of damage. How did that happen?

"Ah, last night, it was raining pretty hard, and it was difficult to see. Well, a deer ran out in the highway in front of my car. I hit the brakes and cut my wheels to avoid hitting it. I missed the deer, but I lost control of the car and ran off the road."

"I see," said the sheriff in a suspicious tone. "Were either you or your wife hurt in the accident."

Dave noticed the he had hesitated before he said 'wife.' 'He must suspect something. How did I get into this mess? Why didn't I just tell him the truth?' Dave thought as he shook his head 'no.'

The sheriff then looked at Pam. "Well, Mrs. Parker, how long have you been Mrs. Parker?"

Before she could answer the deputy came back inside the door. "Sam is back with Sally and Prince, Chief," he said.

"All right, let's go," he said to the deputy. He pulled his pistol from its holster and checked to see if it was fully loaded. Then he looked at Pam and Dave. "We'll have to finish our little talk later. Make yourself as comfortable as you can. I will be back this afternoon. " He stopped. "In other words, don't get lost between now and then. Do I make myself clear?"

"Yes, perfectly clear," Dave said quickly.

The sheriff walked quickly out of the room. Dave and Pam followed him. When Dave opened the door of the office to go outside, he saw them, Sally and Prince. Sally was a very, large, brown and black German Sheppard. Prince was a slim but very tall Doberman. They were lying on the ground, each at the feet of a deputy who held their respective choke chains. When Dave stepped outside of the office door, they both raised and turned their heads toward him. He stopped. In an instant, they both charged. The deputy holding Prince was jerked forward but he was able to hold on. However, the deputy holding Sally, the large Sheppard, was caught completely off guard. The chain was pulled from his hand immediately. The dog was free and charging straight for Dave. Dave quickly stepped back inside. He pushed Pam back and swung the door forward as the ferocious dog dived forward. The door hit the dog in mid-flight deflecting her trajectory slightly. The door was knocked back and it slammed against the wall. The dog hit the floor turning around as she slid to a stop. With teeth snarling, Sally moved forward toward Dave, slowly at first. Pam, standing by the window, quickly turned, and yanked down one of the curtains and held it in front of her as though she were a Matador. She slowly moved toward the dog as she simultaneously stepped in front of Dave.

"When I give you the word duck down behind the curtain, crawl behind the door, and be ready to close it," Pam whispered.

"Okay," Dave said. He didn't wait for her to give the word. He ducked behind the curtain and was already behind the door when he heard her say, 'get ready.' Suddenly she heard a loud shout from behind her.

"Sally, attention!"

The dog froze. Sheriff Davis walked pass Pam, took hold of Sally's choke chain, and said to Pam. "You can put that curtain down now, Mrs. Walker."

"If you don't mind Sheriff, I think I'll hold on to it a few more minutes," Pam replied.

As the sheriff walk out with Sally at his side, he looked at Pam, smiled and said, "Honey, you've really got some balls on you."

"Balls?" Pam said with indignation as the sheriff stepped out into the parking area. She turned toward Dave, who was just coming from behind the door. "Did you hear what he said? I've got balls. If that is his way of complimenting somebody, then he needs to just keep his mouth shut."

Dave went to the door and looked outside. The two dogs were sniffing the seat of the pickup truck.

"I think they got the scent, Chief," said Roy Lee, one of the deputies, as he held tightly to Sally's choke chain.

"Let them go then," Sheriff Davis said.

"But they'll kill him if they catch him," Roy Lee said.

"Now Roy Lee, you know we don't hold to no murdering women molesters in this county. Anyway, they'll probably just tree him if he has any sense at all. Now, let them go!" the sheriff yelled.

The choke chains were removed, and the dogs charged into the woods. The sheriff and all but one of his deputies followed. The one called P. W. remained at the motel. He went to his car and turned his Police radio up so that he could hear it from the registration desk in the motel.

Pam and Dave hurried to their room. Once inside Dave began to get his things together. He put the last few things inside and closed his suitcase. He took it over to the door and sat down on it. He began talking without looking back.

"I don't think I'm going to stick around, here. In fact," he said as he looked through the thin opening in the curtains at the deputy who was standing at the motel front desk, "as soon as that deputy goes to the bathroom, I'm getting out of here. You see, I'm supposed to be at a convention at ten o'clock this morning. If I'm not there, I could lose my job."

"Well, I sure hope you're not planning on leaving me here," Pam snapped "cause if you are, you can just forget that. I'm leaving when you leave."

"I can't take you with me. I'm sorry that's impossible. I can't do it," Dave replied shaking his head.

"Hey, don't nut up on me. All I want to do is to get as far away from this place as I can. Just take me to the next town you get to, so I can catch a bus. Then you can go your merry little way." She paused, "How about it?"

"I can't," Dave said as he turned and faced her, "I'm already getting myself in trouble with the law. I'm not going to get you in trouble, too." Dave turned and began peering through the curtains again.

Pam angrily looked around the room until her eyes froze. There on the table was a flower arrangement, two artificial roses in a small long neck vase. Even the roses caught the mood of the moment. They lean away from each other as if they had just had a fight and were not speaking to each other. Pam walked over to the table, carefully removed the flowers, and laid them on the table, one right behind the other. Then she picked up the vase, turned, and walked toward Dave, who was still looking out through the curtains. Without any warning, Pam came up behind Dave and with her forearm against the back of his neck, pushed the side of his face up against the curtained window, pinning him there. When he braced himself to push back, she brought the vase up to his face and pressed it into his cheek roughly. He froze.

"Before I let you leave here without me, I'll bust your head wide open," Pam threatened. "Are you going to take me?"

"All right, I'll take you." She quickly moved back still holding the vase in her hand.

Dave turned with a frown on his face. He raised his finger and pointing it at her he said, "But you better be ready to move when I say so."

"Okay, I'll be ready," she said softly.

"And another thing, for as long as your riding with me, you've got to do what I say, when I say it, and how I say it. Do you understand that?" Dave growled.

"Okay Dave, you're the boss, boss," she said smiling as she threw her tote bag over her shoulder.

Dave slowly wiped his hand down his face and then took a deep breath and blew it out. He continued watching the deputy through the curtains. 'Will this ever end,' he thought.

A couple of miles away the strange man was running through a path he had found in the wood. He had been moving for about twenty minutes when he heard the sound.

"Dogs," he said softly.

He had figured that they would get dogs to track him. That wouldn't change his plans. He would still circle the motel in a wide arch, double back, get his truck, and leave. Then he would wait for Pam. He looked down at his hands which were clinched around an imaginary neck, Pam's.

No, the dogs were not going to change his plan, but they were going to make it a lot harder to give his trackers the slip. He left the path and headed downhill. He needed to get to some water. He was running at a steady speed even though the ground was very slippery. He ran around a big rock and jumped over a fallen tree. Suddenly his right leg went down into a hole all the way up to his knee. His body twisted around and slammed to the ground. He had been lucky. If he had not been able to get his left leg around and over the hole, the right one would have been broken. As it was, he had twisted his knee. He was not going to be able to move as fast now. He listened. The dogs were much too close. He figured that they must be running free. He wondered what kind of dogs they were. No matter, he had to slow them down. As he pulled himself out of the hole, he thought back to a time when he was in Vietnam.

His platoon was on patrol that day, and everybody had been warned that Charlie was inside the perimeter. He was about ten feet behind the point man and the next man was about ten feet behind him. He remembered looking up at the beautiful blue sky, when he heard the point man scream so loud that they all scattered for cover. He ran up to the point man and looked down. The point man had stepped into a hole and there were two sharp bloody sticks coming up through his boot. It had seemed so grotesque that he began to laugh. A little at first then uncontrollably. Before long, the whole platoon was laughing, even the point man.

Doug laughed as he came back to the present. He looked around him, and then he pulled a knife from his pocket. In a few minutes he had cut three small limbs about two feet long. He sharpened the ends, stuck them down in the hole, and cover the hole with leaves and pine straw. The trap was complete. He continued down the hill.

It was beginning to get light now, and the dogs were getting closer. He was getting panicky now. He heard something. It was running water. Now he could lose the dogs. He began to run faster down the hill. He slipped, fell, and began to tumble head over heels down the hill, over the bank, and into the small creek. He laid there on his back as the cold water flowed around him. The creek was only a few inches deep where he had landed. He took a deep breath and was about to blow it out when he froze His heart began to pound and his eyes became as big as golf balls. There on the bank above his head he saw the white cotton mouth of a water moccasin. The fangs seemed three inches long. Doug laid perfectly still, playing dead. He didn't even dare breathe. The snake uncoiled, slide down the bank, and swam over to the side of his face. It stayed there watching Doug relentlessly. Doug did not even blink. After what seemed like minutes to Doug, the snake crawled onto Doug's shoulder, over his stomach, and down between his legs into the water again. Doug's lungs began to burn. He needed to breathe. He could not hold his breath any longer. He had to breathe. He felt the snake crawl across his leg as the air shot from his lungs. At that same moment he kicked his leg with all his might. The snake sailed into the air over Doug's head.

Doug wasted no time. He was up and had crawled up on the bank before the snake landed on the opposite bank. The snake gave chase but there was no way it was going to catch him now. The snake returned to its den through a hole in the bank of the pond.

Doug could feel his blood pumping in his veins, and he could hardly catch his breath. He had to rest. He slowed to a walk, stumbled, and fell face forward into the wet grass. He tried to push himself up, but he was too exhausted. He rolled over and laid there gasping for air.

The dogs, running down a path in the woods, went pass the place where Doug had left the path. They stopped. They slowly sniffed their way back up the path until they got the scent again. Then down through the woods they went. Sally, the Sheppard, was leading the way. Prince, the Doberman, was right behind her as they approached the booby trap. Sally could tell that the scent was much stronger as she jumped over the fallen tree. Her two front paws went through the leaves and pine straw followed by her head. She screamed an almost human scream as two of the sticks sank into her neck and chest. Her blood flowed down the sticks as she struggled to free herself. Prince remained at her side until her struggle ended. Then, he lowered his head, picked up Doug's scent and ran down the hill toward the stream.

Doug was still on the ground when he heard the dog scream. He jumped to his feet and pulled off his jacket and his shirt. After putting his jacket back on, he dragged the shirt to the left and back to the place where he had been lying. Then he dragged it to the right to a small tree. He pulled the little tree over and tied his shirt to it. Then he went back again to where he had been lying. Then he moved slowly away trying not to touch anything as he moved.

'That will hold them,' he thought, as he pushed through some tall weeds. If he had looked back at that moment, he would have known that his trick was not going to hold them. There at the top of the hill behind him, peering through the grass were a pair of red, ominous eyes. Prince was watching; his teeth fixed in a silent growl as he waited for the right moment to strike.

Doug was going down through the high thick weeds when Prince came out into the open at the top of the hill. Somehow Prince knew that this man was responsible for the death of his mate. Under normal circumstances during a chase, the deputy would always be there holding his lease until the final minutes, when he would hear the sheriff say, "Let them go." Then the deputy would release him, and he and Sally would charge. They would run down their prey and tree him, if he were smart. If not, it would be bloody. Prince would always get there first, sinking his teeth deep into the back of the man's thigh. He would hear the man scream, and then he would taste the man's warms sweet blood. Then Sally would throw herself at the man's chest and he would go down. If the man was lucky, the deputy would get there quickly, to pull them off. Prince would always take another bit. Prince knew it would be different this time. There would be no deputies to pull him off. He was going to punish this man. Prince charged.

Doug was fighting his way through the thick weeds when something hit the back of his thigh with a tremendous force. He turned and saw the large Doberman clamped to thigh. He moaned with pain as the dog tried to tear his flesh from his bone. Doug fell back, throwing all his weight down on the dog. Prince tried to back away, but the weeds were too thick. Prince never released his grip on Doug's thigh, even though he was pinned. Doug slid his hand beneath his thigh and grabbed the back of the dog's neck. With his other hand, grabbed one of the dogs front paws. He bent it back quickly, snapping the tendon in the dog's ankle. Prince howled and when he did, he released his grip on Doug's thigh. Doug quickly moved his leg and grabbed the dogs throat with his other hand. He pressed his thumbs deep into Prince's throat. Doug watched as the dog's eyes rolled to the back of his head. The dog's body grew limp but still Doug did not release his grip. He dragged the dog over to a nearby tree, picked him up, took a deep breath, and swung the dog around as hard as he could. Just at that moment Prince screamed. It was a scream that ended abruptly when his body slammed against the tree. It dropped like a bag of bones onto the ground.

The sheriff and his deputies were standing over Sally's bloody corpse when they heard Prince's cut off scream. Tears filled the sheriff's eyes and streamed away.

"Let go. I'm gonna get that son of a bitch," the sheriff yelled.

They began to run down the hill. They easily found where Doug had rolled over the bank into the stream. They began to run through the path he had made, unfortunately. They soon reached the stream. The first deputy, with his shotgun held high over his head, jumped off the bank into the stream. The moccasin heard him hit the water and came to the entrance of her den. The snake was just about to attack when dirt began to cave in on her head, forcing her back into the hole. The snake's way out was blocked as the next man's boot had pushed a mound of mud in front of her. Suddenly she was trapped. The next deputy, old Billy, did not jump into the creek. He stepped down in the tracks of the man before him. As he did, his boot pushed all the mud away from the entrance of the snake's den. She struck before he knew it. Her fangs sunk deeply into old Billy's boot. As he went forward into the stream, he pulled the snake out of the hole and into the water. Billy felt a sharp pain in his ankle. Wondering what it was, he looked down and sadly confirmed his worse suspicion. Panic shot through him as he watched the large black moccasin struggling to free itself from his boot.

"Snake," he yelled, "I been bit." All the other deputies froze as they watched old Billy kicking his leg to free himself from his newly found companion. Suddenly the snake fell, free. In seconds old Billy had scrabbled up onto the other bank. Everyone else's eyes were on the snake. They lowered their guns and each one felt a rush of excitement as the adrenalin began to flow through their veins. They all shared the same expression. Their eyes bucked and their eyebrows turned down, not in anger but in a devilish grin.

Then the thunder exploded from their guns as they all began to fire at the snake. The pistol and shotgun fire lasted almost ten seconds. All of them had emptied their weapons except the sheriff. The remains of the snake floated in several parts on the surface down the creek. The men looked at the sheriff, who was looking over the hill. The murderer, woman molester, and dog killer was over there somewhere, and he was going to get him if he had to go into the very pit of hell.

Without moving his body or his eyes he said in a low calm voice, "Load up, let's get going." Then he looked at old Billy who was sitting on the bank examining his wound. "Hi ya feeling Billy Boy", the sheriff said with a concerned but stern expression.

"It don't look bad Chief, but I'd kinda like to get back and let the Doc take care of it," old Billy said looking in the sheriff's eyes.

The sheriff turned, "Roy Lee, you and Tommy take old Billy back to the motel. When we get to the top of that hill, I'll radio P. W. and have him call for an ambulance "Let's move."

Dave had been watching the deputy for 45 minutes or more, before he saw him to go to the bathroom. By then Dave was in a tight himself.

"Let's go, now," Dave said softly as he opened the door. They both ran to the car and jumped in. Before she could close the door, he had started the car and they were rolling pass the motel office. For some reason they felt compelled to duck down as they went by. Once on the highway Dave sped up.

"Did you see the deputy come out of the bathroom. Do you think he saw us," Dave asked?

"I didn't see him, but I wasn't looking either. I had my head down."

"Yeah, me too. Well we'd better not take any chances," Dave said, seeing a dirt road up ahead. He slowed the car to a stop just as he passed the dirt road.

"Why are we stopping? We don't need to stop. We need to make as much time as we can," she said as he backed down the dirt road and off to the side where they could see any cars that went by.

"Look, I don't know where I am. Do you?"

Pam shook her head 'no.'

"We need to look at the map and decide which route we need to take. Plus, I want to see if we are being followed," Dave snapped.

"Okay, okay, okay. Here's the map," Pam said as she pulled the map from the dash. "Are you sure you've never run from the law before." Pam smiled.

"Who, me? No way Hosea. I'm Mr. Law Abiding Citizen himself. Just call me L. A. C. for short," Dave smiled.

"Well, Mr. L. A. C., you sure do seem to be mighty cool and calm," Pam said opening the map.

"Me? Not even." Dave said softly as he took one end of the map. There was a silence as they both looked at the map in the dim light before dawn. Pam continued to look at the map.

"Dave, I want to thank you for bringing me with you. I really wouldn't have done what I said. I was just, scared. You understand, don't you?" Pam said looking up at Dave.

Dave looked into her soft blue pleading eyes. Even though deep down inside he really believed that she would have busted in his skull just like she had said, he nodded his head.

"You don't know what scared is. When I saw the hammer fall on that gun that was aimed at my head and when I heard sound of the gun being fired, I was so scared that I swear that my heart stopped beating. You thought I had fainted. No. The medic thought I had been playing dead. Not that either. I actually thought I was dead. I was supposed to be. How could he have missed me at ten feet away. Anyway, when I fell I my head hit really, hard on the floor and that almost knocked me unconscious. That's when I knew I wasn't dead. It doesn't do any good die if you're still going to feel pain. I tried to move. I couldn't move, but I could hear. I heard that lady screaming and then

I heard that man, the murderer." Dave had been looking straight ahead, but now he turned toward Pam. "He called your name." There was silence as they looked each other in the eye. "And, you called his name, Doug. You called him, Doug."

The stare-down ended as Pam turned and looked out of the window.

As the sheriff and his men moved through the woods, the sheriff began to think about Prince. He had heard that awful scream that seemed to come from somewhere nearby. 'If anything has happened to Prince, I'll kill that son of a bitch,' he though angrily. The promise had little time to sink in before he heard his deputy's voice.

"Chief, it's Prince," deputy Logan said.

The sheriff walked up to the tree where Doug had ended Prince's life. The dog's deformed body was a pile of twisted bones and flesh. The terror of the last moment of the dog's life was still molded in his expression. The sheriff kneeled beside Prince and rubbed his head for the last time. A tear rolled down his face, and his breathing became heavy. He cleared his throat and spoke to his men without looking at them.

"We are not going in until we catch him; he's going to pay for this." His voice became louder, "Do you hear me?"

"Yeah, Chief," his men said in staggered voices.

"Well, let's go."

"He went this way Chief, he's headed for the highway," Logan said.

The sheriff pulled his radio from his belt. "P. W. come in." There was no answer. "P. W. come in." There was still no answer. "P. W.!", he said his voice growing louder. There was a pause. The already angry expression grew even more fearful. "P. W., this is Sheriff Davis," the sheriff yelled.

P. W., hearing the sheriff's voice through the radio, rushed out of the bathroom while zipping up his pants. He ran to the car and grabbed the radio phone.

"P. W. here Chief, go ahead, over," P. W. said as he buckled up his belt leaning into the car.

"I told you to stay by the radio. Where in the hell have you been?" "I just went to the john, Chief," P. W. said.

"Look here," the sheriff said calming himself down, " Roy Lee and Tommy are bring old Billy back there. Call the hospital and have them send an ambulance. Tell them that he was bitten by a cotton mouth. You got that!"

"Yeah, I got it, Chief"

"Another thing; when Roy and them, get there, I want you to get your car and patrol the highway between the motel and Route 9. It looks like our boy is headed for the highway."

"Okay Chief," P. W. said as he looked out the window. "Hey Chief"

"Yeah, what is it."

"Parker's car is gone. They must have sneaked off when I was in the john."

"Forget them! Get that car out here as soon as you can, and be careful, this guy is dangerous. Don't take any chances, shot to kill if he looks like he wants to do anything hostel."

"Roger Chief, over and out." P. W. went back into the office and called for an ambulance.

After waiting a long time for a response from Pam, Dave finally spoke. "You knew him, and he knew you. It was you, he was looking for, wasn't it?" He paused for an answer, but Pam continued to look out the window. "Who was he Pam, your husband, your lover. Who?"

"Don't you think it about time we got out of here," Pam said still looking out of the window.

"That's why you were so anxious to leave; cause you knew more than you were telling the sheriff."

"Dave, let's go," Pam said.

"We're going all right, we're going back the that motel, if you don't tell me what's going on."

"You wouldn't believe me if I told you."

Suddenly Dave had a tremendous urge to urinate. He grabbed the keys from the ignition, opened the door, and got out.

"Well, you understand this. When I get back from taking a leak, I'm taking you right back to the motel," he said as he slammed the door.

He went behind a tree and began to unzip his pants. He was really in a tight. He was running in place as he unzipped his pants. "Woo, hold on baby," he said as he pulled his penis from his pants just before the urine began to flow. The urine steamed as it rolled down the tree. "Whew, that was too close for comfort," he said aloud as the water flowed unceasingly. Dave began to sing softly.

"I peed a river, I peed a river, I peed a river over you. Yeah, Yeah, I peed a river o-ver y-o-o-u-u. Sing it Dave!" he laughed.

Behind Dave a figure, was moving through the woods toward him. It was Doug and he recognized Dave. He also saw the car parked in the trees ahead. Doug moved quickly toward Dave who was still peeing. Doug was almost upon him when he stepped on a stick. There was a loud snap. Dave turned shaking out the last few drops of pee. Seeing Doug, Dave almost went into cardiac arrest. Doug was almost growling when he reached for Dave's throat. Before Dave knew what he was doing, he ducked under Doug's arm, grabbed his legs, and lifted. Dave was able to get him off his feet, but Doug's weight and momentum caused Dave to fall back. Dave was able to get enough leverage to guide Dave's head into the tree he had just peed on. Doug was slightly stunned and that gave Dave the time needed to roll away. Dave scrambled to his feet and began to run toward the car screaming.

"Pam start the car, it's him."

Pam hearing the screams looked around. Her mouth dropped open in shock when she saw Doug running after Dave. She unlocked her door, pushed it open, and slid over to the driver's side. The key was not in the ignition.

"You took the car keys," she screamed back to Dave.

Dave pulled the keys from his pocket just before he jumped into the car. He slammed the car door, locked it, and then turned to put the key in the ignition. He nervously fumbled as he tried to push the key into the hole. They fell from his hands to the floor.

"Move out of the way, I'll get them," Pam snapped.

Dave turned toward the window to see where Doug was. Just as he looked, he saw Doug's hand with a rock in it coming straight at his face. He tried to duck as the hand and rock crashed through the window. Dave was able to get his arm up to block some of the blow. But he was still knocked over on Pam who was turning the key in the ignition. Doug reached through the hole in the window, he unlocked the door with his right hand and he open the door with the left just as Pam hit the accelerator. Doug hung on as he tried to get into the car. He had one foot in the door and his arm was still in the window.

Pam reach the paved road burning rubber. The car spun around too far, and Pam hit the brakes. This caused the door and Doug with it, to the swing around as he held on. The door stopped abruptly, slinging Doug against the front bumper and onto the street. Pam threw the car into reverse. She stomped the accelerator again. The tires smoked as backed the car down the street. Then she stumped the brakes and the car slid to a halt.

Dave straighten up in his seat. He swiped his hand across his head and then checked his hand for blood. Then he looked at the road ahead. There in the middle of the road was Doug with that same look of hate on his face. Dave turn to Pam and there was hate and fury in her eyes as well. Dave was just about to speak when she hit the accelerator again. The car lunged toward Doug. He ran toward the woods, but it was too late. Pam turned the car toward him.

"You're going to hit him," Dave screamed, "watch out."

Doug jumped as the car reached him. Dave pulled at the steering wheel, trying to make Pam miss him, but she didn't. She hit his legs as he dove away. Doug hit the ground and laid there, not moving at all, as the car went down the road. Dave looked back at the motionless body on the road. Then he looked at Pam disbelievingly.

"You killed him," Dave sighed. "Well, maybe he's not dead. Stop the car. We've got to go back and see. Oh, God. How did I ever get into a mess like this?" Dave said opening the door not even noticing that the car had not stopped.

"What are you doing, close that door!" Pam yelled as she brought the car to a stop.

"Why did you do that. Are you crazy? Yeah, that's it. You've got to be crazy." Dave was beginning to hyperventilate. "Turn the car around we've got to go back."

"Calm down Dave, before you have a stroke or a heart attack or something," Pam said softly. "What's done is done."

"Oh God, please don't let him be dead." Dave, getting his breathing under control, looked at Pam and said slowly, "We've got to go back."

"And what if he is dead?" Pam snapped.

Dave turned to look back at the body and fear gripped his heart. There running up the road toward them was the strange man. He still had the rock in his hand.

"It's him," Dave shouted. "Go, go!"

Pam gladly mashed the accelerator and the car pulled away. Doug falling behind hurled the rock at the car. It crashed on top of the hood and rolled off. Doug watched as the car pulled around the corner and out of sight.

"I guess he's not dead," Dave said with a little smile on his lips.

"I guess he's not," Pam smiled back.

"Guess what?" Dave said still smiling.

"What?" Pam asked.

"I've got to take a leak," Dave said his eyebrows raised in a look of sympathy.

"You can pee on yourself for all I care. I'm not stopping until we get well, away from here."

"You're the boss, boss," Dave said smiling.

Pam smiled back. But the smiles were short lived because a car passed them going in the opposite direction. It was a yellow late modeled Buick. There was a man driving. He appeared to be in his late fifties. The man looked at their ram shackled car and wondered what hell they had been through. Little did he know that he was headed straight for it.

Before long, the man reached the area where Doug had been hit. He came around the curve and saw a body lying in the street. It was Doug. He slowed and stopped. He got out of his car and ran over to Doug, who was lying face down. He reached down and touched Doug on the shoulder.

"Hey mister, are you okay," he said as he began to turn Doug over. Suddenly, Doug grabbed the man's arm, pulled him down, and rolled over on top of him. Doug clamped his hands around the old man's neck and began to squeeze. There was a look of shock on the man's face as he looked up at Doug. The man's eyes pleaded for mercy. However, they found no compassion in Doug's face. The man's hope began to fade away like the light after a sunset. He had his hands around Doug's wrists but there was no use in struggling. The more he struggled the tighter Doug would squeeze. It was as if Doug was waiting for him to completely surrender and accept death willingly. That is exactly what was happening. The man slowly released Doug's wrists and let his arms fall to the pavement. He slowly closed his eyes for the last time he thought. Just when his last drop of hope was about to go, a shot from a gun rang in his ears.

Sheriff Davis and his deputies had just come out of the woods and they were running down the road toward Doug. Sheriff Davis had fired a warning shot into the air. Even though they were still about two hundred feet away, the sheriff stopped, aimed his revolver at Doug, and yelled, "Get your hands up and move away from that man."

Hope surged back into the man as he opened his eyes and looked up at Doug who was still looking toward the sheriff. Out of the corner of his eye the old man could see the sheriff and his deputies spread out across the street, running toward him. They all had their guns aimed at Doug. Doug looked down at the man beneath him. The man in turn gave Doug a looked of salvation and relief. The man had never been happier in his life. In a second, Doug pushed his thumbs down into the man's larynx and his happiness was over.

Doug picked up the man's limp body and using it for a shield, he hurried toward the man's car. The sheriff fired. The impact of the bullet tore a large hole in the dead man's shoulder.

"Fire, damn it. Don't let him get away," the sheriff screamed as he fired continuously. The deputies began to fire. A shower of bullets and buckshot rained down on Doug. In seconds, the body draped on his shoulders became a mass of bloody flesh. When Doug got to the car, he opened the door, started the engine, and then pushed the body out.

"Shoot at the motor and the tires," the sheriff yelled as the car backed down the highway. Shots hit the windshield and the right front head light, but the car continued. It spun around and sped out of sight.

"I'm out," Logan said putting his revolver back in his holster.

The sheriff who had reloaded, fired a last shot in the direction that the car had gone. The look on his face was one of hate an anguish.

"I'll get you. Sooner or later, I'll get you," he mumbled to himself. "And when I do, you're gonna pay."

His deputies gathered around the man bullet riddled body as he grabbed his radio and began to talk.

"This is one time I'm glad I'm not the Sheriff," Logan said quietly to Sam.

"P. W., come in," the sheriff said solemnly.

CHAPTER 5
ON THE RUN

Dave had finally convinced Pam to pull over so he could take a leak. There were no other cars on the road, so he went just beyond the back door and began to urinate up against up against the car. 'This had to be the final insult to his car,' he thought. "After all you've taken me through, now I show my appreciation by peeing on you. Sorry Ole Pal. It's nothing personal, but I am never in my life, going in the woods again," Dave said softly. He got back in the car and closed the door. It did not close completely. Doug had evidently bent the hinges. He opened it and slammed it harder. It still did not close completely. Then grabbing the door handle with both of his hands, he pulled with all his strength.

"Wham," the door crashed against the car, causing it to rock and spraying little pieces of glass from the hole Doug had put in the window. "That got it," Dave said brushing the glass from his shirt.

"I hope you won't have to go through all that when you get ready to get out," Pam said as she pulled the car back onto the highway.

Dave laid his head back on the seat. He was beginning to get his senses back, but he was very tired and sleepy. Everything was happening so fast. A strange woman was driving his car, going who knows where. A crazy man was trying to kill them both. It was too bizarre to even think about. At least for now, he could relax. With his head still lying back on the seat, he turned toward her. She was so fine to him at that moment. He looked down at her smooth creamy thighs. He could almost see her panties. Her skirt was pulled up way above her knees. 'If only I could make love to you,' he thought in a half dream state. 'All my tensions would be relieved.'

"You can't handle it, so don't even think about it," he heard her say.

'Did she hear me,' he wondered. 'No, she couldn't have, I didn't say anything.' He looked at her face. It was unchanged. She was still looking straight ahead. 'She didn't say anything, my imagination is running away with me. I must be stressed out,' he thought. He closed his eyes again. 'So, I can't handle it. Well, maybe I can't handle it, so what? Is it asking too much for somebody to want me? Why do I always have to feel that I'm the bad guy when I say that I want you? I just want to be wanted,' he thought as he dozed off into dreamland. As he dozed, Pam began to nod.

Her eyelids began to close as her head went forward and bumped against the steering wheel. When she woke up, she was about to run off the road. She swerved back to her side of the highway. Her driving was affecting Dave's dream.

He was dreaming he was an Arabian Sheik who was on his way to the slave market to look over a group of beautiful slaves girls that the local slave trader was selling at a discount. Dave, the Sheik of Parikik, in his dream was being carried in a palanquin on the shoulder of four slaves. He was also accompanied by four servants riding on camels.

"Can't we go any faster, Hasim. I can hardly wait to see the slave girls," Sheik Dave said to his number one servant.

"But Master, you are already low on your front right. If you go any faster you may have a blowout," Hasim said. Hasim was sitting on his camel pointing to the slave on the right side in the front of the palanquin. The slave was slumped over in exhaustion. He was causing the palanquin to be tilted down in the front."I don't care about that. Go faster!" Sheik Dave yelled.

Hasim crack his whip. "Faster!" he ordered. The slaves responded by walking faster. The faster speed caused the palanquin to sway wildly from side to side. Sheik Dave had to hold on tightly to keep from falling out.

Pam at the same time was struggling to stay awake. She was nodding continuously, swerving all over the road causing Dave's head to rock back and forth. She drove past a yellow caution sign indicating a sharp turn ahead. She did not see it. Nor did she see the sign with the large words: REDUCE SPEED AHEAD. She did not see the curve coming up fast until it was too late. When she raised her head, she was only a two or three hundred feet from the curve and she was going much too fast. She pressed the brakes as she approached the curve. Then she saw a dirt road straight ahead. She cut the wheel to the left crossed the center line and slid to stop on the dirt road.

"Oh man, that was close." The motor was still running. Pam cut it off and looked over at Dave. He was still sleep. Pam put the car in park and laid back on the seat. She looked in the rearview mirror and could not see the highways. She felt safe so she closed her eyes.

In his dream he had been going along and the exhausted slave had finally collapsed sending Sheik Dave tumbling out of the palanquin onto the sand.

"What in the name of Allah is going on," Sheik Dave said putting his turban back on.

"You had a flat," Hasim said pointing to the slave lying flat on his face in the sand.

"Look! The slave market," Sheik Dave shouted, jumping to his feet. "We will go from here on camel."

Instantly, they were at the slave market.

"Now these are the finest slave girls from the four corners of the earth," said a short white man with a bald spot in his head. This man, his boss in real life, was a slave trader in his dream. "They have never been touched by a man," the short fat man said with pride. "Isn't that right, Eunuch," the slave trader said to a tall servant near the slave girls.

"That's right master. I never laid a hand on them," the eunuch said raising two handless arms.

The slave trader turned back to face Sheik Dave. "He was caught stealing, three times. The first time, he was demoted from guard to camel keeper, and he lost a hand. The second time, he was denoted to water bearer and he lost another. The third time he was demoted to eunuch and he lost another handy part. He finally learned that crime doesn't pay."

When the eunuch saw that the slave trader was no longer looking at him, he stuck out his tongue at him. Then he looked over at the slave girls, touched his nose with his tongue, and winked his eye. All the slave girls began to smile and giggle. When the slave trader heard the giggling, he looked back. The eunuch put a serious expression back on his face.

"He's the best eunuch I ever had. I haven't had a slave girl to kill herself or run away since he became my eunuch," the slave trader said with pride. "And just look how lovely they are. I have chocolates from Africa," he said pointing to a beautiful black girl at the front of the line, "pearls from the Orient," he pointed to another beauty from Japan. Even though this girl had slanted eyes, Dave knew it was Pam. "And even Lilies from Europe," he pointed to the two blonde white girls at the end of the first line. Dave was not impressed as he continued to walk down the line of slave girls that were chained together by their ankles. Then something caught Dave's eye. Dave could barely see her, so he walked closer. The closer he got the more disturbed he became. There was something familiar about the girl in the back of the second line. When he walked up to her, she raised her head. It was his wife, Carol. Unlike the others, she was not dressed in the fine clothes and her hair was not oiled and combed.

"How much for this one," Dave said.

"This one?" the trader said with surprise.

"Yeah, how much?"

"But Sir, wouldn't you rather have one of the these other, more juicy berries over here," he said pointing to the front of the line.

"No, I want her," Dave said pointing to Carol.

The little fat man leaned over and whispered in Dave's ear. "But Sir, you will not be happy with this one. She is not a virgin, and she has a very unruly nature. She will cause you much grief."

"I want this one," Dave shouted, loudly, and then he crossed his arms.

The little fat man scratched his head and said, "This girl does not belong to me. I sold her to my camel keeper. I'll have to ask him if he is willing to take another girl for her." The trader walked over to a tall dirty man by the camels. Dave recognize him, too. It was Chuckie, the insurance man. The man held up four fingers and pointed to one of the girls in the front of the line. The trader smiled and nodded in approval. Then he walked back over to Dave.

"Narbi is willing to let her go if I will give him the oriental princes and eighty pieces of silver. Now, I am asking for two hundred pieces of silver for the oriental." The trader paused, lowered his head, and then looking up at Dave. "You can have the camel keepers slave for two hundred and ninety pieces of silver."

"I'll take her. My servant will pay you." Dave looked at his servant Hasim and said, "Pay the trader, then take the slave girl, wash her, dress her, and bring her to my tent." Dave got on his camel and watched as the eunuch carried, the oriental slave girl, Pam, back to the camel keeper, Chuckie. She was screaming and fighting to get away, but it was no use. Chuckie, the camel keeper, tied her hands and her feet and laid her on the ground beside him. Pam looked up pitifully at Dave as he rode by. When Dave got back, he went into his tent, sat among his pillows, and waited. Soon his servant dragged the slave girl, Carol, into his tent. Carol was fighting against him all the way. The servant force her down on the pillows next to Dave.

Dave smiled at her and spoke in a calm, pleasant tone, "I am Sheik David, your new master. I'm sure that you will find that I am a kind and gentle master. Here, you will be treated with honor and respect."

"Yeah?" Carol said, "well respect this." She cleared her throat and spat it all in his face. Then she jumped up and ran from the tent yelling, "Narbi, Narbi!"

Dave awoke from his dream wiping sweat from his face, though he thought it was Carol's spit. He opened his eyes. The car was not moving. It was parked on a dirt road. Pam was sleep. Her head was laid back, her mouth partially opened as if to be kissed. She had dirt on her forehead which seemed to ruin the lovely picture that Dave saw. He slid over and wiped her forehead with the sleeve of his shirt. The dirt came off. Now, the picture was lovely. He rubbed her hair back from her face and as he did her face turned toward him, and the side of her face rested in his hand. Then before he knew what was happening, she leaned toward him and fell against him, her nose against his chest. She was still sleep.

"Hold it there, baby. Get control of yourself. I realize that I'm irresistible, but when women throw themselves at me, that turns me completely off," Dave said softly. "Your mama always said you were nothing but a little floozy. She warned me, all right. Hey but I understand. You're just a woman. You can't help yourself."

He turned her face around so that she could breathe. There she was, in his arms so to speak. Her eyes were closed, her lips parted slightly. She was like Sleeping Beauty waiting for a kiss from Prince Charming. A voice inside him said, 'Kiss her.' He slowly leaned forward. He did not notice that a yellow Buick had pulled up behind his car. Dave lowered his lips and touched hers. He wanted to stop but he did not. He pressed his lips against hers as she began to come alive. He felt her tongue move forward. He watched as her eyes slowly opened. They went from drowsy, to puzzled, to alert, to shock. Then with all her strength she screamed.

She pushed Dave away and quickly slid toward her door. Dave was humiliated until he heard the door lock click behind him. He looked around as Doug pulled on the door. It got stuck. Dave screamed. Pam had opened her door and was stepping out. In a fraction of a second, Dave jumped on the seat, and positioned himself like a sprinter ready for the start of the hundred-yard dash. Doug yanked the door open, however, before Doug could extend his arm, Dave dove forward like a swimmer off the starting blocks. He collided with Pam as he went forward. She went down hard as her foot went out from under her. Dave rolled out of the car, over Pam, and onto his feet. When he looked back and saw Doug dive across the front seat of the car. Dave didn't give Pam a second thought, he took off running.

Doug grabbed the side of the seat and quickly pulled himself forward. When his head came out beyond the seat, he saw Pam lying on her back beneath his head. They both froze as their eyes locked. With his chest resting on his hands, Doug ever so slowly brought his knee forward as he prepared to pounce on her like a cat would pounce on a defenseless mouse. Pam stared at his eyes waiting for some type of signal. Then came the moment of truth. Suddenly Doug's eyes grew wild as he was about to attack. That was the sign the Pam had been waiting for. The instant that Doug's head moved, Pam's hand shot forward like a snake. Her sharp fingernails raked down over his eyes leaving three trails of red. That stopped Doug in his tracks, momentarily. However, Doug reached forward and grabbed Pam's hand as she tried to pull it back. Now finally, he had her, he thought. Then came the other claw, straight for his eyes. He was able to save himself only by releasing her arm and using his arm to block her blow. Pam rolled away from the car, but Doug reached forward and caught her skirt. She reached forward, grabbed the bottom of the car door, and swung it around, smashing it against his head. He did not release her. She pulled it back and pushed it forward again. The door bounced back off his head and she pushed it forward again and again. He still did not release his grip.

Doug was able to get his other hand up and he grabbed the door handle. Pam pushed as hard as she could, but she could not move it. Suddenly the door shot forward. Pam looked up and saw Dave leaning against the door. Doug's arm was pinned in the door, but he still would not release her dress. Pam unzipped her skirt and carefully began to slide out of it. Doug hit against the door with his other hand, but he could not free his arm.

"Hurry up," Dave yelled, "I can't hold this door much longer."

Pam pulled her feet out of the dress quickly. Then she jumped up and began to push against the door beside Dave.

"You run for it while I hold him here," Dave said.

"Like this!" Pam said referring to her attire. "At least let me get my skirt."

"Well, how are you going to do that?" Dave asked.

"I'm going to ask him real nice." Pam replied as she moved her right foot back. "Will," she yelled and then kicked Doug's arm as hard as she could. "You," she kicked again. "Give, me, my," she kicked after each word. Then she reached down toward the skirt and yelled, "skirt." After she kicked, she grabbed the skirt and quickly snatched the skirt from Doug's hand.

"See what happens when you ask?" Pam said with a quick smile. She leaned against the car and stepped into her skirt. Dave stared as she pulled her shirt over her hips.

"I told you, you couldn't handle it," Pam said zipping up her skirt.

"You want to bet?" Dave challenged.

"Yeah, I'll bet you."

"It's a bet," Dave said.

Suddenly Doug lunged forward driving his shoulder into the door, knocking Dave back and freeing his arm. "Run," Dave yelled.

Pam looked back to see Doug crawling out of the car. Pam and Dave started running toward the highway. When they reached it, Pam went to the right and Dave went to the left. She was going in the direction from where they had come, back toward the motel. Doug ran to the highway and stopped. He looked at Dave then he looked at Pam. Then off he went at full speed after Pam. Dave looked back and saw that Doug had gone after Pam he stopped. He ran back to his car. The front door on the passenger side was still open so he slammed it shut. He wanted to get into his car, drive away, and forget any of this ever happened, but he knew he couldn't. Pam needed him, and he could not let her down, no matter how scared he was. He started the car, and then backed it onto the highway.

Doug was only about ten yards behind Pam when Dave got the car pointed in their direction. They looked like two sprinters headed into the final turn. Dave pressed the accelerator to the floor, but he didn't think he was going to get to Pam before Doug did.

When Pam heard Doug's breathing getting louder and his footsteps getting closer, she put it in fifth gear. She was kicking hard now. She began to slowly, pull away from him. Then Dave pulled up beside Doug and slowed down to his speed.

"Hey fella, you want a lift?" Dave yelled.

Doug glanced over at him and gave him a scrawl.

"You say you do? Okay, here you go," Dave said softly as he turned the car toward Doug. He bumped him with the side of his car, knocking him off the road, down a small bank into some weeds. Dave sped up next to Pam.

"Hey, slow down speedy," Dave said smiling.

Pam was in no mood for jokes. She was exhausted. She looked back and was relieved that Doug was nowhere in sight. She stopped running. Dave stopped beside her. She fell against the door breathing deep heavy breaths. Her lungs burned and sweat ran down her face. She pulled against the car door. It was jammed. She did not have any strength left. Dave slid over and tried to open it from the inside, but he couldn't. They both looked back at the same time, wondering if they would see Doug. He was not there, but they continued to stare at the crest of the hill anyway. They did not have to wait long. A few seconds later, Doug's body began to appear, as he ran up the hill and onto the road. Pam gave the door one more pull. It did not budge. A look of surrender appeared on her face as she looked into Dave's eyes.

"Get on the hood, hurry up," Dave yelled.

Pam crawled on the hood as Dave moved the car forward. Doug was only able to reach the handle of the back door, but he released it as the car's speed increased. Doug immediately turned and began to run back down the highway toward the yellow Buick.

Once Doug was no longer in sight Dave stopped the car. He got out, and then helped Pam off the hood. He grabbed the handle of the back door. It opened without any problems. He helped her into the back seat.

"I guess I should have tried the back door," Pam said softly.

"I'm just glad to have you here in one piece," Dave said and he kissed her on the forehead. He pulled back and she grabbed his head and pulled it back to hers. She kissed him tenderly on his lips. Then she released him.

"Thank you for coming back for me. You saved me again. You're my hero," Pam said affectionately.

"You'd better lay down for few minutes. Get you strength back. I've got a feeling you're gonna need it. I don't believe we have seen the last of your friend."

"Yeah, let's get out of here," Pam said as she laid down on the seat. Dave ran around the car, got in and sped down the highway.

"You know we're going back toward the motel, don't you?" Pam said.

"What? Is this the same highway that the motel is on?

"Yeah. It's about twenty-five miles from here," Pam said. "But I remember crossing another highway about three or four miles up ahead. If you turn there, we can circle back and give Doug the slip."

"So, his name is Doug," Dave replied. "How well do you know this guy."

"I don't really know him at all. I just know what he told me when I met him."

"Well, what was that?" Dave asked.

"Okay, I'll tell you but just remember I told you that it was weird"

"Yeah, I'll remember," Dave replied.

"It all started yesterday. I had just gotten to work. I worked at this diner just outside of Greenville. I am or was a waitress. Anyway, about four thirty this guy, Doug, comes in and says he's looking for Pam Williamson. I told him that was me. He said that he had a message from my Aunt Mammie. My Aunt Mammie raised me after my mother died. Anyway, he said that she had told him to tell me that I was in danger and that I was to come with him. He would bring me to her and then she would answer all my questions. He said that I shouldn't say anything to anybody, but I should just leave immediately. So, I asked him who he was. That's when he told me his name, Doug Saunders. He said that my aunt read his fortune every week, and they had become good friends. She knew that she could trust him, and since he had to come to Greenville anyway, she asked him to come by and get me and bring me back with him.

I told him that I had to get my purse from the office. However, when I got in the office, I called my Aunt Mammie. The phone rang and I heard her answering machine say:

'Your fortune is yours to know, and it won't cost you a fortune, just an arm and a leg. This is Madame Mammie. What is...'

Then someone, I guess it was Doug, came up behind me, and put a handkerchief over my mouth. That's all I remember until I woke up last night in a dark small box. I didn't know it then, however, Doug had locked me in back of his truck in the tool bin. My hands were tied behind my back, my feet were tied together, and there was tape over my mouth. I could tell that I was in a truck cause the rain was pounding on the box I was in, and water was coming through the cracks. Every time the lightning would flash, I could see a little. I felt around with my fingers until I touched the end of a screw sticking out of the side of the tool chest. Eventually, I was able to work the rope back and forth against it until I could break it. Once my hands were free, I pushed up against the top of the box. It moved a little, but I could tell there was a pad lock on it. I felt the nuts holding the latch. I tried to unscrew them with my hand, but they were too tight. Then I tried with my teeth and I got the nuts started, and then screwed them off the rest of the way with my fingers.

"Is that the highway?" Dave interrupted seeing a road up ahead.

Pam sat up. "Yeah," she said looking at the sign. "SR 37," she said as he turned. "This will take us to Tennessee."

"I'm sorry. You were saying that you were locked in a tool bin, but you got the nuts off the latch."

"That's right. It took a long time, but I did it. Then I pushed the top up slowly until the latch fell down. I peeped out. I had to wait because the truck was moving too fast to jump out of. Finally, he slowed down to make a turn. That's when I pushed up the top and got out as quickly as I could, hoping he wouldn't notice. When I let the top back down, I could see him looking right at me. I was about to jump out of the truck when he hit the brakes. I lost my balance and fell against the tool chest. When I looked up, he was climbing onto the back of the truck. I jumped off on the other side. I started to slip in the mud when I reached up and grabbed the handle of the door. It came open and the motor was still running so I jumped in. By the time he got to the door on the passenger side, I had put the truck in gear. He reached for me as I pressed the gas. He almost fell out, but he hung on. He got one foot inside and swung himself to through the door. At that same, I opened my door and jumped. Doug managed to keep the truck on the road while he reached for the brake pedal with his foot. Then when he pressed the brakes the truck began to slide. It slid off the road into the mud. I hid in the woods and watch until he got the truck out of the mud. He came speeding up the hill till he got to the intersection. Then he started back the way he had come. When he was out of sight, I started down the hill. I figured he would only go so far before he turned around, and when he got back to the intersection, he would try the other way before finally coming the way I had gone. I must have been right, because I had been walking almost a half hour before you came along. At first, when I saw your lights, I thought it was him. I hide behind a tree. Then when I heard the car engine, I knew it wasn't him. So, I ran out to stop you. You know the rest." Pam looked questioningly at him. "Well," she said.

"Well is right," Dave said.

They sat in silence each waiting for the other to say something. Neither one could think of anything. Then after a long silence Pam spoke.

"I've got to go see about Auntie."

Chapter 6
Caught in the Crossfire

A few miles up ahead a Jefferson County Sheriff patrol car pulled out into the middle of the intersection of highway 56 and route 9. Inside Sheriff Davis and his deputy, Sam Sheppard sat in silence. The sheriff was loading bullets into an extra-long clip for an M-16 semi-automatic weapon. He pushed the clip into the rifle and placed it back between his legs. Then he reached for the radio.

"P. W., this is sheriff Davis. Come in," he said.

"P. W. here sheriff, go head chief."

"Me and Sam got a road-block up here at highway 65 and route 9. I want you to let me know as soon as anything come across the horn about this killer," the sheriff said.

"Ahhh, okay Chief."

"You haven't heard anything have you."

"Ah well, not about the killer," P. W. said "Well, what is it then."

"It's about that man you shot," P. W. said.

"What are you talking about. He was already dead. You know that," the sheriff screamed.

"Yeah Chief, that's what we told them."

"That's what you told who?" the sheriff said in a lower tone.

"The reporters from the Nashville Tribune. See, these two reporters came up here as soon as they found out that state assistance DA's father, Harry

Miller, had been killed. And when they saw the body, they started asking questions, and we had to tell them what happened."

"You should have told them that I would answer their questions when I got back," the sheriff snapped. "Who did they talk to; you and who else."

"It wasn't me, Chief. It was mostly Logan. He was talking the most. I didn't hardly say anything, Chief. That's the good Lord's truth," P. W. pleaded.

"Well what exactly did Logan say," the chief said with anger building up in his chest.

"He told them that the suspect was kneeling over Mr. Miller when they and you came out of the woods. They said that when you yelled for the suspect to put his hands up, he held Mr. Miller up and used him for a shield so they would not fire at him. But then you shot anyway. Your shot hit Mr. Miller in the middle of his back. Then you told them to fire, and they did. One of the reporters asked if they were sure that Mr. Miller was dead when you shot."

"What did he say then," the sheriff said nervously.

"He said they couldn't tell and that there was no way that you could have known either," P. W. said cautiously.

"Who said that, Logan?"

"Yeah, it was Logan," P. W. said softy.

The sheriff grabbed his M-16 and started beating the butt against the floor of the car.

"That dirty, stinking, low-down, snake. He's finished. When I get back there!"

"Ahhh, there's one more thing Chief," said P. W.

"What in the hell else," the Chief yelled.

"The county commissioners want to meet with you this afternoon at four o'clock."

The sheriff laid his head back on the seat and closed his eyes. A worried expression appeared on his face as he bit his lips together. Then slowly, that stern calculating expression appeared again. He opened his eyes, raised his head, and put the radio transmitter to his mouth.

"So, they want to have a meeting. Yeah, well if they call back, you tell them that I said, that I'm in pursuit of a dangerous criminal who has already killed two people, one being the state assistant DA's father. If I capture him, before four o'clock, then I will meet with them, if not, I won't. Tell them that I will let them know, as soon as possible, when I can meet with them. You got that?"

"Yeah, Chief."

"Over and out," the sheriff said as he pulled the barrel to his M-16 to his lips. "What about you, Sam. Are you going to back me up?"

"You can count on me Chief. I'd follow you to hell and back," Sam said reassuringly.

"We'll see, Sam. We'll see."

"There's a car coming, Chief," Sam said pointing ahead.

"Yeah, and it's moving pretty fast, too. Come on, let's check it out," the sheriff said opening the door. He left the M-16 on the seat. Sam got out also, but he took his shotgun with him.

"Hey, isn't that the car that was at the motel," Sam said.

"Yeah, that's Mr. and Mistress Parker's car all right. Looks like they had to take a little trip. Why don't you turn on the lights Sam?" The sheriff walked out into the road, folded his arms, and waited.

Dave had not noticed that he was driving so fast, but as soon as he saw the flashing light on the car ahead, he looked down at the speedometer. He was doing 75 mph. He slowed the car as quickly as he could.

"It's him," Dave said.

"Oh no! I don't think my luck could get any worse," Pam sighed.

"Let me do the talking," Dave said stopping the car about five feet from where the sheriff was standing.

"I spoke too soon, it's about to get a lot worse."

The sheriff walked around to Dave's door. "Well, Mr. Walker, fancy meeting you here. Especially, since I told you to stay put."

"I can explain everything, Sheriff Davis," Dave said confidently.

"That good Mr. Walker, because I'd like to hear that explanation. Pull over there and get out of the car. You too Miss, whatever your name is."

They got out of the car and walked over to the sheriff. He was holding open the back door of his patrol car. "Get in!" the sheriff ordered. Pam was about to get into the car. "Wait a minute. Let me see that purse," the sheriff said.

Pam gave him the purse and sat down. He looked through it quickly and thoroughly, then he and tossed it back to her. Then, he turned to Dave.

"Put your hands on the car and spread your legs," the sheriff said slowly and deliberately.

Dave obeyed without saying a word. The sheriff frisked him roughly and pushed him into the car. Then he closed the door, locking them in.

"You're doing pretty, good so far. If you keep it up, at this rate, we'll be on death row by noon tomorrow," Pam sneered.

"I haven't said anything yet," Dave replied.

"That's what I'm worried about. I think that you better tell him the truth. He looks very, angry to me. Don't get him any angrier, please."

"Okay, I'll tell him the truth. All right, are you satisfied?" Dave replied.

"Yes, thank you very much."

The sheriff got in the front seat and looked back at Dave. "Mr. Parker, I have had a real bad day, and to be perfectly honest with you, I've had it up to here," the sheriff said holding his hand underneath his chin. "Now, you haven't been completely honest with me, have you?"

Dave shook his head 'no.'

"But you're going to tell me everything you know, now, aren't you?"

"Yes sir," Dave said softly.

"I'm real glad about that cause you see, if I even think that you are lying to me about anything, I'm going to take you out into those woods and I'm literally, going to kick you so far up your butt that your breath will smell like shoe polish. Do we understand each other?"

"Yes, I understand," Dave said.

"Okay, start talking."

"Look Sheriff, I don't know what's going on here. I'm just a programmer. I'm on my way to a conference. Last night, I saw her standing on the side of the road in the middle of nowhere. It was raining cats and dogs, and there she was. So, I picked her up. How was I to know that some killer was after her. And he's still after her. No matter where we go, he always finds us."

"What are you talking about. Have you seen him since this morning?" the Sheriff said expectantly.

"He almost killed us twice since we left the hotel. I tell you he is still after us. He", Dave stopped in the middle of his sentence.

"He what?" the sheriff said.

"He is up there," Dave said pointing to a car stopped on the crest of the hill straight ahead.

The sheriff lifted the radio speaker to his mouth quickly. His excitement was almost uncontrollable. " P. W. come in. This is Chief Davis. Come in!" He waved his hand until he got Sam's attention, and beckoned for him to get in the car.

"P. W. here, Chief, go head," a voice mumbled through the speaker. P. W. was obviously eating.

"Are Logan and Thompson in position down at 56 and Cartersville Rd."

"Yeah Chief, they just called in," P. W. said smacking between each word.

"Well, tell them that I have spotted the yellow Buick on highway 56 near route 9. I'm going to run him back their way, so they better be ready. Tell them to open fire, if he acts in any way, like he's not going to stop."

"Roger Chief, over and out."

"Let's go," the Sheriff said looking at Sam. Sam turned on the siren and started toward the yellow Buick. "I almost hope he tries to get away."

Dave looked at Pam and said, "They're gonna get him now, and this thing will be all over." He breathed a sigh of relief.

Pam did not reply. She just looked at him as if she could not believe he was talking to her.

"The car is just sitting there. Maybe he's not in it," Sam said as they came closer.

"I don't see anybody, but that doesn't make any sense," the sheriff said his excitement turning into depression.

When the car came within 1000 feet of the yellow Chevy, a head popped up from below the dash and the yellow Buick surged forward.

"It's him, and he's coming this way," Sam yelled.

"Well don't let him get by. Ram him if you have to. We have got to stop him," the sheriff said as he rolled down the window. He pushed the M-16 out the window, leaned his head and shoulder out also. Then he raised the sights of the weapon to his eye.

Pam and Dave looked from the back seat. They both gripped the steel screen that locked them in. The cool wind chilled Dave 's face but his blood was racing hot in his veins.

"He's coming straight for us," Sam screamed.

The sheriff squeezed off five quick shots completely, annihilated the front windshield of the yellow Buick which was still increasing in speed. With only seconds to spare Sam turned the patrol car off the road. The yellow Buick came off the road after them. The sheriff had just gotten his head back inside the car when the two cars collided with a deafening crash. Everything in the car was thrown forward.

Dave and Pam had ducked behind the seat when they saw the crash coming, but they did not escape injury. The impact of the crash had knocked the front seat and Pam and Dave forward. The steel screen that had been above the back of the seat became loose on one side and fell, hitting Dave in the top of the head. There was a big bloody red spot in Dave's head, and he was not moving. Pam's left arm had gone down into the back of the seat and she could not pull it out.

"Dave, Dave," she cried as she shook him with her free hand. "Are you all right."

Dave opened his eyes and began to moan. His head was throbbing with pain. "Yeah, I think so," he said as he grabbed his head. When he felt the wetness, he quickly pulled his hand down to look at it. Just as he had suspected, his fingers were covered with blood. "Oh God, I don't want to die. I don't want to die, " he cried.

"Calm down, Dave. It doesn't look that bad. What about the sheriff and his deputy?" Pam said grimacing in pain.

When Dave raised up, his pain disappeared and was replaced with shock. The sheriff's head had gone through the windshield and it hung there like a bloody Jack that had sprung from its box. Sam, his deputy, was draped over the steering wheel which was partially imbedded in his chest.

"They're dead," he said softly. He was looking at her, but he could still see the sheriff and his deputy.

"Dave, help me. My arm is stuck," Pam whimpered.

"Your arm," Dave said slowly, "is stuck." Then he looked down and saw that her arm had gone into the seat. He began to tear away the cloth on the seat around her arm. When the cloth was pulled back, they could see that her arm was caught between two springs. Dave pulled the springs apart and she pulled her arm free.

"Oh man, that feels so much better. Thanks," she said with a breath of relief.

"Think nothing of it. It was the least I could do." They gave each other a fake smile.

"You sure can pick the weirdest times to be silly," she smirked.

"Well, you just need to be understanding. See, I've never gone through any times like these before."

"What was that?" Pam said.

Dave listened but he could not hear anything.

"There it is again," Pam said raising up to look ahead at the other car.

Suddenly there was a loud cracking sound. It was the sound of the car door of the yellow Buick being kicked open. Pam and Dave both looked in disbelief as an all too familiar figure emerged from the car.

He staggered forward and stopped when he saw them in the back seat of the sheriff's patrol car. There was a gash over his left eye which was partially closed. Blood flowed slowly from the gash down the side of his face. He appeared dazed. He took another shaky step forward, lost his balance, and collapsed beside the yellow Buick. When he fell, they could no longer see him.

"Oh God, I can't believe this," Dave moaned. "We're trapped."

"Why don't you stop whining and see if you can kick that window out," Pam scolded.

"Okay, yeah that a good idea," Dave said slid toward the window. He raised his foot and was about to kick the window when Doug's face popped up on the other side of the glass. His face was twisted and deformed, yet there was a look of satisfaction on his face as he opened the door. Dave kicked at him as he stuck his head in the door. Doug quickly grabbed Dave's leg and began to pull him out of the car. Dave's back hit hard against the ground and immediately Doug went for his throat.

"Now you and your witch are going to die," Doug growled.

Pam got her purse from the floor. She took from it a cigarette lighter and a can of hair spray. Doug had gotten his hands around Dave's neck when Pam began to spray Doug's hair. He looked up and the spray hit him in the face. Then before he could make a move, she flicked on the lighter. The hair spray ignited instantly shooting a two-foot flame into Doug's face. His hair became a torch. He moved back away from the car. Pam followed. He was trying to put out the fire on his head and face. She began to ignite his pants, and then his back. Soon his whole body became a ball of fire. He screamed as he ran off into the woods. Dave was on his feet looking, as the human torch disappeared into the trees.

"Come on let's get out of here," Dave said.

"I'm with you. Go!" Pam said. They began to jog back down the hill toward Dave's car. It was almost a mile away and they were very tired when they reached the car. "Give me the keys," Pam said. "I know where we can go. I'll drive."

He did not ask any questions. He gave her the keys, and after pulling up and out on the door, he got in on the passenger side. He was breathing very heavily. As the car pulled off Dave kept looking back expecting to see Doug come running out of the woods, but he never did.

Dave did not even want to think. He just wanted to clear his head of everything, but he couldn't. The more he tried not to think, the more he thought. He was in big trouble now. The police were after him and he was on the run. He knew that it was just a matter of time before they tracked him down. They always caught the crooks in the movies, and they would get him. Then it would be jail. He was getting very anxious and nervous.

"What are we doing? Where are you going? We need to turn ourselves in now, before it's too late," Dave pleaded.

"Look, we haven't done anything. We haven't been charged with anything. True enough the Sheriff told us that he wanted us to stay at the motel so he could ask us some more questions, but he is dead now. So, his questioning days are over," Pam explained.

"Well it shouldn't matter to you if we go back then, should it?"

"I'm not going back," Pam shouted. "After I get to my Aunt's house, I'll get out, and you can do whatever you want to do."

A somewhat pleasing thought came into his mind. 'I'll ditch her the first chance I get. You think you're tough now baby, just you wait,' he thought as a smirk came on his lips. She looked over at him suspiciously. He laid his head back and closed his eyes. He would have to wait for just the right moment.

Chapter 7
Just One Drink

The paramedics were loading Sheriff Davis' body into the ambulance.

"Wait just a minute there," P. W. said walking over to the corps. He pulled the sheriff's badge from the once proud chest of his former boss and walked away. The flashing lights from the tops of the two state patrol cars, the two patrol cars of the Jefferson County Sheriff's department, and two patrol cars from the Norris County Sheriff's department gave tribute, as the dead officers were taken away.

"We are searching the woods now, but we haven't found the driver of the yellow Buick yet," said the state patrolman to P. W. "He had to be hurt very badly, because there is a ton of blood on the steering wheel and on the seat.

"That's our killer. The sheriff had called in and said that he was in pursuit of this guy. He must have rammed him to stop him from getting away," P.W. said shaking his head.

"Looks like he rammed the sheriff. The sheriff's car was knocked back ten feet. The sheriff was killed instantly when the cars collided. Looks like the driver of the Buick came over to the sheriff's car, after the collision. There's some of his blood on the side of the back door," the patrolman said pointing to the back door. "I wonder what he was trying to do."

"Look, we got to find this guy," P. W. said impatiently. "He killed two people in my county, and we lost two good officers. This here is Norris County, and the Jefferson county line is about mile back down the road. Would you tell Sheriff Crawford that we will send officers to help search the woods tomorrow if you don't find his body today," P. W. said as he took off his deputy's badge and pinned on the Sheriff's badge.

"Okay, Sheriff, I'll let him know," the patrolman said.

"Oh yeah, there were two people, David Parker and his wife, Pam, who were at the motel where our perp killed the clerk. They are wanted for questioning. They are eyewitnesses, and they sneaked off before we could compete our interrogation. Would you put that on the wire, please?"

"Will do, Sheriff," the patrolman said and then he turned and walked to his car.

P.W. began polishing his new badge with his shirt sleeve. "Sheriff Knox. It has a real nice ring to it," P.W. said softly to himself as he turned to the other officers from Jefferson County. "Okay boys, lets wrap it up, and take Chief home."

Pam had been driving for almost two hours when Dave awoke. He looked around at trees and an occasional house. "Where are we?", Dave asked.

"Well, welcome back to the world, sleeping beauty. How was your nap?"

"It was very much needed, thank you. Now, if you don't mind, would you tell me where we are and where we're going," Dave said calmly.

"Yes sir. We are about twenty miles from the state line and in about fifteen more miles we will get to my aunt's house. So, in about fifty minutes I'll be out of your hair, and you can get on with your life," she said with a smile.

"I believe there is a law on the books against leaving the state to avoid prosecution."

"Don't worry about me. I can take care of myself," she said confidently.

"I'm sure you can, but I was thinking more about the other person in this car who would not like to get caught outside of the state."

"You won't. Trust me," she said.

'I know I won't, because I'm not crossing any state line', Dave thought. Just then Dave saw a sign which read, "Joe's Bar", he read aloud. Suddenly he needed a drink. He could taste a Brandy and coke flowing into his mouth.

He moved his tongue as if sloshing it around and then he swallowed his imaginary drink. "Hey, stop at that bar, I need a drink," he ordered.

"What? I don't have time. I've got to get to my aunt's house," she countered.

"I don't care. I want to stop and if you want to stay in this car you had better stop," he demanded.

"All right, I'll stop. You should have told me that you were an alcoholic. I'm going to park in the back. This car or what's left of it can be spotted twenty miles away," she said. She was upset but willing to pacify him at least for a few more minutes. She realized that he had gone through a lot and if she wasn't careful, he might flip out. "Okay, one drink, and then we leave," Pam said pulling the car up to the back of the building. They got out walking swiftly toward the door. "One drink, okay? Okay Dave?

"Okay, Okay, Okay," Dave said as he opened the door and held it open for her. "Come on please."

Once inside Dave grabbed Pam's arm and pulled her to the bar. "A brandy and coke back for me and whatever the lady wants. No, make that a triple," Dave said.

"What's it gonna be, honey", the bartender as he looked Pam over. He was a big man with a belly that hung over his belt. His hungry eyes seem to be looking straight through her clothes. Both Pam and Dave noticed how he was looking at her. "Water, on the rocks," Pam snapped, "and we're in a hurry."

"Keep your draws on there, Honey," he said as he put his hand down on top of her hand and held it. Pam jerked her hand away and moved back from the bar. The bartender gave her a frown. Pam frowned back.

"What about those drinks," Dave said interrupting the mood.

"You'll get your drinks, bub," the bartender snarled as he poured the drinks and placed them on the bar.

"Enjoy you drink, little tits," the bartender said to Pam with a smile as he looked at her small breast through her blouse.

"Thanks, fat boy," Pam said as she turned and walked to a table in the corner of the room. Dave followed nervously. After they had both sat down Dave began to drink the brandy. Pam was still looking at the bartender with hate in her eyes. "That butt hole", she said, "I ought to."

"Oh man, I needed that drink," Dave sighed as he sat the glass down, half empty. It heated up his insides as it found its way to his stomach, and then it exploded into a ball of fire. He hurriedly drank half of his coke chaser in big gulps. He looked at Pam. She was still looking at the bartender. 'Maybe I should leave her here,' Dave thought, 'surely someone would help her.' "Hey," he said loudly to get her attention, "forget about that bartender. Don't we have enough to worry about. People are trying to kill us, the police are after us, and now you want to add a hick bartender to our list of enemies just because he said your tits were small." He gave her a pathetic look. "Anyway, the more I think about it, the more I realize that we need to turn ourselves in. Policemen have been killed, so you know they are going to be after us. No, we can't go any further. We can't cross the state line. I've decided and that's that," Dave said firmly folding his arm.

"If you want to turn yourself in, that's fine. Be my quest, but just let me go to my aunt's house first," Pam said tightening her gripe on his car keys.

Just at that moment three big men walked in the door. They wore blue jeans and work boots. "Set tum up, Joe," the first man bellowed. "The usual," he said as he stopped a few feet away from the bar. He put one hand on his hip and wiped other hand slowly down over his face, stopping on his bearded chin. He was looking at Pam and Dave who had stopped their conversation and were looking back at him. Pam and Dave looked backed at each other when they noticed his stare. The other two men came up to him one on each side. They too were looking at Pam and Dave. Then they looked at an old drunk who was almost passed out at the end of the bar.

"Well Joe, I see we have visitors," the first man said as they all turned back to the bar. Joe had already poured up three shots of whiskey and had them lined up on the bar.

"Smart-ass city folks, Sonny", Joe whispered, "especially that little gal. She's a sassy little bitch."

"Hey Butch, Harv, you heard that, didn't you? We need to show them city slickers that they can't come up here harassing us hill folks." Sonny picked up one of the shots of whiskey, turned it up, and drank it in one swallow. Butch and Harv followed their leader's example, then they all walked toward Pam and Dave, who were talking.

"Look, my Aunt could be in danger, and I'm going whether you," Pam stopped talking suddenly as the three men gathered around their table.

"Howdy folks," Sonny said with a big smile. "This here is Harv and this is Butch, and I'm Sonny. What brings you folks up here to our little town."

"We're just passing through. We saw the sign, so we stopped to have a drink," Dave said cautiously.

"What's your name, Honey," Sonny said looking Pam over. "You know, you could use a little fattening up, but you show is a looker." The three all began to smile.

"If you don't mind," Pam interrupted, "we were having an important and private conversation. So, if you boys would just run along and play somewhere else, it certainly would be appreciated." Pam gave them a quick smile and waited for them to leave. They didn't leave. Each of their smiles turned into frowns.

"I see I'm gonna have to teach you some manners," Sonny said ominously. "Your mouth is a just a little too big for your own good, Baby Cakes."

Dave was getting very nervous. He felt a sudden urge to urinate. The men pulled up three chairs and sat down.

"She was just kidding, fellows. She didn't mean any harm. It's just that we had some important business to discuss," Dave pleaded.

"Important business! You came to a bar to discuss important business," Sonny shouted. "Well maybe I'd like a little of that business myself." Sonny was smiling again as he looked at Pam's legs. Pam showed no fear.

"Let's go Pam," Dave said as he started to get up.

"Sit down, boy!" Sonny snapped as he swung his fist around hitting Dave in the chest and knocking him back down into his seat. "You ain't going nowhere. Here, have some coke." Sonny picked up Dave's coke and threw it into his face. Dave sat there petrified with fear blinking the coke from his eyes.

Just at that moment while they were all waiting to see Dave's reaction, Pam grabbed her glass, swung it around as hard as she could against the side of Sonny's forehead. The glass broke and the jagged edge left a deep cut from the side of his forehead down to his ear. Blood immediately began to run down the side of his face. Everyone jumped to their feet except Dave. He was still sitting there blinking the coke from his eyes. Sonny grabbed the side of his head and then looked at all the blood on his hand. He was shocked as he looked at Pam. She was coming toward him with the jagged broken glass. He reached into his back pocket and pulled out a switchblade. When it popped open, Butch and Harv answered by pulling their switchblades. Sonny tried to drive to knife into Pam's stomach, but Pam's moves were as quick as a cat. She jumped to the side avoiding the knife and at the same time sticking the sharp edge of the glass into Sonny's arm. He cried out as he dropped the knife, turned, and ran into the men's room.

"Look out, Pam," Dave shouted as Butch moved up behind her. Pam turned quickly to face Butch. Harv now turned his attention toward Dave. He was about to stab Dave with his knife, but Dave ducked under the table and went across the floor behind Butch as he ran toward to door. Butch hearing Dave as he went behind him, looked back. That was a mistake. Pam dropped to one knee as she lunged forward, driving her weapon into Butch's genitals. Butch dropped his knife, fell to floor screaming in fear and pain. Dave was already at the door.

"Dave, here catch," Pam yelled as she tossed the keys across the room. The key sailed pass the bar hit the floor and slid over to Dave. He stopped them with his foot. "Get the car and bring it around." Then Pam looked at Harv who was still standing by the table. He looked at Sonny who was peeping out of the men's room. Then he looked at Butch who was still lying on the floor moaning. Finally, he looked back at Pam and began to back away. Pam walked quickly to the door. The bartender was standing behind the bar like a statue. Pam walked past him, the glass still in her hand.

"Here, fat boy," she said as she threw the glass at him. He dived to the floor as it sailed passed his head crashing into a pyramid of drinking glasses. The glasses fell from the counter to the floor breaking into a thousand pieces.

When Pam ran out of the door Dave was just pulling the car around. She jumped in and away they went leaving a cloud of dust in the parking area in front of the bar. It would have been difficult for anyone to read the tag number through all the dust, however, nobody in the bar even thought about it. Harv was helping Butch. Sonny was trying to wrap his wounds. Joe the bartender was trying to get all the glass out of his hair, and the drunk had missed the whole thing.

Chapter 8
A Resting Place

Dave sped down the highway, while regularly, looking up in the rearview mirror to see if they were being followed. His heart was still beating like the peddle of a base drum. His hands were still shaking, and his breathing was very rapid. He looked over at Pam who looked as though she was still angry at that bartender. 'This woman is dangerous', he thought. At that moment, the thought of going to her aunt's house was very appealing.

"How long till we get to your aunt's house," Dave said softly.

A little smile appeared on Pam's face. " Thirty minutes,' she said looking at him out of the corner of her eyes. They passed a sign which read 'Tennessee State Line 5 miles'.

"We'd better go the back way. They might have a roadblock at the state line," Pam said. "Turn right at the next road."

Dave saw a gravel road ahead. "Right here?" he asked.

"Yeah. It takes a little longer this way. I'll tell you how to get there," she said.

Dave followed her instructions. Before long Dave saw a small wood frame house with neatly trimmed hedges on both sides of the front door. There was a sign in front of the house. On the sign was a picture of a hand, and the words, "Fortunes Read."

"Pull in here," Pam said

"I hope we aren't stopping here so you can get your fortune read", Dave said as he pulled into the driveway.

"No. This is my aunt's house," she said smiling. "There's aunt Mammie at the door. Come on."

Dave's mouth dropped open. Aunt Mammie was a black woman. She was medium height with a firm and shapely figure. She had big brown penetrating eyes. Dave watched as Pam ran up to her. They hugged for a long time. Then Dave looked at the sign again.

"A black fortune teller," he said to himself as he got out, " what next?" he whispered.

"Pam honey, I could hardly wait for you to get here. My crystal has been hot as fire, I've been rubbing it so much," Mammie said laughing. "And how are you, honey," Mammie said to Dave as he walked up. "Won't you come in."

"Thank you," Dave said as he followed Pam past the strange woman who was holding the screen door open for them.

"He's a nice one," she said to Pam. "A little thin but nice."

"Be good, Auntie," Pam said.

"Oh, I'm so sorry," Mammie said with a smirk. Turning to Dave she said, "Please, make yourself at home Mr.?"

"This is Dave Parker, Auntie. Dave, this is my Aunt Mammie," Pam said with a big smile as she put her arm around Mammie.

'Yeah right, I'm supposed to believe that this is your aunt,' Dave thought. "Glad to meet you Miss Mammie," he said trying to appear genuine.

"Pam, there is so much to tell you and there is so little time, I just don't know where to start," said Mammie.

"Yeah, I have a lot to tell you, too, but what do you mean, there's so little time?" Pam asked. "I was planning to stay with you for a while. The police may be looking for me. I didn't do anything, but I want to stay out of sight for a while until this thing blows over."

"Police? Is he involved in this, too?" Mammie asked looking at Dave.

Dave wanted to speak up for himself, but he couldn't think of anything to say.

"No matter, you can tell me about it later," Mammie said. "Anyway, you know that anything I have is yours. You can stay here, just as long as you like. But come on in here, and I'll show you why I don't have much time."

Mammie led them into a dimly lit room. In the center of the room there was a table with chairs all around it. In the middle of the table was a crystal ball sitting in a black wooden holder. A lamp hanging down from a chain directed its light directly down on the table and the crystal ball.

'This is more like what I was expecting,' Dave thought. 'She is either a crackpot or a flimflam artist.'

"I think that my time has come. I can see death in my palm," she said holding her hand down on the table where Pam could see. Then she rubbed the crystal. "And look I can't see anything in the crystal past this winter," she said as she rubbed the crystal. It became as a black ball as if it had been dropped into a bucket of black paint. Although Dave saw the ball change from clear to black. He believed it was a trick of some kind. He had heard enough, and he could not hold back his words.

"Now really, you don't believe that palm reading and crystal ball crap, do you?" Dave scolded. Pam and Mammie looked at each other and then back at Dave as if his question was totally ridiculous. Dave shook his head. "You've told those lies to so many fools that you have begun to believe them yourself." Dave did not have any respect for anyone who would take advantage of someone's ignorance and superstitions.

"I was talking to Pam, so butt out," Mammie said forcefully. She then turned back to Pam and said, "he's little, but he sure does have a big mouth." They both giggled.

"Are you sure about this?" Pam said.

"You never can be sure about the future. In fact, I have never been able to see what a person is going to do in the future. However, there have been times, when people ask me if their sick relative is going to recover. In each of those cases, I rub the crystal and think of the person a week or less in the future. If the crystal turns black like it did then, the person does not recover. They die." Mammie said.

"I'm so sorry Auntie," Pam said hugging her aunt tenderly. "How much time do you think you have."

"A couple of days, a couple of weeks, maybe even a couple of minutes, I don't know. But don't worry. I made my own choices, and I lived my life the way I wanted to. So, we just need to enjoy each-others company while we can."

"Sure," Pam said. "Anyway, there may be some other explanation. There's a lot you don't know about that crystal ball, Auntie."

"Now tell me, what's all this about the police," said Mammie.

"This guy came to my job and told me that you were in danger. He said that you told him to bring me back up here. When I tried to call you, he knocked me out an put me in his truck toolbox. I was able to get out and get away. Then I met Dave. I thought I was safe, but he kept following us. He tried to kill us three times. It doesn't make any sense. I have got to find out why he's after me? Who is he?"

"Sit down and put your hands on the crystal," Mammie said. Pam and Mammie sat down. "You can sit too, Mr. Know-it-all," Mammie said to Dave. He obeyed. "Now think of the man who was after you," she said to Pam. "Okay, now remove your hands from the ball."

They both looked into the glass globe. Dave pretended to ignore them and the ball. Suddenly the ball began to glow, and images began to appear and disappear. Dave knew that she was using a trick with the lights. He believed that there was something underneath the table that was generating the images. He had a burning desire to expose this fake once and for all.

"Crystal, wise crystal show us the man," Pam chanted.

That was the last straw for Dave. "Cut the crap!" Dave shouted as he jumped to his feet. "I don't have time for this, I've got to go home, to my wife! This ain't nothing but a piece of glass," Dave said as he picked up the crystal ball and held it out in front of him. The room went dark as the crystal ball began to glow in his hand.

"Don't worry about rushing home, honey. As you can see, your wife is kinda busy," Mammie said pointing to the crystal in his hand.

Dave looked into the crystal and became paralyzed by what he saw. There in the crystal was his wife Carol in the bed with another man. Dave could not see the man's face, but he knew that he had seen the man's head before. 'Who is it?' Dave thought as he stared at him hoping that he would turn around. Tears began to form in Dave's eyes as they changed positions. Dave looked over at Pam with a stunned and pitiful look on his face. Pam looked down at the floor.

"I'm going to pull the car around to the back of the house, Auntie," Pam said sadly as she walked out of the room.

"Pam!" Mammie called and followed her out.

Dave continued to stare at the ball. They were in their third position now. Carol was almost at the point of climax. Their pace quickened. Then her orgasm began. Then his orgasm began. He raised his back in ecstatic pleasure. Dave could now see his face. It was the insurance agent.

"Charles Norris, you son of a bitch," Dave said aloud as Mammie walked back into the room. Dave put the crystal back down in its stand.

"Do you still think it's a bunch of crap?" Mammie asked with raised eyebrows. Dave did not respond to her question.

"Is that something that has already happened or is it something that is going to happen," Dave asked pitifully.

"Neither," Mammie replied fascinated by Carol's passion. "She is gettin' down, isn't she?"

"What do you mean neither," Dave asked impatiently.

"Oh, I mean it's happening right now, honey," she said still looking intensely at the crystal.

Dave took the black cloth that was lying on the table, and covered up the crystal. The room returned as it had been when they first came in. Dave sat down tired, hurt, and depressed. Then, Pam walked into the room.

"You miss it Pam honey. His wife was 'sho nuff' getting down," Mammie said.

"You okay, Dave," Pam whispered putting her hand on his shoulder.

"Yeah," he whispered.

"Here are your keys," Pam said handing him his car keys.

Dave sat in his seat like a zombie, looking at the black cloth which covered the crystal.

"Auntie, why is this guy trying to kill me?" Pam said.

"Well, as we were trying to find out before we were so rudely interrupted," Mammie said as she removed the black cloth from the crystal ball. There in the crystal were Carol and Chuck having intercourse again. "They're at it again," Mammie said in surprise. "Don't they ever get tired?"

"Stop it, stop it!" Dave screamed.

"Okay honey," Mammie whispered sympathetically, "but I'm not doing it. You are. Just Stop thinking about her." Mammie reached over and gave Dave's ear a hard pull.

"Ouch," he yelled as the crystal went clear again.

"Okay, Pam rub the crystal and think about," Mammie stopped. She suddenly got a deathly cold chill that shook her entire body and left her shocked with fear.

Pam noticed her shake and she also became afraid. "Are you all right, Auntie," Pam said.

"Yes, it was just a chill. I have been having them more and more often. It is real scary."

"Maybe you should go see a doctor," Pam suggested.

"Please! I'm not crazy," Mammie replied. "Rub the ball." Pam began to rub the ball.

"Pam," Mammie whisper, "if something happens to me, go down to Tipton and notify L. W. Zackery.

"Who is he?" "He is the pastor of the Church of Christ in Tipton," Mammie whispered.

"A preacher?" Pam said loudly.

"If I had wanted everybody to know, I would have put an article in the paper."

"Sorry Auntie. If that's what you want, that's what I'll do."

"Thank you, Pam. That makes me feel better."

"Look!" Pam shouted.

There before them within the ball was Doug. The crystal seemed to expand into a huge globe of light. There was a rainbow of light beams within the globe. Suddenly the beams disappeared, the room went dark, and there on the table in miniature was Doug, standing in the woods. He was standing in the shadow of someone or something.

A voice whispered softly, "You failed."

"I'll get them. They haven't gotten away yet," Doug explained. The shadow moved down reviling Doug's face. He was burned on most of his head. The eyelid of his right eye had been burned off and the other eye was a swollen with third degree burns. He could barely see. Most of his shirt had been burned and his right hand which stretched out before him was as black as old coals. A woman's hand with nails like those of a cat appeared in front of him.

"The price for failure is death," the voice said.

Doug turned to run, but immediately his body was hurled forward as if by a strong wind. He went flying through the trees until his arms hit a limb that sent him into a spin. He hit another limb and his neck was broken. Finally, his body landed flatly against a large tree and fell to the ground. Just as suddenly as before, the scene disappeared, the room returned to normal, and the crystal in the middle of the table was a black ball. For five seconds, they all looked at the ball expecting to see something else. Then Pam and Dave looked at Mammie.

"That 'thang' never did nothing like that before," Mammie said looking just as surprised as they were.

"I guess we don't have to worry about Doug anymore," Pam said almost sympathetically.

There was silence as everyone looked back at the crystal.

"Is anybody hungry besides me. I tell you, I'm starving. Come on, let's see what we've got to eat in here," Mammie said as she started walking toward the kitchen. "We'll get back to the crystal later." Mammie covered the crystal with the black cloth.

No one objected. Pam and Dave followed her quietly. While Pam and Dave seated themselves at the dining room table, Mammie walked into the kitchen. She turned on the radio and the music of Michael Jackson came beating out of the speakers. Mammie occasionally danced and sang along.

"Billy Jean's not my love," she sang as she put the food on the plates. She danced over to the table with a plate in both hands. She put a plate on the table in front of both Pam and Dave, did spin and then danced back over to the stove.

"I still got my old moves, Honey. In fact, I just might be getting a little better," Mammie said with a laugh.

The music came to an abrupt stop. " And now, here's a new bulletin. The bodies of two Jefferson county sheriff officers were found on Route 9. They were apparently killed in a head on collision with another vehicle. The state patrol is looking for the driver of the other vehicle. He is believed to be seriously injured. Anyone having any information concerning the whereabouts of this person should call the state patrol office immediately. Now, here is more of the music you love the most."

Mammie turned the radio off, got her plate, and returned to the table. They ate with very, little conversation. When Dave had finished, he pushed his chair back from the table, slid down in his chair.

"That was great, ma'am," Dave said rubbing his stomach.

"All my friends call me Mammie," she said with a smile.

"Okay Miss Mammie. I didn't even know how hungry I was until I started eating," Dave said drowsily.

"Well, you have been through a lot," Mammie said in a soothing voice.

"And I am so tired, so tired," he said slowly.

"I have a bed ready for you," she said.

Mammie and Pam helped Dave into a bedroom, and they laid him down gently. Pam took off his shoes and Mammie covered him with a blanket.

"Auntie, did you put something in his tea?" Pam asked.

"Yeah, but it was just a little nectar," Mammie laughed. "He should be out for the rest of the night. Come on? We need to get back and see what the crystal can tell us. There is something mighty scary about that last scene we saw. We could be in some serious trouble."

A few minutes later they were seated at the table in front of the crystal ball.

"I'm ready when you are," Mammie whispered.

Pam took a deep breath and blew it out slowly. "Okay, here goes nothing," Pam replied as she began to rub the crystal. "I'll concentrate on that hand we saw last time."

"Okay crystal do your stuff," Mammie said excitedly.

"Show us Crystal, why are these things are happening. Show us why," Pam whispered.

Instantly the room went was black. Pam and Mammie sat silent and motionless until the face of a woman appeared in the crystal. They could not see the face clearly. There was a dark hood over her head casting a shadow over most of the face. Gradually, the scene expanded as the crystal changed into a large mist. The woman was lying in bed and there were three figures standing around the bed.

"You must find her and kill her," the woman said in a sinister voice. "She is draining my power and my strength. Doug failed. He had her and he let her get away. Consequently, he is no longer with us. I will not accept failure." Her voice became louder. "Do you hear me!" she screamed. They all nodded in silence.

Each person standing around the bed had on a black robe with a hood that covered most of their face. Pam was trying to see their faces, but she couldn't.

"Go get that bottle on the table in pantry, Jake," she said with a cough. The one she had called Jake, turned and Pam could see his face for a moment. As he walked into the next room, he passed shelves filled with jars, boxes, and animal cages. There were birds, rats, snakes, and other animals that Pam could not see clearly. Jake went to the table in the middle of the room and picked up a bottle containing a dark thick liquid. He took it back to the woman lying in the bed. She took it from him and drank about a third of it. Her eyes began to glow from within the dark shadow of the hood. Then her whole body began to shake as her eyes rolled to the back of her head. After several seconds, the shaking stopped. When her eyes returned to the front, she got up quickly, walked into the next room, took a cage off the shelf, and sat it on the table. Inside the cage, a large copperhead was coiled and ready to strike. She opened the top of the cage and quickly shot her hand down into the cage, pinning the snake's head down against the bottom of the cage. Its tail immediately coiled around her arm as she pulled it out of the cage. The fangs of the snake were long and wet with venom. She grabbed a cloth covered beaker and placed it near the snake's fangs. It aggressively bit into the cloth sending its venom into the jar. She dropped the snake back over into the cage and closed the top.

"Jake, prepare yourself for a trip," she commanded. "Tomorrow, I want you to leave and don't come back without that book." She turned the beaker up to her lips and drank the venom. "Kill anybody that gets in your." Suddenly she stopped. She placed her fingers against her forehead and began to concentrate. Everything around her went black and her hooded head grew larger and larger. Then she slowly began to pull her hand away from her away from her face.

Mammie hurriedly covered the crystal with the black cloth, and the lights in the room came back on, and everything was back to normal in the crystal room at Mammie's house.

"What do you make of that," Pam said as they got up to leave the room.

"You're in serious trouble." Mammie said. "Those were witches and it sounded like they tried to kill you once and they are going to try again.

"Why! Why me?" Pam pleaded.

"Do you have that book that they were talking about?

"No! " Pam snapped. "Not unless they are talking about," Pam hesitated, "my diary. But, what would they want with that?"

"I don't know," Mammie said, "but we can talk about it in the morning. I need some rest, honey. This is a bit much for the old girl to take in one sitting." Mammie walked into her room and closed the door without looking back.

"Good night," Pam said and she went to her room.

CHAPTER 9
THE CRYSTAL

The portion that Mamie had put in Dave's tea only made him have nightmares. He kept seeing his wife Carol in bed with the insurance man. Dave awoke with a start as he sat up in bed. The light of the moon was enough for him to see around the room. He saw a candle and a box of matches on the dresser. He got up slipped on his shoes, got the matches, and walked to the door. Carefully he opened it trying not to make a sound. He crept down the hall. He stopped in front of the door of the crystal ball room. He slowly opened the door, walked in, and closed it behind him. He did not turn on the light, so he was in total darkness. He took a match out of the box and lit it. The shimmering light pointed the way to the table. He sat down in the chair just before he had to blow out the flame. Again, he was in total darkness, but he remembered where the ball was. He reached out, removed the black cloth, and began to rub it. Instantly, a miniature room appeared on the table. It was Dave's bedroom.

Carol and Chuck were lying in the bed. The room was dark, but Dave could tell that Carol was sleeping in the insurance man's arms. Dave jumped when the phone beside his bed in the image began to ring. Carol and her lover awoke. Carol turned on the lamp by the phone. They looked at each other.

"Don't make a sound Chuckie, okay?" she said looking at him suspiciously.

"Sure, I'll be as quiet as a church mouse," he said with a little smirk.

She picked up the phone and intentionally dropped it on the nightstand. She finally got it to her ear and said in a half sleep voice, "Hello."

"Hello, Carol? Is this Carol?" a man's voice said.

"Yes. Who is this?" she said surprised that it wasn't Dave.

"This is Thomas Moore. Sorry to disturb you at this hour but I was kinda worried. Tell me, is Dave there by any chance," he said.

"No, he left Sunday night, Thomas. He isn't there with you," Carol said in a worried voice.

"No, and J. T., I mean Mr. Monroe is really upset. Dave was supposed to make a presentation this afternoon and he never showed up. I was just calling to see if something had happened."

"I don't know what could have happened. It was raining badly when he left. I hope he didn't have an accident," Carol said. She had begun to worry.

"Well, I didn't mean to get you upset. I'm sure he'll show up. He probably just had some car trouble. You know how those small-town service stations are. I'm sure you'll hear from him soon. When you do, tell him to come up with a good excuse or he might not have a job," Thomas warned.

"Okay Thomas, and thank you for calling," Carol said and hung up the phone.

Suddenly the image began to expand. It engulfed the entire table, and Carol and Chuck became almost life-size.

"What's the matter," Chuck said sitting up in the bed. He was a handsome man with big muscles. Dave's small chest and arms were no comparison. Dave suddenly felt very inferior as he looked at Chuck's body. Carol, still looking at the phone said, "You'd better leave. Something may have happened to Dave. He may even be on his way back home."

"I thought he was going to be gone for a week," Chuck said angrily.

"Well, he's not at the convention. He never got there." Her voice began to shake as tears filled her eyes. "And I'm worried about him," she said turning toward Chuck. "So, you have got to leave, right now!" she demanded.

"Wait a minute, baby," Chuck said as he slid over to her and put his arms around her. "He'll call."

"No," she screamed pushing his arms away and jumping up from the bed. "Don't touch me, just leave!" she screamed. She walked over to a chair where his clothes were. She picked up his pants and threw them in his face.

"What in hell is wrong with you," he said as she picked up his shoes. She threw one that hit him in the chest as he tried to protect his head. Then she threw the other one. This on hit his face and blood began to come from his lip.

"You filthy tramp!" he said as he looked at the blood on his hand that he had wiped from his mouth. He looked at her with anger in his eyes. Fear shook her heart as she watched him charge at her. She had no time to run. His strong hands clamped around her arms. "This ain't your henpecked husband. You don't treat me any kind of way. Not Chuck," he growled as he swung her into the air and down on the bed. Before she could react, he was sitting on top of her. His legs had her arms pinned down. "So, you want to get violent, do you?" he said raising his hand to slap her.

"No! Please, don't," she pleaded as his hand came down across her face. Carol screamed.

Dave became filled with rage. He was so angry, the tears that formed in his eyes turned to steam before they could turn into drops. "I'll kill you," Dave screamed, forgetting where he was. Dave grabbed a pair of sharp scissors off a nearby shelf and dived forward at Chuck. As he dove, his feet came out of his unlaced shoes. As Dave's hand went closer to Chuck's neck and the scissors went closer Chuck's chest, his hands went into the image. His body followed. The room went dark.

Mammie walked down the hall and turned the doorknob to the crystal room. She thought she had heard a scream. She opened the door and turned on the light. Everything looked normal. She turned off the light and was about to go out when she realized something was not right. She turned on the light and looked at the crystal. The black cloth was not on it. It was lying on the table beside the crystal. "Somebody has been in here," she whispered. "It had to be numb nuts," as she grabbed the black cloth. Her foot hit something. She looked down and saw Dave's shoes. "Numb nuts." As she began to cover the crystal, she froze. She began to blink her eyes. She dropped the cloth and began rubbing her eyes. Then she lowered her head closer to the crystal. "Lord have mercy on my soul," she yelled. "How did you get in my crystal ball."

Mammie covered up the ball with the black cloth, slowly, pulled it off again, and looked at the crystal, hoping that she would not see Dave. "No, no, no, no, no" she yelled, each 'no' louder than the one before. "Pam! Pamela!" she screamed. "Get out here, right now."

Ten seconds later, Pam opened the door and stuck her head inside, "What's wrong Auntie?"

"Your little boyfriend is in my crystal ball," she said forcing herself to speak softly.

"What?" she said as she leaned down toward the crystal. Her eyes and her mouth got wider the closer she got to the crystal. "Where is Dave?"

"He's inside the crystal," Mammie said unbelievingly.

Pam ran out of the room. She came back a minute later. "He's not in his room. Did he sneak out?

"No! He sneaked in. Don't you see. He's trying to get out with a pair of scissors no less," Mammie said closing her eyes.

Pam watched, as a miniature Dave pointlessly hit the scissors against the inside wall of the glass of the crystal. She watched as he became exhausted and slid to the round bottom of the ball.

"How do we get him out!" Pam became frantic.

"I don't know," Mammie said disgusted. "How did he get in there."

"Okay. Let me rub it. I'll think of him and maybe it will open up and he can come out," Pam reasoned. She closed her eyes, thought of Dave, opened her eyes, rubbed the crystal, and waited. Nothing happened to the crystal. However, inside the crystal Dave was throwing himself from side to side against the walls of the crystal. He finally, he put the scissors in his back pocket and collapsed on the round bottom.

"Auntie, do something!" Tears begin to run down Pam's face. Mammie stood there, trying to think of something. "Okay. If you won't do anything, I will," Pam said angrily as she stomped out the room.

"What are you going to do?"

Pam said nothing. She went to the kitchen, took a hammer from a drawer, and returned to the crystal room. When Mammie saw the hammer in Pam's hand, Mammie moved to block her path to the crystal.

"Don't do that. If you break the crystal, he could be lost forever."

"Move Auntie," Pam screamed as she swung her aunt out of her way with one arm. Mammie went crashing into the wall. Pam raised the hammer up and brought it down toward the crystal with all her might.

"No! Pam. Don't." Mammie watched as the hammer reached the crystal.

What Mammie expected to happen, didn't. The crystal did not explode into a thousand pieces. Instead, the crystal turned into a large image on the table. The hammer and Pam's arm went into the image. Then her shoulder and head went in. Her whole body was about the fall in when Mammie grabbed her around her waist with one arm and the doorknob with her hand and began to pull her back. Inside the image, Dave saws Pam's head and arms falling toward him. He grabbed her arms. When Mammie pulled Pam back out, Pam pulled Dave back out. Then, the crystal returned to its normal state. They all stayed where they were. They were all exhausted. Mammie still holding the doorknob and Pam tightly around her waist. Dave was on his knees on the floor, still holding Pam's arms tightly. Then the hammer which was still in Pam's hand dropped to the floor. They all moved at the same time. Mammie released Pam and the doorknob. Dave released Pam's arms. Pam turned toward Mammie and hugged her.

"I'm sorry, Auntie," Pam said. "Did I hurt you?"

"No, I'm alright," Mammie said turning her head from side to side. "My wall, however, may have my body print on it," she said looking at the wall. "You did it, honey. I don't know how, but you got him out."

"Carol!" Dave yelled, remembering the scene that had caused him to get trapped in the crystal. Dave jumped up knocking over the table. The crystal fell to the floor. He pushed past Pam and Mammie, and then went to Mammie's telephone.

"What's wrong with that boy. He acts like he may have a few screws loose," Mammie said setting the table back up.

"He didn't even say thank you," Pam said sitting the crystal back on the table.

When Dave got to the phone, he dialed his number. After four rings, Carol answered.

"Carol, are you all right," Dave asked.

"Dave? Of course, I'm all right. Why wouldn't I be?" she said calmly. "You sure did pick a strange time to call to see if I was all right."

"Oh, I'm sorry dear. I had a bad dream and I just wanted to check on you," he said confused. "Are you sure everything's all right?"

"Yes, everything's fine. Enjoy your trip and don't worry about me. Call me tomorrow. I'm too sleepy to talk now, bye." The phone clicked before Dave could respond. Dave hung up the phone. He turned around. Pam and Mamie were still standing in front of the crystal room door looking at him suspiciously.

"She was sleep, by herself," Dave explained even though they had not asked. "That crystal ball is a bunch of bull. I don't know how you do it, hypnosis or something, but I knew it was a trick," he argued but no one wanted to argue back.

"I'm going to bed, honey, like you need to do," Mamie said shaking her head. "And don't come sneaking out here no more, fooling with my crystal, and tearing up my house." Mamie handed him his shoes, turned, and walked toward her room. "You need to do something about that boy, Pam. He ought to be locked up somewhere. He ain't got no home training, and if that was a long-distance call, you gone pay me for that," Mammie's voice trailed off as she closed her door behind her.

"What's the big idea Dave," Pam snapped. "Nobody's asking you to believe anything. She can't help cause your wife is screwing around on you.

I ought to," Pam stopped, raised her hand, and pointed her little finger at Dave.

Dave's anger turned to shame. " I'm sorry," Dave said looking down at the floor. Pam lowered her hand.

"Not as sorry as you're going to be," Pam said as she turned and walked to her room. The door closed behind her.

Dave stood there for a few minutes. He was drained, and exhausted. His hand was shaking, as he reached into his pocket and pulled out his car keys. A frown appeared on his face as his eyes went from side to side scanning the room. He slowly walked to his room and closed the door. "I've got to get out of here," he said to himself.

CHAPTER 10
THE DISCOVERY

The next morning when Pam got up Mammie was already making biscuits.

"Hi ya honey," Mammie said. "Did you have a good night sleep."

"Pretty good," Pam said softly. "I had a lot of things on my mind."

"Your boyfriend, knuckle brains, is still sleeping, but that's good cause there is something that we need to talk about." Mammie looked at Pam with one eyebrow raised.

"Let me tell you something. You boyfriend is planning on cutting out the first chance he gets."

"Number one, he's not my boyfriend, and number two, I don't care what he does. He can go sky diving over Mount St. Helen during an eruption for all I care. I'd even pack the chute for him."

"Oh, really now," Mamie said squinting her eyes.

"I can't forgive him for talking to you like he did last night," Pam argued. "If I hadn't promised you, I would have zapped him right there on the spot."

"Now Pam, you know it wasn't as bad as all that. The boy didn't mean all that stuff. Anyway, you know how men are. They can screw around all over town and say it's okay, cause they are men, but soon as a woman does it, she's the worst whore that ever was. I mean they just go berserk." Mammie laughed. "He didn't mean no harm honey. You do like him, don't you?" Mammie said closing one eye and looking at her with the other.

"Don't you put the eye on me," Pam said holding up both hands in front of her face, blocking Mammie's stare. She lowered her hands only when

Mamie turned away. "Maybe I am being a little hard on him. He can be sweet at times." A little smile came on Pam's face.

"Sweet? You mean he's got a little sugar in his blood," Mammie said as she held out her hand and began to shake it.

"No!" Pam said assuredly but then a frown appeared on her face. "I don't think so."

"Just kidding honey," Mammie said. "But he is planning on ditching you. I picked up on one of his thoughts."

"Yeah, I know. He wants to turn himself in. He wants me to turn myself in, too. I told him to bring me here and then he could leave." Suddenly sadness fell over her like a shadow. "So, he can go anytime he wants, back to his wife or wherever. That's not my concern anymore." Pam's anger of the night before was beginning to return. "He didn't tell me he was married."

"You aren't in love, are you?"

"I guess not," Pam said.

"Well, I hope not.

Carol and Chuck laid in the bed both facing the ceiling. Neither said anything and both wondering what the other was thinking.

"Look," Chuck said coldly, "I'm sorry about slapping you. But I just lost my temper. I don't like being pushed around. If you want me to leave, ask me nice, and don't go throwing my clothes and my shoes in my face. You'll make me mad." There was a frown on his face as the words came out.

Carol cleared her throat, "Okay." This had been the first time, that she could remember, that she had ever been slapped. She was a little angry, a little hurt, and very scared. "You didn't have to hit me that hard." Her voice trembled and she hesitated as she tried to regain her composure. "I didn't mean to burst your lip. I never would have been able to hit your head if I had been aiming at it," she explained. They turned their heads toward each other.

"Friends?" Chuck said smiling.

"Friends," Carol said forcing a half smile.

"All that fighting has gotten me in the mood again," he said as he rolled over toward her. He put his arm across her and tried to pull her closer to him. She pushed his arm away saying, "I don't feel like it, Chuck."

"What!" he said loudly. Then a smile appeared on his face. "Well, don't worry about it, baby, I just might be able to make you change your mind, that is unless you still want me to leave."

She thought for a moment. "I guess you can stay as long as you behave yourself."

"Sure, I'll be the perfect gentleman," he said as he laid there. "Tell me, what kind of man is your husband in bed?"

"He's absent from the bed. I don't even like him touching me. He's not a real man. He doesn't have any animal in him like you," she said. "I have to tell him everything. He's more like my child than my husband. The only thing that he does good is signing his check and giving it to me." She hesitated, "And that's all he needs to do."

"You mean you don't have sex at all," Chuck looked surprised.

"Very seldom and then it only lasts a minute. I make him climax as quickly as possible when we do." Then the tone of her voice changed. "But he's okay otherwise. That's why I haven't left him. He has been very, nice to me. He paid for my last years in college and he help me pay for an apartment, too, before were married. My mother loves him. She probably should have married him. She said, 'Carol, you got yourself a real good man. You better marry this one. He's dependable.' So, I took her word for it. She was right. He is dependable. I haven't had to worry about anything," Carol said. She wondered if Chuck was half as dependable as Dave.

"Yeah, but do you love him?

Dave woke up around noon. He had a slight headache. He looked for his clothes but could not find them. He was sure that he had put them at the foot of the bed. He looked under the bed. He didn't see his clothes, but he did see something else. It was a pull ring to a door.

"I wonder what that's for," he said softly. He looked toward the head of the bed. His shoes were still there. "They took my clothes, to keep me here," he said to himself. He put on his shoes, and quietly pushed the bed across the room. Then he grabbed the pull ring and lifted the door in the floor. There was a ladder going down into the dark hole. Dave looked around the room and saw the matches were back on the dresser. He lit one and began to climb down the ladder in nothing but his shorts, his t-shirt, and his shoes. He had to light another match before the first one went out. He had gone down about ten feet when it happened. The rung he had just stepped on broke, and he fell into the darkness.

"Ahhhhhh," he screamed for a short moment. His scream came to a sudden end as he hit the muddy bottom of the pit. Fortunately, the pit was only about fifteen feet deep. He was not hurt although his bottom was sore from the landing. He felt around for the matches but couldn't find them. He felt something else. It seemed to be a box. He also felt something else. It was soft and round. Suddenly the soft and round thing shot away from his hand and went under his leg.

"Ahhh," he said as he jumped to his feet. He felt for the ladder, found it, and began to climb up. He climbed over the broken rung and out of the darkness. He was a mess. There was mud all over him and his shoes and his underwear. He closed the trap door and pulled the bed back over the door. Then he heard a voice at the door.

"Dave, are you awake?" There was a knock on the door.

"Just a minute," Dave said jumping into bed. "Okay."

Pam walked in with his clothes. They had been washed.

"Here are some clean clothes, a washcloth and a towel. You can get a shower, now. When you get out, breakfast will be ready," Pam said smiling. "Mamie went into town, so we have the place all to ourselves at least until three. Isn't that nice?" She laid the clothes down on the dresser. She had on a silk robe and he could see the outline of her bikini panties through it.

As she turned to face him, her thigh came through the split in the robe. She was so beautiful. Suddenly he began to desire her.

"I thought about what you said last night, and I decided to forgive you and let you make it up to me," she said as she walked over to the bed. She untied the belt of her robe and it fell open. "Did you really mean it when you said you can't resist me," she said as she pulled the robe off and let it drop at her feet.

'Holy Cow,' Dave thought as his eyes began to bulge out of his head. "What are you doing? Put that robe back on!"

"Why?" Pam said surprised. "Don't you want to make love to me?"

"No!" Dave snapped. "I told you, I'm a married man. I can't do that." He covered his head with the sheet.

Pam was embarrassed, hurt, and furious. She spread her arms away from her body and balled up her fists. She stared angrily at Dave. Then she stumped once on the floor. In an instant, her robe was back on to her body, and the whole house seemed to shake.

Dave felt the house shake, so he peeped from beneath the sheet at Pam. 'Her robe was back on,' he thought, 'How did she do that so quickly.' Pam gave him a very, angry stare, which gave Dave a cold chill. He quickly pulled the cover back over his head. Then Pam realized that her robe was back on, and she couldn't remember putting it back on. She looked back at Dave. Her anger was gone now. In fact, she almost wanted to laugh at how stupid she was and how stupid he looked hiding there under the covers.

"You biscuit eating basketball," Pam stopped in the middle of her sentence. She noticed a couple of muddy fingers holding the covers. She walked closer to the bed and noticed that Dave's feet had an unusual appearance under the covers. It appeared to her that he had shoes on.

Dave could hear her walking toward him. His eyes began to open wider and wider and his ears strained to hear her movements. He was tempted to raise his head from under the covers, but he was too scared.

Pam quickly grabbed the covers at the foot of the bed and pulled them up. She exposed his muddy shoes and legs, not to mention the sheets.

"This is unbelievable," she said disgustedly. "How in the world did you get all this mud on you?"

Dave threw back the covers and sat on the side of the bed looking straight ahead. Pam looking at all the mud on the sheets began to shake her head.

"What is wrong with you," Pam asked. "Where did all this mud come from. You've probably got mud in the crack of your."

"Shut up!" Dave snapped cutting her off. "you want to know where I got the mud from. I'll show you where it came from," Dave said pushing the bed over. There was the pull ring covered with mud. Pam looked at it and then back at Dave as he pulled open the door. There is something down there. It felt like a small chest. And there is probably a tunnel to that crystal ball room, too." Dave beckoned for Pam to move closer. "Why don't you just go on down there and see for yourself, Miss Smart butt."

"Okay," Pam said. "Let me get a flashlight."

She was only gone a few minutes before she returned with the flashlight in her hand. She had put on a pair of jeans and a tee shirt. Dave had already started down the ladder. His head was just above floor level as he waited for her. "I'll go down first. Give me the flashlight," Dave said.

"Here, hurry up. Auntie will be back soon. "

"Oh! I thought she was going to be gone all afternoon," Dave replied.

"Well, now I have other things to do before she gets back, like wash sheets," Pam sneered.

Dave went down. He knew that one of the rungs was broken so when he reached it, he stepped to the next one. When Dave reached the ground, he pointed the light up toward Pam. Pam started down immediately. When Pam was about to step on the broken rung, Dave moved the light away from the rung and moved away from the ladder anticipating her fall.

"Come on down slow poke. I thought you were in a hurry?" Dave said.

Pam's foot reached the broken rung and she shifted her weight to it. There was a crack and Pam fell. Her bottom hit the muddy floor with a thud.

"Wow," Pam moaned.

"You're not hurt are you," Dave asked sarcastically.

"No, I'm all right, I guess," Pam said.

"You wanted to know where I got all the mud from?" Dave pointed the flashlight beam on her. She was filthy. Dave held out his hand as if showing off a prize-winning hog. "Walla." There was total vindication on his face.

"Okay, okay," Pam said with a little smile on her face. "Where is the chest." Dave shined the light around the floor. "This must be an old well."

"No, it's not deep enough," Pam said. "This hole is only about the size of an outhouse hole."

"You mean this ain't mud," Dave sighed.

"Look!" Pam said. "There!" Pam said. The light was shining on a small chest half submerged in what Dave was still hoping was mud. "Come on, let's get it out of here."

Pam and Dave began to pull the chest out. Pam stopped and stood up as though she had heard something.

"What is it," Dave whispered looking up. "Is somebody coming? What did you hear?"

"I didn't hear anything. I felt something cold and piercing like the eyes of a cat," she murmured in a strange voice. "Come on, let's get out of here. Leave that stupid box." Pam began to climb out of the hole.

Dave pointed the flashlight at the chest. Excitement began to grow in him. He began to breathe more rapidly. He grabbed the latch, paused for a moment, and then pulled open the top of the chest. Inside was a book with one word written in big gold letters on the cover "Witchcraft." He laid the flashlight across the open chest and held the book in its light. He opened it and began to read the table of contents. He began to read aloud, "Spells, Portions, Roots, Transformations, Sight. What is this mess?"

"Hold the light," Pam yelled. She had reached the point where the rung was broken, and she couldn't see. Dave pointed the light to the ladder just ahead of her. "Come on, get out of there, now," she said as she climbed back onto the floor of Dave's room.

Dave heard footsteps as Pam walked out of the room. He looked up just in time to see it. The trap door was closing.

"Pam," he yelled. However, his yell was drowned out by the slam of the trap door. Then, he heard something. It was a voice, laughing. He spun around shining the beam of light all around the hole, but he saw nothing. There it was again, but this time it was louder. It was coming from up in the room. He found the ladder with the light and went to it quickly. He dropped the book into the chest and climbed the ladder as fast as he could. When he reached the top of the ladder, he tried to push open the door. It would not move. He began to beat on it with the flashlight. Then, as if he hadn't known something else was going to happen, something else happened. The light began to flicker as the flashlight began to fail. Dave turned his attention to the flashlight.

Pam was in the bathroom running water to get it hot for a shower when she decided to go back and check on Dave. She walked back to his room and the door was closed.

"You don't have to worry I won't bother you anymore. I can take a hint," she said through the door. She turned to walk away when she heard a knocking sound. She opened the door and looked in. The bed was back in place, the room looked normal, but where was Dave?

"Dave!" she called. There was no answer. Then she saw something that she could not believe. The bed began to raise up on one corner. Then she heard Dave's voice.

"Pam! Will you get this bed out of the way, please!"

Pam could only see Dave's nose and lips because he was only able to open the trap door a few inches because one of the legs of the bed was holding it down.

"Dave," Pam shouted as she walked toward him. "How did you manage to get yourself into this mess. On second thought, don't answer that. I don't even want to know. Sometimes, I swear, you can." Her sentence was cut off. A nylon stocking went down past her eyes and around her neck. A man, who had come from behind the door, pulled the stocking ferociously, forcing her back against him and cutting off her air. She tried to scream but could not.

She tightened the muscles in her neck. Then she reached back over her head with both hands and was able the scratch his face slightly. The pressure on her throat increased as he lifted her off the floor. Her eyes began to roll to the back of her head. She was about to pass out. She tried to summon the energy for one more try, however, her arms begin to fall forward slowly, and her body began go limp. Then she felt it, her last chance. He placed his chin on her head, loosened his grip on the shocking. He quickly wrapped the stocking around his hand two times, as he prepared to give her the final choking pull. She could feel the blood flow back into her brain. Quickly, she brought both hands up and clamped his head. Her fingernails digging deeply into the sides of his face. He tried to pull back, but he couldn't. She had him. The pain was almost unbearable, but he kept his strangle hold. Pam's little finger came out of his face and curled like a snake in front of his eye. Fear surged through him as the finger surged forward into his right eye. His reflexes were automatic. He released the stocking, grabbed Pam's hands, and pulled her hands away.

Pam dropped to the floor, and then jerked her arms free. He swung and hit her in the lip as she quickly rolled away from him. She hit the bed and knocked the leg off the trap door. The man put his hand over his eye and then looked at his hand. It was cover with blood. He growled at Pam as hate surged within him. He grabbed a chair and started toward Pam when Dave's head appeared from under the bed. Dave was squeezing out of the trap door which was still under the bed. The man, seeing Dave, threw the chair at Dave's head. Dave was barely able to get his arm up in front of his head in time to block the blow as the chair landed partially against the bed and partially against Dave's arm. The man looked at Pam once more. He took a deep breath and let out a scream of anguish. Then he turned and ran out of the door. Pam just lay there with her back against the dresser, holding her neck. She was still dazed. Dave pushed the bed over far enough for him to get the trap door up. He climbed out and ran to the door. He saw that the kitchen door was open, so he walked cautiously to the kitchen. Once there he went outside and ran around to the front of the house. He saw a black sedan speeding up the dirt and gravel road leaving a cloud of dust behind it.

There was something different he thought as he looked at the front yard. 'The post,' he thought,' and the sign with the hand on it is gone.' Dave came back in the house, locked the doors, and began to check the house. After he had checked all the rooms, he came back in his room. Pam was standing in front of the mirror looking at her neck and her lip.

"Are you all right?" Dave asked. "Who was that? Why was he going to hit you with that chair? Did he lock me in the well?" Dave hesitated. "Is somebody else trying to kill you?"

"I'm going to get a shower," Pam said touching her slightly swollen lip with her fingers. There was a sad frown on her face. Dave wanted to hug her, but he didn't.

Instead he said, "Let me get in there first, I got to pee."

"Go!" she said.

When he returned, he had a sad look on his face. "You left the water was running in the shower. I turned it off. However, there is probably not any hot water left," Dave said softly.

"Does my lip look really bad," she said as she tried to blink the tears from her eyes. This time Dave went to her and hugged her.

"No! It's not too bad," Dave said consoling her. "Anyway, you're still the prettiest girl I know." He pulled back from her and looked her in her eyes and said, "Do you mind if I take a shower with you, please."

"No, I don't mind," she said and gave him a little smile. "But what about your wife?"

"Oh No!" Dave shouted. "I forgot to call Carol," Dave said as he ran out of the room.

Carol walked back and forth in front of the telephone. She stopped, reached for the phone, and then pulled her hand back.

"Where is he," she said aloud putting both her hands against her head. She walked away and then back toward the phone. This time she picked it up and started to dial. She let it ring fifteen times, but there was no answer. She slammed the phone down on the receiver and let out a short scream of anxiety. She walked to the door of the bedroom.

"Please!" she pleaded as she turned and looked at the phone. At that moment it began to ring. She ran to the phone and quickly picked it up. "Chuckie?" she said anxiously.

"I have a collect long-distance call for Caroline Parker from David Parker; will you accept the charges?" the telephone operator said monotonously.

"Yes, I'll accept," she said disappointingly.

"Carol, how are you doing, honey?" Dave said. "Whose Chuckie?"

"Chuckie? What are you talking about?" she said slyly.

"You said Chuckie when you answered the phone."

"No I didn't. I said yucky. There was mushed roach under the phone when I moved it," she said convinced the she had lied her way out of the situation. "Are you in Knoxville now, and do you still have a job?"

"No. I haven't gotten there yet. I'm having some problems," he said.

"Problems! Well did you call Mr. Monroe and tell him you would be late?" she asked. "Anyway, what kind of problems are you having?"

"No, I haven't called yet. You see the car," Dave hesitated.

"The car? You and that blasted car. Forget about that piece of junk. You need to call your boss right now! So, go ahead and do it. You can call me back later," she scolded. "Sometimes, I just don't know about you, or what's going on in your mind? I swear sometimes I think that you don't have sense enough to come in out of the rain. Do you have a pen?" she waited for his reply.

"Yes," Dave whispered even though he did not have one.

"Write this down. Number one. Call Mr. Monroe. Number two. Look in the yellow pages under car rental and rent one. Number three. Take your stupid butt up to the convention while you still have a job. And number five.

Called me once you get settled in your hotel room. Goodbye Dave," she waited.

"You missed number four," Dave whispered.

"No, it didn't. I decided it would be better if I skipped number four."

"Go ahead, tell me," Dave ordered. "Don't be shy."

"All right then. Number four. Take your thumb out of your butt! Goodbye Dave," she said in a louder voice.

"Goodbye," Dave said softly and he slowly placed the phone down. "Bitch!" he said after he had hung up the phone. He stood there looking straight ahead as if in a trance. He did not know what he was thinking of. Too many thoughts were going through his subconscious mind.

"You can get a shower now, Dave," he heard Pam say. "Throw those shorts out once you get in the shower and I'll wash them with the sheets."

Dave looked down at himself. He had forgotten he was still in his muddy underwear. He hurried down the hall toward the bathroom.

Chapter 11
The Visitor

An hour later, Mammie drove her car up to her house. She was glad that she had taken down her sign because she had her grandson with her. She had written her daughter-in-law and asked her to tell him that she wanted him to come to see her. Mammie wanted to see him before she died, and here he was. He was a lot like her son, his father, who had died at the early age of 28. She had been so proud of her son all his life. She had loved him more than anything in the world. And he had loved her. She remembered not long after Pam came to live with her, she had gotten a letter from Sarah, her son's wife. The letter had said that her son had died of a heart attack. Sarah was pregnant with Jason at the time, and she had almost lost Jason because of the stress. Sarah never had much to do with her after her husband died. It was as if she blamed Mammie. Sarah never allow Jason to visit his grandmother. She would allow him to call her, which he did often until he graduated from high school. Then he would only call only once or twice a year. Mammie had never seen him in person, but she would often check on him with the crystal. If he knew all the times, she had spied on him, and all the things that she had seen him do, he would never speak to her again.

"Yeah, Gramma, I'm sorry I stopped calling and writing but you know how it is. You can get pretty busy dealing with all the bull in this world," Jason said interrupting her thoughts.

"No apologies necessary, Jasse honey. We'll just sit down to night after dinner and have a nice long talk. You can tell me about everything that I missed," she said smiling.

"That's a bet," he said as she drove the car around to the back of the house. She parked it right next to Dave's car. Jason was all eyes as he looked the car over.

"Now let's see. They had a 20% off sale at the Demolition Derby, and you got there late. No?" Jason said with a smile. It was a warm happy smile.

"Would you believe, I have guests," she said with a smirk.

"Oh, great! I always wanted the meet Bobby Allison."

"No. It's my adopted niece, Pamela Williamson and a friend of hers," Mammie said more seriously.

"Wow! Two chicks. Gramma, you didn't have to go to all that trouble. How old are they?" Jason said excitedly.

"Down boy! Sit Fido!" Mammie said. "Her friend is a man, a white man."

"Oh no! One of those mixed couple. They better get out of Tennessee fast. Come to think of it, they should have left last week." Jason looked back at their car. "So that's what happened to the car. The Klu-Klux got a hold of it. I hope they weren't in it at the time."

"I see you haven't changed a bit. You still love to laugh and be happy, and I am so happy that you are here," Mammie said. "However, they are in a little trouble, and they'll be leaving soon, so don't ask too many questions. Okay?"

"Sure! What kind of trouble?"

"What you don't know will help you," she said.

"Okay, okay. Your wish is my command, Gramma," he said getting out of the car. He got his suitcase. "They're not in trouble with the law, are they?"

"I've got to hurry up and get some food in that mouth of yours," she said shaking her head.

"Yes! Speaking of food, what's on the menu for tonight?" Jason said as he followed Mammie up the steps to the kitchen door. They walked to the door. The screen door was leaning off to the side. The top hinge was broken.

"What happened to that! It was okay when I left this morning," Mammie said with a frown on her face. "And the door jamb is damaged, too. That white boy had something to do with this. He's been a pain ever since he got here."

"There goes the neighborhood," Jason said shaking his head. "Gramma, now I thought you knew that interracial families don't make it too good in the hills of Tennessee."

Mammie quickly turned her head toward her grandson and frowned with one eye closed. Jason quickly covered his eyes with his forearm and turned away from her.

"Just kidding Gramma, just kidding," Jason said and then he peeped on eye over his arm. "Shoot, I can fix that thing in no time." He smiled at her.

Mammie smiled back. She wondered how he knew to cover his eyes to protect himself from her evil eye. 'He knows more about me than I thought he did,' she thought. She grabbed his head with both hands and kissed him on the forehead. "You're the best grandson I ever had."

"That good since I'm the only one you ever had," he replied. They both laughed. They walked through the house into the living room.

"What did your mother tell you about me before you left," Mammie said with a concerned look on her face.

"Gramma, you know that a mother and a son can discuss some pretty confidential stuff. And Mama told me not to tell you anything that we talked about. So, I know you wouldn't want me to violate that trust. I wouldn't do that anyway, just like wouldn't tell Mama anything that you and I discuss in confidence. You can understand that, can't you?" he said apologetically.

"Cut the crap, Jasse!" she said closing one eye.

"Okay, all right, I'll tell you, but don't get upset with me if you hear something that you don't like," Jason warned.

"All right. I won't get upset. Why should I get upset? Nothing that daughter-in-law of mind says or does surprises me. She takes my son away from me where I can't protect him. Then when something happens to him, she blames me. Then she forbids me from seeing my grandson until he's a grown man."

"Gramma!" Jason yelled. "You're getting upset!"

The sound of Jason's yell was heard by Pam and Dave who were in Pam's room talking.

"What was that! "Dave said jumping to his feet. Dave went to the door put his ear up to it and listened. "Someone is in the living room."

"It must be Mammie," Pam said. "We'd better go and tell her what happened." Pam got up, walked to the mirror, and looked at her lip. "It's getting darker." She frowned.

"Come on." Dave walked out of the door as Pam followed. He tipped down the hall toward the living room.

Jason was sitting on the sofa looking down at his knees. "She told me that you had probably flipped out with all that witchcraft crap. She said you think you are going to die soon even though you're in good health, and that's why you wanted me to come as soon as I could. She said that you go through this same death trip every seven years or so. She told me not to worry about it. Mama also told me not to let you put the evil eye on me." He closed one eye and looked at Mammie, mimicking her evil eye expression.

At that moment, Dave and Pam walked into the room. "Mammie, somebody came in," Pam stopped speaking when she noticed the other person in the room. There was silence for about ten seconds as Pam, Dave, and Jason looked each other over. Then the silence was broken.

"I want to introduce both of you to my grandson, Jason," Mammie said with a big smile. "He just arrived from Chicago."

Without smiling but with a pleasant look Jason said to Dave, "How are you?"

"Okay I guess," Dave said.

"Glad to meet you," Pam said reaching out her hand to shake his.

"The pleasure is all mine," he said as he quickly looked her over. 'She was fine,' he thought, 'white or not. She wasn't flat behind either. She must have some black blood in her somewhere down the line.'

They shook hands and looked at each other for longer than usual. Dave immediately became jealous. He wanted to say something, but he could not think of anything.

"By the way, I noticed that the screen door was hanging on for dear life,' Mammie said.

"Oh yeah Auntie, I need to tell you about that later," Pam said making a gesture toward Jason.

"How about now. It's okay, you can talk in front of Jason. He might as well know what's happening around here. He's going to be here for a while," Mammie said.

"Okay then. While you were gone, a man came into the house and attacked me. He tried to strangle me to death. He almost got me, but I was able to get to one of his eyes. That saved me," Pam said. She took a deep breath and raised her eyebrows.

"Well where were you when you were attacked," Mammie asked.

"I was in Dave's room."

"Well, where was Dave when all this was going on?" Mammie asked.

"He was in the room," Pam paused, "under the bed."

Everyone looked at Dave in astonishment.

"What were you doing under? No, disregard the question," Mammie said. "Pam, did you get a good look at him. Do you think you could identify him if you saw him again?"

"I couldn't see to well then. I almost lost consciousness, but he won't be hard to find without this," Pam said holding a sealed plastic sandwich bag. Inside the bag was a punctured eyeball. Everybody stood gathered around her bag. Then, they all looked at Pam in disbelief.

"Well, he hit me in my mouth. See what he did to my lip," she said. She pulled her lip out so that Jason and Mammie could see where it had been cut on the inside.

"That Dude has got to be sorry that he tangled with you," Jason said backing up to his seat. He looked at Pam as if she were Al Capone's mean stepmother.

"Had you ever seen him before," Mammie said. She seemed very worried.

"No. I don't think so. Why?" Pam asked.

"Come on," Mammie said as she got up and started walking toward the crystal room. "We don't have much time. Bring that eye."

They all followed her into the room. Pam and Mammie sat down on the same side of the table while Jason and Dave stood behind them.

"Okay Honey, think about the man that attacked you and once you get a picture of him rub the crystal," Mammie said.

Pam closed her eyes and concentrated. Then laying the eyeball on the table, she rubbed both hands over the crystal. Jason looked suspiciously at each person in the room as they looked intently at the ball as if something was about to happen.

"Flipped out on all that witchcraft crap, huh," Mammie said turning her head back toward Jason. Jason said nothing. They all waited. Nothing happened.

"That's strange," Mammie said. "It usually goes black if a person is dead. It didn't do diddly." She thought for a moment. "Rub the eye on the crystal."

Pam took the eye out of the bag and rubbed it on the crystal. When Pam removed the eye, the crystal began to glow, and the room got darker. Suddenly the room went black and then a man in a phonebooth appeared in a circle of light in the middle of the room where the crystal ball had been.

"That's him!" yelled Pam.

Jason fell back against the wall in shock. "What in the hell is this?" he said.

"Be quiet, Jasse," Mammie said.

They could see the man life size from the waist up in the phone booth. He had a new bandage over his right eye. He was dressed in a black turtle-neck sweater with a black skull cap on his head. He began to speak.

"I found her. She was very close to where you said," the man said. "No. I almost killed her, but she got away," he paused. "I would have, but she poked my eye out," he growled and slammed his fist into the side of the phone booth. "Don't kill her?" he yelled. "What about my eye?" He put one hand over his bandaged eye and leaned against the side of the booth. There was a terrible frown of hate on his face. Hot tears rolled down from his left eye. "I didn't get it?" he paused again. "All right, I won't kill her until get it." There was another pause. "Why do you want to know where she is? I told you, I'll take care of her," he said with a concerned look on his face. He suddenly pulled the phone away from his ear and looked at it in disgust. A voice could be heard from the telephone.

"I said, where is she! I won't to know right now!" the voice screamed.

Mammie looked at Pam. "Give me that eye, quick!"

Pam dropped the eye in Mammie's hand. Mammie quickly opened the draw in the table and pulled out a long needle with a devil's head on the top. She put the pointed end up to the eye.

The man in the booth was speaking. "All right, all right! I just asked. She's..."

Mammie stuck the needle in the eye. Instantly, the man in the phone booth stopped speaking. He dropped the phone and putting both hands up to his bandaged eye socket, he fell back against the door in terrible pain. He could barely scream the pain was so great. He sank down in the booth groaning and squirming. He open the door to the booth and stumbled and fell out the door. He began to pull at the bandages. He tore at them with both hands, throwing them in all directions until his eye socket was totally uncovered. Blood began to run down his face. He crawled to his feet and ran toward the black sedan Dave had seen earlier. Mammie pulled the needle from the eye. Instantly, the man fell against the black sedan in relief as the pain subsided. He laid there over the hood taking deep breaths. Then he got into the car and began to drive down the highway.

"I got to get to a hospital," he sighed.

Mammie covered the crystal with the black satin cloth and instantly the room returned to normal.

"That ought to hold him for a while," Mammie said. Everybody was still looking at the black cloth that covered the crystal ball. They all seem to be in a trance.

"Hey!" Mammie yelled. The trance was broken. "I better put this eye in the freezer. It might last a little longer. We may just need it again," Mammie said getting up to leave the room.

"Look," Dave said seriously. "It's been nice and all. I really enjoyed my stay, but I'm supposed to be at this convention in Knoxville. I really need to be getting up there."

"I know what you mean brother," Jason said softly, cutting his eyes all around the room as if he expected the pictures on the wall to start talking.

"Ya'll go and sit down at the dinner table. I'll be there in a minute," Mammie said calmly. "I'll bring you something to drink."

They all went into the dining room and sat down in silence. Then Pam spoke.

"Why are they trying to kill me," Pam asked knowing that no one could answer.

"I told you that we should have turned ourselves in to the police. That's what we still should do. In fact, I'm going to do it even if you don't. Look the police will be able to protect you," Dave argued. "We could leave tonight and go to the nearest State Patrol office, and turn ourselves in. How about it?"

"Sounds like a pretty, good idea to me," Jason said, "If you leave right away, you'd probably be gone by the time the next bunch of thugs show up looking for you."

Mammie made sure that all her guests were in the dining room, then she closed the door and walked back to the crystal ball table. She opened the draw of the table again. This time she took a jar of clay from the draw. She began to mold it into the shape of a man whose head was almost as big as his body. When she was satisfied with its shape, she pushed her thumb into it to make a place for the eye. Then she put the eye in the space. She carefully removed the cloth from the crystal. Instantly, the man appeared. He was driving down the highway. There was not much traffic. Mammie held the clay doll in her left hand and pulled the devil head needle from the draw. She pushed the needle into the chest of the clay doll. Immediately, the man began to hold his chest and moan in pain. She removed the pin and his pain was gone. Mammie dropped the pin back down in the draw and closed it. She took a deep breath and then grabbed the doll's head with her right hand and began to twist. There was a cracking sound as if the clay doll had real bones in its neck. Mammie was straining to break the dolls head off. She pulled with all her strength until the head came off. To her surprise, blood gushed up from the dolls neck. She dropped the dolls body on the floor and watched as the blood continued to flow from the doll's neck. Suddenly she felt a sharp pain on one of her fingers. She screamed out in pain and held out her hand out in front of her so she could see the problem. The head that she had just pulled from the doll now looked real and now it had teeth that were embedded in her finger. She tried to pull it off, but the more she pulled the harder the little head bit down. Its face was one of anger and hate. She screamed as she knocked the head against the edge of the table. It still held on. She ran out of the room through the dining room and into the kitchen. Pam, Dave, and Jason jumped up from the table and ran behind her into the kitchen.

"What in the world is going on in here? What is that thing?" Jason asked, looking wide-eyed at the little man's head clamped to Mammie's finger. Mammie took a big knife from the sink and stabbed the head. The knife went through the top of the head and into the counter. Still the head would not turn her finger loose. She tried to pull the knife up, but she was too weak now and getting weaker.

"Help me," she screamed.

Jason grabbed the knife with both hands, rocked it back and forth, and pulled it out. Jason raised the head up. He grabbed the little head's chin and pulled it down. Mammie pulled her finger out of its mouth. Pam had already turned on the burner of the gas stove.

"Put it over here," she yelled.

Jason lower the head at the end of the knife into the flame. It began to burn. Jason pulled the head out of the flame. It was still snapping at the end of the knife. He put it back into the flame again.

Pam had a feeling that something was happening in the crystal room. She slowly backed out of the kitchen while everybody's attention was focused on the head. She went into the crystal room. She removed the black cloth. There on the table was a miniature scene. The black sedan was stopped in the middle of the highway. A car came up and skidded to a halt narrowly missing the black sedan. A young couple got out of their car and walk up to the black sedan. They could see a man inside with his head against the side window.

"What's wrong with him?" the young girl said.

"I don't know. It may be carbon monoxide poisoning," the young man said. "I'd better open the door."

He pulled the door open and the man's body fell forward toward him. The young man reached out to catch him. When he did, the man's head rolled off his shoulder. The young man jumped back as the head, hit against the door, bounced on the pavement, and rolled down into the ditch beside the road. The girl started to scream. The young man backed away from the body slowly as another car stopped.

On the floor at Pam's feet, crawling toward her was the doll's body. She felt it crawl onto her foot and she jumped back. She kicked it off her foot. As she did, the body in the car fell out of the car. Pam grabbed the doll's body and ran toward the kitchen.

"Burn it up, quick," she screamed as she ran through the kitchen and out the door. "Get some paper, and that head!"

Jason brought the head and Mammie brought some lighter fluid. Pam threw the body down on the ground. Jason threw the knife with the head on it down beside the body. Then Mammie gave Pam the lighter fluid and some matches. Soon there was a large flame. They all gather around it. None of them wanted to take any chances and let that little creature get away.

Miles away, a crowd watched as a man's body and his decapitated head burst into flame and burn to ashes. Soon the black sedan was in flames. The crowd ran back to their vehicles and move them back. They watched as the flame grew higher and higher. Suddenly there was a tremendous explosion. There was a simultaneous explosion at Mammie's house. It knocked everyone in the circle to the ground. The doll's body was gone.

"Oh man, this is too heavy for me," Jason said looking at Mammie. "How's your finger, Gramma?"

"It hurts like the devil. How do you think it feels?" Mammie said and then she smiled. "But it will be okay, thanks honey. You too, Pam," Mammie said still showing the signs of pain on her face.

"I need a drink," Dave said.

"Hey, you said it, man," Jason began to smile. "You got any alcohol, Gramma."

"Not the kind you want," Mammie said.

"We're going to town to get some. Okay if I use your car?" Jason said to his grandmother.

Mammie thought, "Okay. Me and Pam need to have a little talk anyway. Now, if you get into any trouble, use your head. If anybody bothers you, tell em that you're Miss Mammie's grandson. Okay?" Mammie said. She reached into her dress pocket and threw him the car keys.

"All right, see you later, alligator" Jason said as he strutted to the car.

Pam and Mammie walked into the house as Jason and Dave drove away. When the two women reached the living room, Mammie spoke.

"It's happening, isn't it?" Mammie said. "You're changing."

Pam stopped, but she didn't turn around. "What are you talking about, Auntie?"

"You're using your powers," Mammie said.

A frown appeared on Pam's face. "What powers!" A picture on the wall straight ahead of Pam suddenly tilted.

"Those powers," Mammie said. Then she grabbed Pam by the arm and pulled her around. "You can't fool me child, I raised you. I know what makes you happy and I know what makes you sad. I know when you are trying to hide something, too. So, answer my question or else," Mammie said with one eye closed.

"Okay, Auntie, Pam said calmly looking up at Mammie's evil eye.

Mammie opened her other eye and her mouth fell open in surprised that Pam had not turned away from her evil eye.

"Well!" Mammie said batting her eyes and looking away from Pam. "Why don't we just sit down over here on the sofa."

Pam sat down slowly. "Look, if this is about what happened this afternoon. I mean about what happened between me and Dave, what I was doing in his room? You know."

"No, I don't know." Mammie said. "But since you mentioned it, what were you doing in the room that I so graciously allowed him to sleep in."

"That's not what you wanted to talk about?" Pam answered.

"No, it wasn't, but I insist that you tell me," Mammie said.

"Oh, we were just talking."

"Yeah right! Not if you had anything to do with it," Mammie smirked. "Anyway, you can tell me about that later. What I want to tell you now, is much more serious." Mammie paused. "I guess I need to start at the beginning." She took a deep breath. "I know you don't remember your mother because she died when you were a baby."

"No, but sometimes when I dream, I see the shadow of a lady with long hair blowing in the wind," Pam said.

"Your mother had long hair," Mammie paused again. "Well she didn't die like I told you. She didn't die of cancer. Your mother was murdered. She was killed by witches."

"What?" Pam said in astonishment.

"Your mother was a witch. I've tried to keep it from you until now because I thought that if you didn't know about it, you wouldn't be affected by it. But I see I was wrong. How long have you known about your powers?"

"Since I was nine." Pam said softly. When I was in the fourth grade there were some boys who used to follow me when I left school. They would pick at me. They would say, 'Your Mama is dead, I hit her in the head.' It used to make me so mad. And this one boy, Timmy Thompson was the leader. I hated him."

"Timmy Thompson? Isn't that the boy that was killed?" Mammie said suspiciously.

"Yes, that's the one," Pam said coldly. "I remember that day very well. He and his gang followed me after school. They were calling me names and I just ignored them, but then Timmy Thompson threw a rock and hit me in my back. So, I decided to run through the woods to get away from them."

Pam sees herself as a child. She is nine years old and she is running into the woods. A group of little boys were standing on the dirt road where she had left the road and went into the woods. One of the boys, Timmy Thompson, says, "Come on, let's get her."

One of the other boys said, "I ain't going in those woods."

"Forget about her!" another boy said. "Why did you have to hit her with that rock?"

"Come on, let's get outta here!" the last boy said as the others shook their heads in agreement.

"Go home then, I'll get her myself," Timmy said and then he ran into the woods. He saw her running down a small path through the trees. It was late spring and there is new growth all around. Little Pam follows the path to the right and goes out of his sight. "I'm gonna get you," he yells and throws a hand full of rocks in the direction that she had gone. The rocks sprayed the area all around and she ducks behind a tree. Not far from where she is standing, a bobcat is lying in her den with her new cubs. Some of the rocks hit near her den. The bobcat hears the sound of Timmy yelling, and she come out of her den. There directly in front of her, fifteen feet away is Pam. Pam sees the cat and the cat sees her. They are both frozen for a few seconds. Then the cat breaks the trance when she shows her teeth and snarls.

Pam raises her hand as if she has a rock in it. She decides that she will pretend to throw at the bobcat. She hopes that her actions will make the bobcat run away. She flings her arm forward. The cat did not run, but something else happened. It falls backwards as if it has been knocked to the ground. When Pam sees this she instantly starts to run back toward the street. She is moving at full speed when Timmy sees her coming his way. He ducks behind a tree. He hides and waits for her to get closer. When she is almost to him, he sticks out his leg in front of her and she trips and falls hard against the ground and rolls head over heels. He comes up to her with a stick in his hand.

"I told you, I was gonna get you," he said. He pulls the stick back and is about to hit her when something happened.

"What happened, child?" Mammie said interrupting the image that Pam had seen in her mind.

"I didn't say anything, and I don't know why I did it, but I raised my little finger and pointed it at him. Then I projected a thought to him," Pam said.

"What thought?" Mammie asked impatiently.

"I thought, 'Look behind you.'" Pam said.

Now Pam can see herself back in the woods.

Timmy looks as if he has just received her thought. He turns his head around just in time to see the bobcat dive toward him. Pam was already running when the claws of the bobcat hit Timmy's side below his raised arm. The stick he had been holding flew into the air. Pam hear his screams as she ran toward home. She did not look back. The image of her childhood experience fades from her mind and she returns to present.

"They found him the next day. The bobcat had killed him and eaten parts of his body. Some of the men in the community hunted down the bobcat and killed her and her cubs. After that, the kids in school never bothered me again," Pam said.

"So, you've been using your powers all this time," Mammie said. "Did you know about your mother?"

"No, I didn't know she was a witch, but I had a hunch that my mother may have been gifted and that I may have inherited her gift," Pam said.

"What gift is this?" Mammie asked.

"Well, I can move things with my mind," Pam said.

"Like the picture?" Mammie asked.

"Well, yeah, but that was an accident, Pam said. "I can't lift anything up in the air, but I can push things. It's like blowing, only you don't use air you use mind waves. Making that picture tilt was about as much as I can do with my mind by itself. However, if I use my mind and my body at the same time, I can get more power."

"What do you mean?" Mammie asked.

"I mean, if I was going to hit somebody and I used my mind along with my fist, I could get a lot more power into it," Pam gave a little smile. "I know that it doesn't sound like much, but it really comes in handy sometimes. I can hit things pretty hard and not even skin up my knuckles."

"Yeah, that's like having a pair of brass knuckles. I could have used that on knuckle brains last night," Mammie said smiling.

"Dave? What did he do now?" Pam said.

"I need a break from talking and thinking about knuckle brains," Mammie said holding her head.

"So, do you think I really did inherit my mother's gift?" Pam said excitedly.

"Well, it looks like you have inherited some of her powers," Mammie said. "I don't know if I would call it a gift. It's beginning to look more like a curse to me. Anyway, I have more to tell you, so listen carefully. When I met your mother, she was looking for a live-in housekeeper. She was pregnant, in fact, she looked overdue to me. She was walking so wide-legged that I thought that the baby's head was already half-way out. I mean she was really making me nervous. She had been living here for only a couple of weeks when she hired me. She told me to get everything ready for the new baby. I had been living here for a few days, and then she said she was going back to Massachusetts to take care of some business. She said that she would be back in two days, but it was two weeks before I saw her again. A Taxicab pulled up and she came running up with a baby, you. I knew something was wrong because the Taxi didn't leave. When she came inside, there was this look of sorrow on her face."

It's twenty years earlier. Mammie and Pam's mother is standing in the living room with a newly born baby in her arms.

"Here take her," Pam's mother says. "I don't have much time. I'm depending on you to take care of my baby till I get back, and I don't know how long that will be. I've got to leave her with you. No one must ever find out that she is mine or they'll kill her."

"Whose gonna kill her? What are you talking about?" Mammie asked.

"I got involved with these devil worshipers, witches. I went to this ceremony and they gave me something to drink. They must have put some drugs in my drink because it made me hallucinate. I don't know what happened after that. The next day they said I was going to be the mother of the supreme Witchhead. They moved me to this beautiful big house. They gave me everything I wanted. They treated me like a queen. Two months later

I found out that I was pregnant. They told me that my child would have great powers. I really didn't mind what had happened because I had everything I wanted, and I knew my child and I would be well taken care of. Then one day I heard my doctor and nurse talking outside my door. The nurse said that she wasn't sure, but she thought she heard two heartbeats. Then the doctor said that if there were twins, the second child would have to be killed, because if they were both allowed to live, they would eventually fight for control of the coven. He said that all the witches would be caught up in that fight. They would have to choose which one they would follow. Then there would be a war to the death. All those on the losing side would be put to death. Then he told her to be sure that she notified him if she heard more than one heartbeat again. I began to wonder if I was going to have twins. The next day I went to a clinic and asked a doctor to check to see if I was carrying twins. He said that he heard two heart beats. I knew then that I had to do something. I couldn't let either one of my babies be killed. I decided to run away. I went back and stole some money out of the safe. Then I left. I came down here and bought this house. I was hoping I would be able to hide here, but no matter where I go, they keep finding me. I went to New York City when the baby was due. I found this man who I paid to pretend he was my husband. He took me to the hospital and paid the hospital bill with a cashier's check made out to the hospital. Then I had the babies, Tamera and Pamela. Pamela was born second. I'm leaving her here with you. If they catch me, I'll tell them that she died. I don't know what they'll do to me but I'm still the mother of the supreme Witchhead. I'm sure they won't hurt me."

Pam's mother takes Pam into the nursery that Mammie prepared. She looks all around the room that is filled with baby toys. There is a bassinet on rockers a play pen and a rocking chair in the middle of the room. The walls were covered with nursery rhyme wallpaper. Pam's mother looks very, pleased.

"It's beautiful," she said as tears rolled down her cheeks. She takes Pam out of the blanket that she has been carrying her in and lays her down in the bassinet. "My precious little Pamela, Mommy loves you," she says kissing her one last time. Then she looks around the room until she finds what she has been looking for. It is a doll about the size of Pamela. She wraps it in the blanket and turns and quickly walks toward the door. "Take care of my baby," she says, not looking back as she goes out the door. Mammie stands at the door until the Taxi is out of sight.

Mammie's memory fades, and she is back in the present. "That was the last time I saw your mother, but her words have always stuck in my mind."

"What words?" Pam said.

"If they find out about you, they'll kill you, because you were born second," Mammie said.

"I have a twin sister," Pam said looking straight ahead.

"Yeah, and that's why these people have been trying to kill you!" Mammie shouted. "They're witches!"

"A twin," Pam said again.

"Well, maybe we'd better continue our talk tomorrow," Mammie said watching Pam carefully. "Better get you some rest honey, you've had a very busy day."

"Okay, Auntie, I'll see you in the morning," Pam said as she walked very slowly to her room. "I'm a twin," she said softly as she closed the door behind her.

Chapter 12
A Game of Pool

Jason and Dave had been going down the highway for about thirty-five minutes in silence. It took that long for the shock of the events at Mammie's house to wear off.

"You and Pam are pretty tight, huh?" Jason said.

"Well, yes and no," Dave said.

"Oh! It's one of those, yes in the bed, and no in the streets situations," Jason replied.

"No! I don't mean that!" Dave surprised himself at how loud he had responded. "I mean, yes I like her, but no, I don't have any claims on her. We don't, we aren't, intimate or anything."

"Really now," Jason said smiling. "Interesting."

A frown appeared on Dave's face. "How much farther is it anyway?"

"I think there's a bar a few more miles down the road," Jason said. "Just hold on Davy boy, we'll be drinking big time in a few more minutes." There was silence again for a few minutes. "Hey man, that sure was some freaky stuff with that crystal ball and that head. Man, oh man, it took me out."

"Yeah," Dave said, "that was freaky, but you can't imagine what I've been through since I met Pam. It has been one nightmare after another. In just three days, two different goons have tried to kill us, and they came pretty darn close, too. One of them shot me in the leg and tried to pull my head off my shoulders."

"Yeah, I kinda noticed how beat up you were looking," Jason said.

"I can't believe that this is really happening. I have a wife and a job to see about."

"Well, what do the police want you for?" Jason asked.

"As far as I know, we are just wanted for questioning." Dave replied.

"What do they want to question you about?" Jason persisted.

"Look, I don't feel like talking about it. Do you mind if we just drop the subject?"

"Hey, what I don't know won't hurt me." Jason pointed ahead. "Look I think that's the place." Up ahead was a sign, 'Joe's Bar'.

When Dave saw the sign, he shouted. "Oh no!"

"What is it?" Jason asked.

"We can't go in there," said Dave. "Pam and I were confronted by three thugs yesterday. We had to fight our way out of there. I know I would be recognized in two seconds."

"Don't worry. You just stay in the car. I'll go in and buy the liquor and come right back." Jason said pulling into the parking lot. "I'll leave the key just in case you need it."

Jason got out of the car, walked up to the door, and went in. Dave sat nervously looking around continuously. He did not have to wait long for trouble to arrive. A pickup truck drove up and parked two cars down from the car he was in. Two men got out noisily.

"I don't give a damn. The first person that laughs at me will get his teeth knocked out," the man in front said.

His voice sounded familiar to Dave. 'It couldn't be,' Dave thought. He ducked down and peeped over the door waiting for them to walk by. Seconds later they came into view. It was them, Sonny and Harv. There was a bandage on the side of Sonny's head.

"Hey Sonny, I don't want no more trouble. I've had enough to last me for a while," Harv said.

"Ain't gone be no trouble unless I see them two butt-holes again," Sonny said ominously.

Dave ducked down lower on the seat. When he did his left hand accidentally hit the keys that were hanging from the ignition. Sonny stopped instantly. He was standing directly in front the car. Dave's heart began to pound like a set of Timpani drums in a symphony orchestra. He sank down to the floor as he watched the keys swing back and forth.

"Did you hear something," Sonny asked looking around suspiciously.

"Something like what?" Harv replied.

"I don't know," Sonny said as he began to walk toward the door of the car where Dave was. "Whose car is this? I ain't never seen this here before." Sonny was almost at the open window of the driver's side.

"I hope it ain't no more of them city folks," Harv said.

Sonny stopped in his tracks. "Well let's just have a look see," Sonny said turning around. "It might just be our friends, Mr. and Mrs. Buthole. And I tell you this, if it is, I'm gonna make them wish that they'd never been born. I'm gonna cut his nuts off and ram them down his throat."

Dave put his hand protectively over his genitals when he heard Sonny's remark.

"And that gal, I'm gonna take her in the woods, tie her to a tree, and have myself balls of fun," Sonny said smiling. "I get mad every time I think about them." Sonny balled up his fist and slammed it down on the hood of the car.

The loud noise scared Dave so much that he almost lost control of his bladder. Now, he had to pee really, bad. He squeezed his legs together as hard as he could. He knew that he couldn't wait much longer. He slowly zipped down his pants as quietly as he could.

'Mammie please forgive me,' he thought to himself.

"Well don't think about them then," Harv said. "Let go get drunk."

"Might as well," Sonny said smiling. They both walked toward the door and disappeared inside. Dave peeped over the dash as soon as he heard the bar door close. He hurried as fast as he could to get out of the car. Seconds later he was on his knees peeing underneath the car next to Mammie's.

"That was close," Dave said. Then he thought about Jason, a black man, in that bar with those rednecks.

When Sonny and Harv walked in, Jason and Joe, the bartender were talking. Joe looked turned his attention to them immediately.

"What'll be?" Joe said.

"Two cold ones," Sonny said.

Joe popped the tops on two beers and placed them on the bar.

"Put it on our tab," Harv said as he picked up the beers and walked down to the other end of the bar where Sonny had already gone.

Jason watched Harv as he handed Sonny his beer. Jason also noticed that Sonny was giving him a very cold stare. Jason turned back toward the bartender.

"Look I'm willing to pay double what it's worth," Jason said.

"How many times do I have to tell you, I don't sell liquor by the bottle. This here's a bar, not a package store, boy," Joe said looking down slightly at Jason. There was a little smirk on Joe's face. "So, why don't you just get on about your business." Joe smiled.

Jason looked Joe in his eyes. It was a cold confident stare. Joe's smile turned stern.

"Well, since you put it that way, I guess I'll have a double Hennessy on the rocks and maybe a game of pool," Jason said as he walked toward a pool table in the corner of the room.

"The table is out of order," Joe said quickly.

Jason put his money in the slots on the side of the table and pushed. The balls fell just as Jason had expected. Jason began to rack the balls.

"The man said that the table was out of order. Ain't that what you said, Joe," Sonny said in a very loud voice.

Joe nodded, "Yeah, that's what I said all right."

Jason continued to rack the balls. Sonny any Harv got up from the bar and started walking toward Jason.

"I think what Joe is trying to say more or less is we don't want no blacks in here, so get." Sonny paused and waited for Jason to respond. Jason said nothing. He calmly walked over to the cue rack on the wall and picked out a cue stick. He laid it on the table and rolled it back and forth.

"Hey boy, did you hear me talking to you," Sonny said as he and Harv split. Sonny went around the table to the left and Harv went to the right. Jason slowly reached his hand into his back pocket. Seeing this Sonny and Harv stopped. They both simultaneously reached into their back pockets and pulled out their switchblade knives and switched them open. Joe bent down behind the bar and pulled out a shotgun.

Jason slowly, pulled a fifty-dollar bill from his pocket and laid it on the table.

"I'll play anybody in here a game of eight ball, my fifty against a quart of Cognac. There was a pause as Sonny and Harv both looked at the fifty-dollar bill lying on the table. "If you're scared holler redneck, I mean red rock," Jason said calmly.

"I'll take you on," Sonny said, "but you're leaving as soon as the game is over, one way or another," Sonny warned.

"All I want is the liquor, and then you can kiss my behind goodbye," Jason said.

Sonny beckoned Harv with a head motion. Harv walked around the table to him. Sonny whispered something to Harv. They both put their knives back into their pockets, then Sonny looked at Jason and said, "Okay, my break."

"That's okay with me," Jason said. "Just one thing. Here's my fifty, where's the bottle."

"Joe, get me a bottle of that Cognac," Sonny said.

"Hennessy," Jason said.

Joe reached behind the bar a got a quart of Hennessy Cognac and tossed it to Harv. Harv sat it on a nearby table.

"Your break," Jason said as he chalked up his stick.

Sonny grabbed a stick and moved to the cue-ball to the center of the table. He aimed carefully and then he pulled back the stick and drove it forward. There was a loud crack as the balls scattered in all directions. Two balls fell in the pocket, one high ball and one low ball. Sonny looked at Jason and winked his eye, then he turned his attention to the balls on the table. Sonny made the five-ball in the side and set up on the two-ball in the corner. Then he made the two, the seven, and the four in the same corner. That left only the three, the six, and the eight-ball.

"You're in trouble now, Sambo," Sonny said with a chuckle. "You don't mind if I call you Sambo do you." Sonny took aim.

"No," Jason said calmly. Sonny took aim. He began to move his stick back and forth toward the cue ball. "I don't mind." Sonny was just about to shoot when Jason said, "Peckerwood."

The shot was too hard. The ball hit both rims of the side pocket and came out. At the same time the cue ball continued to roll. It kissed off the thirteen ball and hit the eight ball which was only inches away from the corner pocket. All eyes watched as the eight-ball moved toward pocket.

"No, don't do it!" Sonny begged as the ball went up to the edge and fell over. Sonny caught the ball before in could go down inside the table.

"You don't mind if I call you Peckerwood do you?" Jason said picking up his money.

"Put that dam money down, the game ain't over. The eight ball goes on the spot," Sonny said as he slammed the eight ball down on the table. "Now shoot, Nigger!"

Jason looked from Sonny, to Harv, to Joe. They were all frowning at him. He put the money back down on the table and walked to the pool table and looked it over.

"I see that we're playing by hillbilly rules," Jason said. He made the ten ball in the corner, the fifteen in the side, and the fourteen in the other side. He walked around the table chalking up his stick. He shot the nine ball with bottom english and backed it up for perfect position on the twelve which he made easily. He banked the eleven, cross corner. That left him with a very difficult shot on the thirteen ball. Sonny looked up at Harv smiling and shaking his head up and down. Then he looked at Jason.

"I got you now, Sambo," Sonny said. "You did pretty good for a nigger, but you shoudda known not to go up against a white man."

Jason never looked up as he hit the cue ball with bottom right english. They all looked on in amazement as the thirteen-ball hit two rail and went into the side pocket. The cue ball rolled to a stop a foot away from the eight ball, leaving Jason with a straight shot in the corner where Sonny was standing.

"Right there," Jason said pointing to the corner pocket with the cue stick. Then he took aim. Sonny started moving back and forth behind the pocket trying to throw Jason's concentration off. He even put his hand in the pocket. "Miss, miss, miss!" Sonny chanted.

"You might want to more your hand," Jason said. Sonny left his fingers in the pocket and turned his head. Jason hit the ball solidly. The eight-ball shot across the table. Sonny snatched his hand up out of the pocket just before the eight-ball slammed against the back of the pocket.

Jason picked up his money and the bottle of Cognac. There was a little smirk on his face as he turned back toward Sonny. To his disappointment, and dismay, he saw Sonny swinging his cue stick at his head. Jason fell back and hit the floor as the stick sailed pass his head. The stick knocked over a glass candle jar on a nearby table.

"Hey, Sonny watch that!" Joe yelled.

Harv and Sonny had Jason hemmed in.

"Give me that bottle," Sonny demanded.

"Sure, here take it," Jason replied. "Forget about the bet. I'll just go somewhere else and get something to drink."

"You'll go somewhere else, all right, but you ain't gonna feel like doing no drinking," Sonny said. "Not with a busted mouth, you ain't." Sonny suddenly pulled his knife and began to move toward Jason. Jason began to back away. However, before he knew what was happening, Harv grabbed him from behind. Sonny walked up to Jason as he closed his knife.

"Now, look here. I want you to go back and tell all your friends that this here bar is off limits," Sonny said pointing his finger in Jason's face.

Jason thought of what his grandmother had said before he left her house. He repeated the words in his mind. 'Now if you get into any trouble, use your head. And if anybody bothers you, you tell 'em that you're Miss Mammie's grandson.'

"This is what you'll get if you come back," Sonny said as he drew back his fist. Instantly, his fist shot forward toward Jason's nose.

'Use my head,' Jason thought as it became quite clear to him what he must do, so he did it. At the very last second, he lowered his head forward causing Sonny to strike the top of his head. There was a loud cracking sound.

"Ahh," Sonny yelled holding his hand. "I think I busted my hand."

"Hey man, I better warn you," Jason said hoping it would make a difference. "I'm Miss Mammie's grandson, and if anything happens to me somebody's going to be in big trouble."

Harv immediately released his hold on Jason

"Let's go Sonny," Harv said. "You heard what he said. Miss Mammie, the root lady is his grandmother."

"I don't give a dam," Sonny screamed pulling out his knife again.

"Don't do it, Sonny," Joe yelled. "I don't want no killing in here. At least, take him outta here."

"Stay outta this, Joe," Sonny warned.

Joe said nothing else.

"This is for my hand," Sonny said waving the knife in front of Jason.

Suddenly, a glass candle holder flew across the room and hit Sonny in the back. Sonny turned around and looked at Joe.

"Dam it Joe! What did you do that for?" Sonny said trying to rub the spot where the glass jar had hit him.

"I didn't do that," Joe said.

"It was Miss Mammie. She did it," Harv said backing away from Jason.

Just at that moment, a crackled voice was heard from across the room near the door. "Leave my grandson alone."

All eyes turned toward the side of the room where the voice had come from. While everyone else was looking away, Jason pulled a single edge razor blade out of his back pocket. He took the cardboard protector off and creeped up behind Sonny. He grabbed the hand that Sonny had the knife in and when Sonny turned around, he put the razor blade up to Sonny's eye. Sonny froze.

"Don't move!" Jason said softly. "Don't even breathe." Sonny stopped breathing.

"Close the knife and slide it in the side pocket." Jason held on to Sonny's wrist as he did as Jason had instructed. "Good boy," Jason said turning his head toward Harv. "Now you. Put your knife in the pocket." Harv did it. "Now Sonny, unbuckle your belt and take off your pants."

"What?" Sonny yelled.

"You can either take them off or I'll cut them off," Jason threatened. Sonny did as Jason said while Jason held the blade to his closed eyelid.

"Now, tie the legs in as many knots as you can, and then drop them on the floor," Jason said. Sonny obeyed. "Now, how about walking me to the door, honey," Jason said as he got behind Sonny. He put the blade to the back of Sonny's neck. Then he got the bottle and pushed Sonny toward the door. Joe still had his hands on the shotgun, but he did not move. Jason stopped when he reached the bar.

"Empty that gun," Jason said standing behind Sonny.

Joe slowly picked up the shotgun, opened it and pulled both shells out and threw them over the bar.

"All right, it's empty," Joe said. "Now, get out of here."

"With pleasure," Jason said. It's amazing what a person has to go through just to buy a bottle of liquor these days. Isn't it, Joe?"

Joe said nothing.

Jason looked toward some tables near the door and yelled, "Okay, let's go gramma."

"I'm coming," the crackled voice said. Then Dave crawled out from beneath the table where he had been hiding, and he ran to the bar. "Let me have a coke," Dave said as Jason moved past Joe. Joe poured a coke and set it on the bar.

"It's him," Sonny said surprised to see Dave.

"It's on him," Dave said pointing to Sonny. Then without warning he threw the coke in Sonny's face. Some of the coke splashed on Jason.

"What are you doing?" Jason asked as he released Sonny and started toward the door.

"I'm repaying a debt," Dave said as he ran pass Jason and out of the door.

Sonny ran to the door. He saw Dave and Jason get into their car. Then he looked around on the floor until he found one of the shotgun shells. Then he ran to the bar and grabbed the shotgun that was still in Joe's hands. Joe would not release it.

"Give me the gun, Joe, before they get away" Sonny yelled.

Joe released the gun reluctantly. Sonny put the shell in and ran out the door. The car was already out of sight. Sonny just stood there steaming. He ran back in the bar.

"Get my pants and let's go," Sonny ordered.

"Hey sonny, come on. Just forget about it. He won fair enough." Harv pleaded.

"I ain't forgetting nothing. They made a fool out of me. I'm going at em," Sonny scowled. "Are you coming?"

"Yeah," Harv said regretfully. "I'm coming, but I got a feeling I'm gon be sorry."

Sonny looked at Joe and said, "You got some more shells."

Joe put a half-filled box of shells on the bar. Sonny picked them up immediately. He took his knotted pants from Harv.

"You drive, while I untie my pants," Sonny said to Harv as they rushed out of the door.

Joe stood there for a minute just staring at the door. "There's got to be a easier way to make a living," he said.

Chapter 13
Back in the Woods

Only a few miles away Jason and Dave were speeding down the highway. Only they were not going back to Mammie's house. They were going in the opposite direction. Dave kept looking back to see if they were being followed.

"If you don't mind," Dave said calmly, "I'd like to ask you a question." He didn't wait for a response. "Where in the heck, are we going? Mammie's house is back that way!" he shouted.

"You see anything back there," Jason said.

"No, it's clear," Dave said looking back. To his surprise Jason slowed the car to a stop.

"What are you doing, now?"

"I ain't running from those punks no more," Jason said angrily. "We're going back there and kick some butt." Jason began to back off the highway as if to turn around.

"We, ain't doing nothing." Dave was getting panicky. "I'll get out right here. You can go back and kick all the butt you want. Stop the car! Let me out of this car! You're crazy!" Dave reached for the handle of the door. Before he could pull it, Jason reached over and grabbed his other hand.

"Calm down Davy boy," Jason said smiling. "I might be crazy, but I ain't no fool, and I ain't that crazy. If my guess is right, it won't be long before those hillbillies will be coming down this road like bats of hell. So, we'll just pull up here in these trees and wait for them to pass. Then we'll backtrack it home."

"You really had me worried there for minute," Dave said greatly relieved.

"Give me that bottle, "Jason said. "I'm sho nuff ready for a drink now." Dave handed the bottle to him and he quickly opened it. He turned the bottle up and took two big gulps. "Ahhhh. That's mighty strong medicine, Kee-mo-sob-bee," Jason said as he handed the bottle back to Dave. Dave took a swallow and immediately started coughing.

"You can say that again, Ton-toe," Dave said with a smile.

"We sure could use that coke, you threw in Bozo's face," Jason said taking the bottle from Dave. "Was that the guy you were telling me about?"

"Yeah. Pam and I were assaulted by those two, and one more the other day," Dave said. "You saw that bandage on his head. Well, that happened when Pam broke a glass on it."

"Yeah?" Jason said surprised. "Why did she do that?"

"Well, those goons came over to our table and started making some wise cracks, so Pam said, 'why don't you boys run along and play with yourselves.' That was it. They started getting rough then. Bozo threw my coke in my face and that's when Pam hit him."

"Then what happened?" Jason was fascinated.

"Well," Dave took another drink, "then all three of them pulled their switchblades on us. So, Pam drops to one knee and drives the broken glass into one of the other guy's groin."

"In his nuts," Jason said putting both hand over his genitals.

"Yeah, in the nuts," Dave said. "He wasn't there tonight."

"I bet. He's probably in the hospital waiting for a nut donor," Jason said and they both laughed.

"Then, Sonny, Bozo as you so lovingly call him, came at Pam with his knife. She ripped his arm open with the broken glass and he ran into the mens room." Dave was shaking his head up and down.

"Well, what about you?" Jason asked. "You took on the other guy?"

Dave turned the bottle up again, but this time it was not because he wanted another drink. He did not want to answer Jason's question. He lowered the bottle.

"I've got to take a leak," Dave said looking away. He didn't want Jason to know that he had been hiding under the table during the whole episode. He pulled the door handle and the light inside the car came on.

"Close the door!" Jason snapped.

Dave turned back toward Jason. One of his legs was already on the ground.

"What?" he said.

"Close it! It's them!" Jason said.

Dave pulled his foot inside and quickly slammed the door shut. The sound of the door slamming seemed like thunder inside the car. Jason could only guess how loud it was outside. Jason just looked at Dave. He wanted to say something to really insult Dave's intelligence, but he didn't. He just shook his head from side to side and looked up toward heaven.

The truck that Dave had seen Sonny drive up in at the bar speeded by. Dave and Jason could see that the person on the passenger side had a shotgun.

"Did you see that gun?" Dave said.

"Yeah," Jason said. "I just hope that they didn't see that light."

"They kept going," Dave said. "They didn't see it."

"Maybe, you're right," Jason said. He thought for a minute. "I meant to thank you for what you did back there in the bar. You really saved my bacon." Jason smiled. "I thought I was going to have to kill somebody just to get out of there. Thanks."

"Sure," Dave said. "You would have done the same for me."

"Hey, I don't know if I would have been that dramatic. Coming in there like Boris Karloff. Unreal." They both laughed. Jason reached up and cut off the top light switch. "Go ahead and take that leak. We'd better get going before they turn around."

The grass was high near the car, so Dave went about twenty feet away from the car near a large tree where the grass was low. He felt much safer unzipping his pants where he didn't have to worry about something crawling in.

"I've been here before," he said to himself thinking about the last time he had to pee in the woods. He began to urinate, and urinate, and urinate. "Oh no, another river," Dave said as the urine splashed against the base of the tree. He finally finished and was about to zip up his pants when he heard something that sounded like voices. Instinct made him duck down as he looked all around him. Then he saw what he had heard. It was Sonny and his partner. They were creeping closer and closer to the doors of Mammie's car. One was on each side. Dave wanted to yell out and warn Jason, but it was too late. Sonny had the shotgun in one hand. He opened the car door where Jason was sitting with the other. At the same time, Harv reached for the door handle on the other side. No sooner had Sonny opened the door, he pushed the barrel of the gun against Jason's head. Immediately Jason fell away from Sonny down toward the seat. He quickly brought his forearm up and knocked the gun away from his head. When Jason hit the gun, Sonny accidentally pulled both triggers and the shot gun fired. The shots blew out the window on the side where Harv was about to enter. Glass and buckshot exploded threw the window as Harv fell to the ground screaming. The kick of the shotgun had drven the butt of the gun hard against Sonny's ribs and he had dropped the gun. Jason seized his opportunity. He kicked Sonny in the chest as hard as he could. Sonny fell backwards to the ground. Jason jump from the car, ran over Sonny, and into the darkness of the woods.

"Harv! Harv! Are you all right?" Sonny yelled getting to his feet.

Harv was lying on the ground trembling. "Yeah, I guess so," Harv said as he began to feel himself with his hands hoping that he would not find any wet spots. He didn't.

"Well, come on! Let's get him," Sonny said as he reloaded the shotgun. "He went down here," Sonny said as he started down a small hill.

"All right I'm coming, but you watch it with that gun. You almost killed me," Harv complained.

Dave watched as they both disappeared down the hill. Then there was another shot.

"There he goes," Dave heard a voice yell out from farther away. Dave ran to the car. The keys were still in the ignition. He started the engine and quickly drove back onto the highway. He knew he had to get back to bar. He remembered there was a phonebooth outside the bar. He had to get back there and call the police before it was too late.

In almost no time, he was at Joe's Bar. He slid the car into the parking lot, jumped out, and ran to the phonebooth. He dropped his money in and pressed "O."

The operator answered, "Operator."

"Give me the police!" Dave yelled. "This is an emergency! Hurry!"

"I'll connect you with the Sheriff's office," the operator said calmly.

There were a few rings and then another female voice answered. "Sheriff's office, Barnes county."

"Look, you need to send a car out here to Joe's Bar. There's a homicide attempt in progress," Dave pleaded.

"Who am I speaking with, sir," the woman replied in a very disinterested tone of voice.

"My name is Dave Parker," Dave said impatiently.

"David Parker?" the woman replied as though surprised to hear his name. "We'll send a car out right away. Exactly where are you now," she said but this time with considerably more interest.

"I'm outside Joe's Bar. I don't know the name of the highway.

"We know Joe's Bar. Stay right there till the car arrives," she said.

"Okay, but hurry," Dave pleaded. "It may already be too late."

The finger of the woman that Dave had been talking to pressed down on the phone receiver post once and released it. Then she immediately began to dial. A man answered.

"Hello."

"Dutchman?" she asked.

"Yeah," he replied.

"It's Sibal. I'm glad I caught you before you left. I've located David Parker. He's on highway 58, at Joe's Bar. Get out there ASAP and find out as much as you can from the locals. I'm going to pick him up and bring him in for questioning. I'm sure I'll be able to find out where Pamela is, if he knows. I'll check back with you tomorrow morning if I don't get to talk to you tonight."

"All right, Sibal. I'll get up there right away. Remember, we have a deal. We take her together and we share the reward," Dutchman said.

"I remember," she said coldly. "Just make sure you stick to the agreement." She hung up the phone and rushed into the next room. "Sheriff, we've got trouble out at Joe's Bar."

Chapter 14
The Arrest

Jason was lying in the ditch beside the road when Sonny and Harv walked by going toward Sonny's truck.

"Come on, Sonny, their car is gone. The other one got away," Harv said. "Forget about them. We've done enough."

"Yeah, okay," Sonny said smiling. "He could be anywhere in those woods. I guess I taught them a listen they won't forget."

When they had passed, Jason got up and started running down the highway. He wanted to put some distance between himself and them. He didn't know what, but he knew something was about to happen. He didn't have to wait long. A few seconds later, he heard an agonizing scream in the distance. It was Sonny.

"I'll kill you for this," Sonny cried looking at the tires on his truck. They were all flat. The valve stems had been cut off. Tears filled his eyes. Hate streamed up in him. He pointed the shot gun toward the woods and began firing. He reloaded and fired in a different direction. He kept reloading and firing until he was out of shells.

"I swear, I'll get you for this," Sonny growled softly as he looked into the woods. Tears rolled down his face, as he walked to the truck. "Get in!" he said to Harv. Harv said nothing. He just obeyed. He had never seen Sonny this mad before. Moments later they were flapping down the road doing five miles per hour on four flat tires. They were headed back to Joe's Bar.

Back at the bar Dave was pacing back and forth in front of the phone booth when he saw the flashing red and blue lights. As the sheriff's car neared the bar, Dave ran out to flag them down. Sibal got out of the car first. She unbuckled her gun holster as Dave hurried toward her.

"David Parker?" she asked.

"Yes! We don't have any time to waste. We've got to..." Dave's mouth froze as Sibal pulled her pistol, put it against Dave's head, and cocked the hammer.

"Shut your mouth, boy," Sibal ordered. "Put your hands on the car and spread em." She pushed him up against the car roughly, and kicked his legs apart as Sheriff Harris looked on in shock. Sibal kept the gun up against his head as she frisked him from the waist up. She pulled his arms down one at a time, and cuffed both hands behind his back. Then she holstered her gun and continued to frisk him. She slid her hands down the outside of both legs. She checked his socks. Then she brought her hands up the inside of both legs until she reached midway of his thighs. There she stopped. Dave breathed a sigh of relief. Then she raised up and without warning she brought one of her hands up between his legs, hitting him hard in the groin and grabbing tightly.

"Ahhhh," Dave moaned as he closed his legs on her hand and slumped over the car.

"You're not hiding anything in there are you," she said slyly.

"Nooooo, nooooo! I don't have anything, please," he moaned. He was in real pain.

"We know who you are, Parker. Because of you and that girl two police officers are dead now." She paused. "Now I'm gonna ask you just once and I want the truth. You got that?" she said squeezing his genitals harder.

"Yes ma'am, I got it," he pleaded.

"Where is the girl, Pamela," Sibal growled.

"She's at her aunt Mammie's house about twenty miles east of here." Dave was almost in tears. "That's the truth."

Sibal released her grip, opened the back door of the patrol car and pushed Dave in. He fell forward on the back seat and just laid there waiting for his genital to stop aching. Dave was glad to be in the safe confines of the patrol car. He could hear the two officers arguing outside the car.

"What do you think you're doing," the sheriff said. "You don't do that kind of stuff in public." He paused. "If that ever happens again your through. Do I make myself clear?"

"Yes sir," Sibal said nastily. She turned her back to him and walked toward the bar. Joe was standing in the door looking in amazement. The sheriff opened the front door of the police car, got in, and turned toward Dave who was still lying face down on the seat.

"Hey, you all right back there," Sheriff Harris said.

Dave did not raise his head. He kept his tear-filled eyes away from the sheriff. "No, I wouldn't say that I'm all right," Dave said.

"Well, at least you can talk," Sheriff said with a little laugh. "You know, I hear that you have less problems in life without your nuts, two less problems." The sheriff laughed again.

"Look Sheriff, what about my friend. I called you because some guys were trying to kill him," Dave said.

"You called us?" Sheriff Harris asked.

"Yes. I reported a possible homicide in progress. That dyke took the call," Dave snapped.

"Watch your mouth, now. Officer Smith might not like it if I was to tell her what you said," Sheriff Harris cautioned.

"Well, what are you going to do about my friend. He could be dead by now!" Dave said.

"We'll take care of everything," the sheriff said confidently. "But first tell me what happened."

As Dave was telling his story, a black sedan pulled up to the parking lot. A tall man in a dark suit got out and went into the bar. Once inside he saw

Joe and Sibal talking. He walked pass them and sat down at a nearby table with his back turned.

"Yeah, they came in here, him and a black guy, and they started a fight with some of my regular customers. They broke up some chairs and some glasses," Joe explained.

"You say he was with a black man?" Sibal asked.

"Yeah. They left here together. When that one came back the black guy wasn't with him." Joe tried to look very, serious.

"Had you ever seen the black guy before," Sibal asked.

"No, but he said that he was Miss Mammie's grandson," Joe said. "Miss Mammie is the local root lady. Some folks around here believe in the stuff."

"Where does this Miss Mammie live," Sibal asked.

"She lives right across the state line off highway 157. You'll see a big rock about ten miles after you cross over into Tennessee, then you take the first dirt road on the right. Her place is about a mile down that road." Joe caught himself. "Or maybe it's the second street on the left. At least that's what folks say. I never been there myself."

Sibal paused for a moment and looked around. "Joe," she said in an especially friendly voice. "You've got such a nice place here." Then she looked him in the eye and her voice became more serious. "Joe, why do you think the guy I got out there in the car called my office to report a possible homicide in progress?" Joe's eyes lit up. "Ah, well, you see," Joe stammered.

"Don't lie to me, Joe." Sibal's voice was very threatening now. "I'd have to lock you up as a possible accessory to murder and anything could happen to this place while you were in jail. It could be hit by lightning and burn to the ground. That would be a pity." She raised her finger toward his face. "I want you to start over. This time I want the truth, from the time they first came in here until now. You got that Joe," she said poking him in the nose.

"Yes, ma'am, I got you, loud and clear," Joe said humbly. "Well, it really started yesterday. The white guy came in here with this girl. She was a real bitch. She couldn't take a joke. Ya know what I mean." Joe told her everything. After Sibal had finished questioning Joe, she walked over to the table where the man in the dark suit was sitting. She stood beside him with her back to Joe.

"We've got Dave Parker out there in the car," she whispered. "He says that the girl, Pam is just across the Tennessee line at a root lady's house. Her name is Miss Mammie. I'm gonna take Parker in for questioning, and as soon as I get an exact location I'll beep you. Where will you be?"

"I'll wait here for a while," he said. "Something might turn up. Maybe someone will come in who knows where this Miss Mammie lives. If I find out anything, I'll call you."

"Look, Dutchman, we made a deal," she said. "Neither one of us is to try to take her alone."

"I hope you remember that when you find out her location, "Dutchman said. Their conversation was interrupted by the loud talking of the men coming through the door. It was Sonny, Harv, and the sheriff.

"Hey, they slashed my tires. What are you gonna do about it, "Sonny yelled.

"Did you actually see anyone slash your tires," the sheriff asked.

"Wasn't nobody out there but me and Harv and them two. Common sense should tell you that it had to be one of them, Herbert," Sonny snapped.

"Well, tell me why did the one out there in my car call me and say that you two were trying to kill his friend."

"Sheriff, that Sambo put a razor to my throat," Sonny said. "You think I'm gonna let him get away with that."

"What happened to the black guy anyway," Sheriff Harris said. "What did you do with him."

"Nothin, compared to what I'm gonna do to him," Sonny said kicking over a chair.

"You'd better calm down, Sonny, or I'll have to take you in and lock you up for disturbing the peace," the Sheriff Harris said.

Sonny turned and walked up to the sheriff. He looked down at him and said, "You and who else, Herbert?" Before the sheriff could respond Sibal spoke.

"Me, fool!" she said pulling her revolver. Sonny turned around and looked down the barrel of her 38. Her thumb slowly, pulled back the hammer and the loud sound of the click echoed around the room as the hammer locked into firing position.

"Say one more word and I'll blow your brains up against that wall, punk," Sibal said forcefully squeezing the trigger.

Nobody said anything. They all watched her finger as it pulled the trigger slowly back. There was an expression hate on her face. It was as if she wanted him to say something just so she could blow his brains out.

"It's okay, you can put your gun away, officer Smith," the Sheriff said fearfully. "I have everything under control."

The sheriff hoped that she would follow his instructions, but he really had his doubts. Her eyes looked like the eyes of a lunatic. Sibal still had the gun aimed at Sonny's nose as she continued to squeeze the trigger. There was another click as the trigger went back all the way. Fortunately for Sonny she was still holding the hammer with her thumb. She let the hammer forward slowly while Sonny watched. He was praying that her thumb didn't slip. When the hammer was again resting against the firing pin, she pulled the pistol back from his nose and placed it back in her holster. Sonny took a deep breath and blew it out slowly.

"Harv!" Sheriff Harris yelled. "What happened to that black guy?"

"We tried to catch him, but he got away," Harv said quickly. There was fear in his eyes as he cautiously watched Sibal. He most definitely, did not want to do anything to provoke that crazy woman deputy. "He's still back there in the woods somewhere. Sonny took a few shots at him, but I don't think he hit him. Anyway, while we were going after the black one, the other one got to the car and drove away. We ran back but we were too late. I guess that when the black one must've cut the tires." He paused. "That's all we did, Sheriff. That's it."

"All right, Harv," the sheriff said. "I hope for your sakes, that this black man is not hurt." Then he turned to Sibal. "Okay Smith, let's take Parker and go look for this black man."

Sibal immediately began walking to the door and Sheriff Harris followed. When he went by Sonny, he tipped his hat. "Sonny," he said with a little smile.

Sonny did not move. He was still in a state of shock. Soon the patrol car was moving down the highway.

"Let me buy you boys a drink. You look like you could use one," the man in the dark suit said.

"Hey mister, I'm sorry but I'm closing up," Joe said shaking his head.

"Don't be so formal. My friends call me Dutch," Dutchman said putting a hundred-dollar bill down on the bar. "I'm sure you can stay open for just a little longer, can't you?" Dutchman said still smiling.

"Sure Mister, I mean Dutch putting the bottle and three glasses on the bar.

Dutchman poured up three glasses and handed them to Sonny and Harv. They all drank up. Then Dutchman poured again.

"Look fellows. I'm a private detective and I'm looking for this woman. She goes by the name of Pam. She is a friend of that guy that the police had in the car. The police are looking for her and there is a reward on her head. Now, if you guys could help me find her and take her in, then there will be something in it for you. Say, about a thousand apiece," Dutchman said. "Are you interested?"

"Yeah," Sonny said patting the bandage on his head.

"A thousand dollars?" Harv asked.

"Yes, at least; it could be a little more," Dutchman paused. "Now, my sources say that she is staying with a Miss Mammie, the root lady. Do either of you know where she lives?" Dutchman asked.

"Yeah, I know I can take you right to her," Harv said.

"Okay fellows, let's go!" dutchman said as he got the bottle and stood up. "If you have any weapons, you'd better bring them. She's pretty dangerous."

"You don't have to tell us that, we've seen her before," Sonny said, "And I'm gonna even the score."

The three of them walked out, leaving Joe at the bar. When he passed the telephone, Dutchman thought about the agreement that he had with Sibal.

'I can take her myself, and the credit will be all mine,' he thought. 'Tamera will make me a grand wizard.' He smiled a sinister smile.

They all walked to the black sedan and drove away.

Chapter 15
Burn It Down

Mammie had mixed up a slimy brown and green potion in a pot on the stove. The potion, a thick and lumpy glob, was bubbling.

"Ah! smells absolutely horrible. It must be ready," Mammie said with a laugh. She stirred it a few more times. She then untied the cloth around her finger. The cloth dropped into the trash revealing a swollen and infected finger. It looked as if it had been unattended for weeks instead of hours. She stuck the finger down into the bubbling potion.

"Owww! You son of a biscuit eating basketball player," she moaned pulling her finger out. It was covered with potion. She washed off her finger and examined it. It was no longer swollen and infected. The infection had been sucked out, leaving the finger wrinkled as if it had been in bath water for a long time.

"Oh Mammie, you're just too much," she said to herself. She poured a cup of tea and then she walked out of the kitchen toward Pam's room. "Pam?" Mammie said knocking lightly on the door.

"Come on in Auntie," Pam said anxiously.

When Mammie opened the door, she saw Pam sitting on the bed wearing a T-shirt and panties. Her nipples were protruding on her small but firm breasts. Mammie smiled as she sat down on the bed beside her.

"My little Pamela is growing up. Why you must be every bit of a double A cup now," Mammie said with a chuckle.

"I beg your pardon," Pam said poking out her chest. "These big mamas are D's. I don't know what you're talking about," Pam said imitating Mammie.

They both laughed as they sat there looking at each other. Suddenly a strange look came over Mammie's face.

"What's the matter, Auntie," Pam said.

"I got that death chill again, child," she said when the feeling had passed. "It seems to come more and more frequently. I guess my time is almost up."

"Auntie, why do you keep talking like that. You're in great shape. You'll easily live another sixty years.

"Wait just a minute! Another sixty years? Why you little rascal," Mammie smiled pointing her finger at Pam. "I wish I could live to see sixty," she said. "Here, I made you some yellow root tea just the way you like it."

"Thanks, Auntie," Pam said smiling. "This is just like old times."

"Yes, it is, honey," Mammie said.

Pam drank it all and handed the cup back to Mammie.

"Thanks, that was good," Pam said.

"Good for whatever ails you," Mammie replied.

"Auntie," Pam said in a serious tone of voice. "I've got to ask you something, and I want you to tell me the truth."

"Of course, honey. You know I wouldn't lie to you."

"Get real, Auntie," Pam said. "You've been lying to me all my life. First you told me that my mother had died of cancer, then you told me that my mother had been killed by witches. Well, if the last time you saw her was when she left me here with you, how do you know that she is dead?" Pam asked.

"If you're asking if I saw her dead body, no I didn't," Mammie replied. "Anyway, I only lied to you to protect you."

"Well, how do you know that my mother is dead?" Pam demanded.

"I received a package from her about a month after she left. The package contained the crystal ball and a letter. In the letter she said that she was in danger. She said that if they caught her, they would make her tell them where you were. She said that she couldn't let them take her alive. She said that she would kill herself before she would let that happen. There were also instructions on how to use the crystal. One of the things she said was if I thought of someone and rubbed the crystal and the ball turned black then that meant that the person was dead." Mammie stopped.

"Well, did you try it?" Pam asked, knowing the answer already.

Mammie shook her head up and down sadly. "I've tried it several times with several different people. Every time the crystal went black, it meant death. You want the truth, here it is. Your mother killed herself because she didn't want the witches to find you."

"How do you know that?" Pam cried. "You said you didn't see her body."

Tears welled up in Mammie's eyes. "I saw what happened to her just before she died. I saw it in the crystal."

"How did she die?" Pam asked.

"Are you sure you want to hear this," Mammie cautioned.

"Yes," Pam said after swallowing.

"I usually checked on you mother every evening after dinner. Well, one night I woke up with you mother on my mind. I couldn't sleep. So, I went to the crystal room to see if she was all right. When the ball lit up, she was running up some stairs. There were some men running after her. After running up several flights she finally reached the roof. I could see that she was in a large city on the roof of a tall building. She ran to the edge of the roof and there was nowhere to go. The men had her cornered. She put one leg over the wall at the edge of the roof. The men told her that all she had to do was tell them where the other baby was, and they would let her go. She didn't say a word. She just fell backwards off the roof, and the crystal went black." Mammie raised her eyebrows and looked at Pam sadly.

"Is that why she sent you the crystal, so you would know when she was dead," Pam questioned angrily.

"Yes," Mammie said, "that, and she said that the crystal would block their ability to sense you."

"What do you mean sense me?"

"They're witches!" Mammie said. "They can do stuff like that! That's why those men tried to kill you. When you left here last year the crystal couldn't block their sensors. They were able to sense you and they eventually located you."

"Why did this have to happen to me?" Pam said sadly. "Why couldn't I have been born like everybody else?"

"Honey, your life didn't just begin when you were born. Life is a continuation of everything that came before. And you are not only a continuation of your mother physically, but your situation in life is a continuation of her situations. It is what your mother did and her parents and all who came before them, and you, who made this situation. The sad thing is there will be many other situations created by others and ourselves. Many will be good, and many will be bad. You have to do all you can, to make good situations so that others, the ones who come after you, won't have it so bad. You have to do the best you can be and let the chips fall where they may."

"The chips?" Pam snapped. "In this case the chips are my life?"

"No honey, you'll be all right," Mammie said. "All you have to do is leave here and take the crystal with you. They won't be able to find you as long as you keep it near you." Mammie paused. "There's one other thing."

"Will you stop?" Pam signed. "That's the third time you've said that. One more 'one other thing' and I'm going to scream." There was silence for a minute. "Well, what is it?"

"You can't ever use you powers, cause your sister will be able to sense you and then they'll start hunting you again." Mammie stopped as if waiting for a reply.

"But I really don't use them that much, Auntie." Pam told on her.

"Who's lying now?" Mammie said. "That's probably how they found you, honey."

"But, that's how I make a living," Pam replied.

"How's that?" Mammie said.

"I work at this café, waiting tables. When I take people their change, sometimes I make them think that I have given them more money than I really did. I keep the rest. I usually make about a hundred dollars a day in tips. I wouldn't be able to survive without pushing."

"Pushing?" Mammie said.

"That's what I call it," Pam said. "I push their minds into thinking what I want them to think."

"Well, if you want to live a long normal life, cut out the pushing," Mammie warned. "Are there any other powers that you haven't told me about?"

"Just one," Pam said.

"I'm almost scared to ask," Mammie said closing her eyes.

"I can see in slow motion," Pam said.

"You can see in slow motion? How does that work?" Mammie asked.

"Well, I don't know how it works. It just happens," Pam said. "The other day this man tried to stab me with his knife. I saw the blade coming at me in slow motion. I moved out of the way and stuck him in the arm with a broken glass before he knew what had happened. I didn't try to do it, it just happened."

"Hmm, you see in slow motion." Mammie quickly reached her hand forward and slapped Pam's face. Pam's mouth dropped open. "Yeah, I see what you mean."

"Dog, Auntie," Pam said. "That hurt."

"Sorry," Mammie said. "Just testing. It seems that this one is just developing. You could have more powers but let me tell you form experience. Some things are better left alone. Nothing comes free in life. Sooner or later you will have to pay. Take it from me, find you someone and settle down and live a normal life. Don't get caught up in this witchcraft mess. It's not worth it. I know. It cost me a son." A tear rolled down Mammie right cheek. "My family shunned me. My daughter-in-law wouldn't let me spend any time with my grandson. I could only write him. Now, he's grown up and I missed all those early years of his life." Mammie expression changed from regret to pleasure as she looked into Pam's eyes. "If it hadn't been for you, I just don't know. You and my Jason are the only important things in my life. That's why you have to leave first thing in the morning."

"What!" Pam said. "We can stay a few more days, can't we?"

"No, I'm afraid not. There's no sense in taking any chances," Mammie looked toward the door and listened. "Where are those two? I sure will be glad when they get back." Mammie looked worried.

"Me too." Pam said.

"You'd better get some sleep cause I've got a feeling that they are not going to be in an condition to drive in the morning." Mammie said shaking her head.

"In the morning!" Pam said surprised. "You still want us to leave tomorrow?"

"Yes!" Mammie answered, "first thing in the morning." Pam was hurt and her face showed it.

"There's one more thing," Mammie said.

"Ahhhhhhhhhhh!" Pam screamed.

"Would you mind sleeping where nucklebrains slept last night. The bed in your room is much bigger and they are going to have to sleep together tonight. I'll change the sheets."

"Don't bother," Pam said. "I've already changed them," Pam said grabbing her clothes and shoes. She walked past Mammie and went out of the room. Mammie followed.

"You'd better lock the door," Mammie said. "You wouldn't want a couple of drunks accidentally getting into bed with you."

"Good idea," Pam said.

"Now give Auntie a hug before you go to bed." Mammie walked over to her and they hugged each other. Then Mammie walked to the door and stopped. Without looking back, she said, "I don't want you to leave, but it's got to be this way."

She closed the door as she went out. She heard the door lock as she entered the crystal room. She knew that Pam would be sleep soon because she had put something in her tea.

Only a hundred feet away, three men were creeping toward the house.

"Let's go," Dutchman said as he began to run carrying two large cans of gasoline. Sonny and Harv followed. Sonny had the shotgun and Harv had a crowbar. They sprinted across the yard bending down as low as they could. They regrouped at the corner of the back porch.

"Are you sure this is the place," Sonny asked Harv.

"I guess so, it's the only one on this road," Harv said nervously.

"It's the right place," Dutchman said sitting one of the cans down on the ground. "Now listen, we take the girl alive but be careful. She is very, dangerous, and watch out for that root lady, too," Dutchman warned.

"I've been waiting for this," Sonny said. Then a sinister thought came into his mind. "Is it okay to have a little fun with her before you take her in?"

"Sure fellows; it might help to loosen up her tongue," Dutchman said smiling. "Harv, take that crowbar and open up that door. When you get it open, we will have to move fast. We don't want anyone to get away."

"Okay! Let's do it!" Sonny said excitedly.

"Yeah, I got something for you Miss Pam," Harv said holding the crowbar out from his groin.

They went to door, the porch squeaked as they gather around the door. When Mammie heard the squeaking on the porch, she walked out of the crystal room and stood in the hall expecting to see Jason and Dave come in.

Suddenly, instead of a key turning the lock, there was a loud crack as the wood around the door was torn loose and the door flew open. The three intruders stood paralyzed in the door as they faced Mammie who was still standing in the hall. In her hand Mammie had the crystal which was covered by the black cloth she had been using to polish it.

"Get her!" Dutchman scouted.

Mammie ran up to the door of where Pam was sleeping. She quickly removed the cloth from the crystal, rubbed it and sat it down in front of the door. Then she concentrated. Immediately a light began to glow from the crystal. Mammie turned and walked confidently back toward the intruders who had just started down the hall. Sonny and Harv were about to grab her when she gave them the evil eye. Harv and Sonny stopped dead in their tracks. They dropped their weapons, began holding their stomachs and started moaning in severe pain.

"Don't look at her eye," Dutchman said putting the gas can down and grabbing the shotgun from the floor. He aimed the gun at her and continued walking toward her. She gave him the evil eye even harder, but he kept coming. He poked the end of the shotgun in her stomach causing her to bend over and moan in pain.

"So, you want to give me the evil eye," Dutchman said coldly. "Well, we'll have to do something about that he said holding the shot gun barrows under her chin. "Sonny! Cut a strip out of that tablecloth and tie it over her eyes. Harv, bring that chair with arms over here.

Sonny moved cautiously as he did as Dutchman had asked. Once her eyes were covered, using the barrows of the shotgun, Dutchman pushed her down in the chair Harv had put behind her.

"Tie her to the chair," Dutchman said.

Sonny reacted instantly, cutting more strips from the tablecloth.

"No! Use coat hangers. Look in that closet," Dutchman ordered as he leaned down and put his mouth up to Mammie's ear. "Where is the girl, Pamela?" he said.

"She left! About hour ago. We knew you were coming. We just didn't know it would be this soon," Mammie said.

Dutchman looked toward the hall as if he had heard something. "She is lying! Search the house! She's here somewhere!" Dutchman said. "Don't let her escape!"

While Dutchman tied her arms to the arms of the chair with coat hangers, Sonny and Harv started going throughout the house checking rooms, closets, underneath beds and everywhere, but they found nothing. They checked everywhere except the room where Pam was. They did not check it because they didn't see the door to her room. When Mammie had put the crystal in front of the door she had thought of the wall beside the door. Therefore, all they saw was an image of a wall projected by the crystal. When they had finished their search, they came back to the living room.

"Nobody's here," Sonny said.

"Ahhh," Dutchman growled. He was furious. "Where did she go?" Dutchman shouted.

"I'll never tell," Mammie said assuredly.

"Root lady, you'd better tell me what I want to know," Dutchman warned. "If you do, I'll make it quick and painless. If you don't, you'll die a slow and very painful death." He paused. "Where is Pamela?"

Mammie rocked her head from side to side and tried to imitate Pam in her mannerisms and voice. "I am Pamela," Mammie said coldly. Dutchman frowned. "Bring me that gas," he said.

When Harv handed him the gas can, he raised it over her head and began to pour.

"Where is she?" he snarled.

Mammie spat the gasoline from her lips as fear swept over her. The wall image in front of Pam's room flickered, but no one noticed but Mammie.

"Ah, she gone. She headed west about four this afternoon," Mammie said. Her voice was beginning to tremble. "She said that she was going to LA to visit some."

Her sentence was cut short as more gasoline was poured over her head. Mammie almost choked as some of the gas went into her mouth and throat. Dutchman lowered the can and gave it to Harv.

"Douse the place," Dutchman said.

Immediately Harv began to pour gas over the furniture in the kitchen, the dining room, and the living room. He ran out when he was in the hall. When the can was empty Harv came back into the dining room. He hit the can with his fist.

"That's all the gas," Harv said. "I just had enough for these three rooms."

"There's another can outside but I don't think we'll need it in here," Dutchman said as he walked into the kitchen on his way out of the house. "Burn it down, her included," he said without looking back. "The girl got away."

Sonny walked up to Mammie. "Well, looks like your fortune telling days are over," he said.

Harv came back into the room with a burning rag on the end of a broken chair leg.

"Come on Sonny, let's get her out of here," Harv said. "I don't think we ought to do this."

"Gimme that torch," Sonny said taking the torch from Harv. "So, you think you can give me the evil eye and get away with it. Well, I tell you what I'm gonna do. I'm gonna burn that evil eye right outta your head."

He pulled down the blindfold down from Mammie's eyes and pushed the torch toward her face.

Suddenly from Mammie's mouth, shot a small stream of gasoline. It went through the flame of the torch immediately turning into liquid fire that landed on Sonny's face and head. Instantly, the flame engulfed his head. Harv froze in disbelief as Sonny dropped the torch and began screaming. He began running around the room wildly. When the torch hit the floor, there was a loud woosh sound as Mammie instantly became one gigantic flame. Mammie pushed her chair back and rolled toward the wall. She squirmed until her mouth was over a floor heater vent. Two little flames rolled in opposite directions on the gas paths to the other room two rooms that had been doused.

"Woosh, woosh," was their reply to the first flame's call. When the flame in the dining room died down, Sonny and Mammie laid motionless on the floor. They both were covered with flames. Harv had become a moving torch. He continued to try to beat the flames off his body, but he was only fanning the fire. He tried to scream but when he inhaled, he swallowed the flame and seared his vocal cords. He ran for the window. He knew that he had to jump through it before the smoke poisoned him. He got to the window and jumped as hard as he could. His arms went through the glass only to be stopped by the burglar bars on the outside of the window. His head hit hard against his arms and slid downward onto the jagged edges of broken window glass. His pain ceased.

Dutchman had been pouring gasoline into a bucket and throwing it against sides of the house when he saw the house light up. He had completely circled the house and was about to throw the last bucket on the house when Harv crashed through the glass into the burglar bars. Flames, nourished by the air, immediately jumped out of the window, touched the gasoline, soaked walls, and spread quickly around the house.

Dutchman moved back quickly as heat grew in intensity. As he sat the bucket of gasoline down, he saw the lights of a car coming down the road. He quickly ran back to the road, got in his car, and drove away with his lights off.

Inside the house Pam, still asleep, began to cough. She awoke to see a room filled with smoke. She looked at the window and flames were licking against the glass. She grabbed her pillow and pushed it firmly against her nose and mouth as she rolled off the bed onto the floor. Then she pulled her pants from the foot of the bed and quickly put them on. When she had put on her shoes, she pulled covers from the bed and crawled to the door. She threw a part of the blanket over the hot doorknob and slowly opened the door. Flames immediately blazed all around the door. She kicked the door shut and crawled away from the door. As she did, she could hear a loud cracking sound coming from above her. She looked up. A crack appeared in the middle of the ceiling and quickly spread across splitting the room in half. Both sides of the ceiling began to sag, and flames danced down through the split. Pam slid herself quickly across the floor to the bed. She had remembered the well. She kicked the bed over and raised the trap door. Quickly she threw the covers and the pillow down into the darkness. Then she followed shutting the trap door over her. All she could do now was wait it out and hope that there would be enough air. She sat down on the covers and made herself as comfortable as she could. Then she thought of her Aunt.

"Auntie," she sobbed softly as tears streamed down her face.

Chapter 16
The Warning

The car screeched to a halt on the road in front of the house. It was the sheriff's car. Jason and Dave were in shock as they pressed their faces against the window of the back seat. They watched giant flames leap from Mammie's rooftop high into the air and disappear into the darkness above, while smaller flames danced along the gutters.

"Hurry up! Let me out!" Jason yelled. "My Gram mama might be in there."

"If your grand-mammy is in there, she's a crispy critter now," Sibal said nastily.

Suddenly there was an explosion and a ball of fire.

"My car," Dave sighed.

"All we can do now is wait for the firemen to get here," the sheriff said. He had called for a fire truck when he had first seen the fire while driving down the road. He got out and opened the back door. Jason and Dave got out quickly. Jason ran toward the front door, but he could not get within ten feet because of the tremendous heat. He ran around to the side door. The kitchen was in total flames. He slowly walked around to the front of the house again. Dave was still standing in the front yard near the patrol car. Sibal and the sheriff were looking around for evidence.

'Maybe they weren't here,' Jason thought as he looked at the burning house. Then his eyes caught something in the window. "What's that!" he yelled, pointing. "In the window."

Sibal ran over to him and looked. The sheriff and Dave came over, also. They all strained to make out the black figure in the window.

"What are you talking about," Dave said. "I don't see anything."

"It's a person's head," the sheriff said. "Was there anybody here, besides your grandmother and this person, Pamela."

"Not when we left," Dave said sadly.

"Well, this was no accident. I found this gas can over there by that bush. Somebody set this fire," the sheriff said, "And not long before we got here. I'm pretty, sure I saw the brake lights of a car, when we were coming down the road."

"We never should have left," Dave sighed. "Maybe they would still be alive." "We don't know that they were in there," Jason insisted.

"I wouldn't get my hopes up too high, if I were you," the sheriff said.

"They're both toast. Can't you smell that burning flesh?" Sibal said as she walked away. "They're both dead, accept it."

"You lowlife, stinking...", Jason began but was grabbed on the arm and pulled by Dave.

"You don't want to mess with her, Jason," Dave wispered. "She's crazy."

Sibal turned and looked at Jason with hate in her eyes. "Your mouth just got your behind in trouble," she hissed under her breath.

"Parker!" the sheriff called. "I need for you to fill out a report on that car of yours. The form is in my car. Come with me."

Dave and the sheriff walked back to the patrol car. Sibal and Jason continued to stare at each other. There was a definite hate connection.

"So, you're a tough guy, right?" Sibal asked.

"I can take care of myself, and I don't have to hide behind a badge or a gun to prove that I'm a man," Jason said.

"So, you think that I'm hiding behind my badge and my gun," Sibal said smugly.

"No! I think that you are a cold-hearted, good-for-nothing, bitch."

"Is that so?" Sibal snarled. "Well, one of these days, and it won't be long, you and me, are gonna go at it. And when that happens, you can just forget that I'm a woman." Sibal was strangely calm.

"I don't have to forget that. I never thought that you were a woman in the first place."

Sibal turned and walked away. She didn't want Jason to see how angry he had made her. She wanted very badly to kill him right then. However, she knew that she would get her chance.

Jason watched her as she walked around the house. Then, something made Jason look toward the door. He thought he saw something moving. He walked closer to the door and then it happened. A flaming silhouette appeared in the door. Somehow Jason knew it was his grandmother. The flaming figure ran down the steps away from the house and fell to the ground in front of him.

"Gram mama," Jason yelled as he took off his jacket and began smothering the flames from her head. Once those were out, he began working his way down. She raised her charred and blistered head slightly.

"You're in danger," she whispered. "Only the crystal can save you." Her head fell back hard against the ground. One of her ears which was solid carbon broke off and fell in the dirt. Jason had stopped smothering the fire at her thighs when she spoke to him. Her legs were still aflame, so he threw his jacket over her legs and leaned down to where her face had been.

"Where is Pam?" Jason pleaded.

Her black charred lips opened to reveal a badly blistered tongue.

"She is in the house," Mammie whispered in obvious agony.

Jason looked up at the house. It was one big flame now. There was aloud cracking sound and then the entire roof fell in.

"Witches, witches," coughed. "Witches!"

"Witches?" Jason said aloud. When he turned his attention back to smothering the fires out on Mammies legs, he noticed that his jacket was on fire. Quickly he threw it away from her, got up and began to stump out the fire. He reached down to pick up his smoking jacket when Sibal walked up with a bucket.

"Watch out," she ordered. "I'll put the fire out with this water," she said as she threw the liquid from the bucket into the air. It spread into a sheet and fell over Mammie's entire body. Suddenly the whole area where the liquid had fallen, including Mammie's body, and one leg of Jason's pants burst into flame. Jason and Sibal jumped back from the blaze. Mammie's flaming body sat up with her arms spread out. She shook violently for several seconds and then fell back down.

"Ahhhh," Jason screamed. "You threw gas on her!" Jason had hate in his eyes, as he stared at Sibal.

"Excuse me! I thought it was water," Sibal snapped.

When Jason had smothered the fire on himself, he turned back toward Mammie. The smell of her burning flesh was almost too strong to bear. He rolled Mammie over on her stomach. When the flame had died down, Jason reached and caught Mammie's shoulder and pulled her over. Then he continued the roll her until the fire was out. Then he sat there leaning over her. He could not make out any of her facial features. A tear fell from his face onto hers. Suddenly her hand reached up, grabbed him by the head, and pulled him down to where her lips had been.

"Beware. Danger will be near you when you hear this," she whispered releasing her grip on his head.

"Hear what?" he asked.

Then without warning her hand slammed against his left ear causing his ear to ring. Jason grabbed his ear as Mammie's arm fell back to the ground. She was dead.

"Oh God, please don't let her die, please," Jason sobbed.

Dave walked over and put his hand on Jason's shoulder. "I'm really sorry," Dave said sadly.

"I had never really had a chance to get to know her," Jason whispered. "This was going to be my first real chance to spend some time with her. Why did this have to happen?" More tears flowed down his face.

"Do you think, Pam?" Dave stopped.

"She dead," Jason said. "She was inside. Gramma told me."

Tears welled up in Dave's eyes and sorrow gripped his heart. Their solitude was soon broken by a fire truck's siren. The fire truck came charging down the dirt road. It was followed by a police car. A few minutes later an ambulance arrived.

It didn't take long for the firemen to put out with was left of the burning debris. The sheriff and Sibal met the other officers when they got out of the car. They laughed and shook hands. Dave saw them point in his and Jason's direction.

Then the firemen began to go through the ruble. The paramedics came and put Mammie's body in a body bag and put her on a rack in the ambulance.

"We got one," yelled a fireman from inside the skeleton of a house. Soon they were coming out with a body. It was burned beyond recognition.

"Oh no," Dave said. "It must be Pam."

One fireman had the legs and one had the arms as they made their way through the burnt wood. The fireman holding the legs tripped and was about to fall backwards when the other fireman jerked the arms to keep him from falling. However, when he did, he pulled one of the arms completely out of the socket. The first fireman regained his balance.

"Wait a minute," the second fireman said. "Let me get rid of this," he said holding the arm up in the air. He drew back and tossed the arm into the air. It sailed high above the debris as Dave and Jason watched. It hit the ground on the elbow, bounced up against the ambulance and came to rest up against the tire.

"Good shot," said the paramedic at the ambulance. He picked up the arm and tossed it in a body bag.

Dave felt sick. "How could they treat her body like that," he said in a trembling voice.

The policeman, Sibal, and the sheriff walked over to the body and began to examine it. The sheriff said something, and they all began to laugh. Sibal walked over to the body bag. She took out the arm and began to examine it. She was looking at the hand. Then she walked back over to the sheriff and gave it to him. They all talked a while longer then they walked over to Dave and Jason.

The sheriff, who had been laughing and joking moments earlier, changed his expression to one of remorse. "That body they found was the body of a man," the sheriff said. Dave and Jason both breathed a breath of relief.

"This is Sargent Hilliard of the Hapeville County police department," the sheriff said. Sargent Hilliard nodded, and they returned his nod. "We're in his jurisdiction now. We have already told him why we're here, and how we found things. We have come to the conclusion, that after your little run in with those guys at the bar, they figured out where you were staying. Then they came out here and burned your grandmother's house down with your grandmother and probably this other woman inside. Somehow one of the perpetrators was killed in the fire."

"Hey fellows," one of the paramedics yelled. "We got another one. We got some more roasted nuts."

"Make that two perpetrators killed in the fire," the sheriff said. "And since someone had to be driving that car I saw, then there had to be at least three of them."

"Are you going to need us for anything?" Dave asked.

"As far as I'm concerned your free to go," the sheriff said. "Do you need them for anything, Sargent Hilliard."

"Can you give me any more information on this Pamela?" Sargent Hilliard asked.

"I've already told him everything I know," Dave said.

"I just met her," Jason said. "When can I have my grandmother's body.

"I'm not sure," Sargent said. "Maybe two or three days. Are you going to be around for that long?"

"No, I'll make funeral arrangements and then I'm leaving. I'll be back for the funeral. Sheriff Harris already gave you my address and phone number. Just call me when you're through with the body and I'll notify the mortician to go and get it."

"All right," Sargent Hilliard said. Then he thought. "what about the other body, that is if we find it."

Neither Jason nor Dave said anything.

"Well, I guess that's it for now," Sargent Hilliard said. "I'll be getting in touch with both of you when this case goes to court, that is if it goes to court."

"Sheriff?" Jason asked. "Can you take us back to the bar so I can get my grandmother's car. And could you tell me where the nearest motel is?"

"Yeah, and a car rental company, too," Dave added.

"Of course, that won't be a problem at all." The sheriff smiled. "In fact, we're ready to leave now."

They all loaded back into the patrol car and headed back toward bar. When they arrived at the bar, Jason got the keys from the sheriff. Then, he and Dave got into the car and went to look for the motel that the sheriff had told them about. It was located just outside the city limits. Before too long they were walking into the room.

"The sheriff was right. It's not the Ritz, but it's fairly clean, and the bed is very, comfortable," Jason said lying back on the bed. "Are you sure that wouldn't rather get some rest before you head back home."

"No sir, I'm getting away from here as soon as possible." Dave said emphatically. "Do you mind if I use your phone? I need to call my insurance company."

"Sure, go ahead, but when you get through, I need to talk with you." Dave looked at Jason suspiciously.

It didn't take long for Dave to give the necessary information to his insurance company. Then he sat down and waited for Jason to speak.

"Look, there's something that you need to know before you leave." Jason said.

"What is it?" Dave asked.

"My Gram mama told me something before she died," Jason paused. "she said that I was in danger. And if I am in danger, you are, too. The witches know who we are now. They are not going to rest until we are dead."

"Listen", Dave said. "I don't mean you any harm, but I don't believe in that witchcraft stuff."

"After all that has happened, and everything you've seen?" Jason asked.

"As far as I'm concerned, this has all been a bad dream that is going to end today, cause today, as soon as possible, I'm leaving this place. Tonight, I'll go to sleep in my bed and when I wake up, I'm going to forget all of this ever happened."

"Well, you do what you want to do. I'm going home for a few days. I'm going to get all the supplies I need, and then I'm coming back. I'll find out who's behind my grandmother's death. I hope that I'm wrong. I hope that this ends right here for you." Jason paused. "Anyway, is there anything that I can do for you before you leave," Jason asked.

"Yes, could you give me a ride to a car rental place?" Dave asked.

"Now?" Jason asked.

"Yeah! I want to bet out of here before anything else happens," Dave said.

"Sure, let's go," Jason said opening the door.

"Wait, I have a present for you," Dave said reaching down into his coat.

"You're kidding, right?"

"This has always brought me good luck," Dave said as he pulled his lug wrench out of his coat sleeve. He handed it to Jason with both hands.

"Well. What can I say?" Jason said taking the shiny wrench. "I'll keep it with me always." Jason smiled. "You ready."

Chapter 17
The Fight

A black sedan pulled up and parked across the street from the Discount Car Rental Company. The man outside watched as Jason and Dave went inside. He had a dagger, jaded with emeralds in his hand. He was using it to clean his nails. There was a sinister look in his eyes as he looked toward the car rental office. He didn't notice the car that had come up behind him until he heard the quiet click of the car door closing. He looked in his rearview mirror and saw the red and blue lights atop the car even though it was dark. He looked in the side view mirror and saw an officer from the stomach down to the middle of the thigh. The officer had reached the back of his car and was moving closer. He put the dagger in his right hand and slid it underneath his thigh. Then there was a tap on the window. He began rolling it down as the muscles in his right arm tightened. Once the window was down, he knew what he would do.

'It would have to be quick,' he thought. When he had gotten the window only halfway down, he heard a familiar click. It was the sound of hammer of a 38-caliber revolver locking into the firing position. He froze.

"Put your hands on the steering wheel or I'll blow your brains out!" a female's voice said angrily.

"Sibal?" he said relieved.

"Get your hands on the steering wheel, now!" she screamed. He released his grip on the dagger and did as she commanded.

"What's that you got there under your leg Dutch?" Sibal said. "Move your leg over, real slow like." He slid his leg over, exposing the dagger. "You weren't going to use that, on little ole me, were you?"

"I didn't know it was you," he said.

"Well, did you know that we had an agreement? Hmmmmmmm?"

"Look, I had to act fast. I didn't have time to get in touch with you. I had to act then, and still I was too late. Pamela got away."

"What?" Sibal was disgusted. She put her gun back in her holster.

"She wasn't in the house. We looked everywhere. So, we burned it down."

"So, who was it that we found in the ruble?" Sibal asked.

"The yokels from the bar," Dutchman said. "Somehow, those idiots got caught in the fire. Saved me the trouble of having to kill them. The way I got it figured, one of those two knows where she is. I'm betting that it's Parker. I'm going to follow him. If he doesn't meet up with her, I'll kill him and come back here."

"Sounds good," said Sibal. "I'll follow Jason. He's got a big mouth. If he doesn't make contact with her in the next couple of days, I'll shut that big mouth for good."

"Hey, there they come."

"Remember, we have an agreement," Sibal said. "We share the credit."

"Don't worry. I'll remember. Just make sure you do."

Dutchman watched as Dave and Jason shook hands. Then Dave got into a 1998 Ford Escort. Dave drove out of the parking lot and down the highway. Dutchman followed. Jason got into Mammie's car and headed back for the motel. Sibal followed.

Within fifteen minutes Jason was back at the motel. Jason walked into his motel room turned on the light, and then cautiously scanned the room. He closed the curtains first, and then he closed the door. He raised his arm and tightened his grip on the lug wrench that he was holding out in front of him. Then he moved toward the bathroom checking every possible hiding place as he moved forward. The bathroom door was closed. He slowly and quietly crept up to it. Standing against the wall beside the door with the lug wrench held over his head, he turned the doorknob and pushed. He watched as the opening door revealed more and more of the bathroom. He didn't lower his arm until the door hit the inside wall. There was only one other place to check in the bathroom, and that was behind the shower curtain. He stood at the door and holding the lug wrench out toward the middle of the curtain, he pushed the curtain back until he could see completely beneath the it. He saw nothing but an empty tub. He took a deep breath and blew it out slowly. He was about to turn and walk away when a he heard a voice in his mind. It said, 'Look behind the curtain, dummy.' He placed the lug wrench at the end of the curtain and quickly pulled them to the wall. There was nothing.

"Now, let's just check this place out, thoroughly," Jason said aloud. He quickly walked back to the door and put the latch on. Then he propped a chair against to doorknob. At that point, he began to check the drawers, pulling them completely out. He looked carefully at every piece of furniture for any electronic listening devices or anything else that seemed suspicious. He even pulled all the covers from the bed, checking them and the pillows for snakes. He had heard that witches put snakes in peoples bed, and he was not about to take any chances.

After he was sure that his room was secure, he threw the lug wrench on the floor, and remade the bed. He then began to take off his clothes so he could get a bath. After taking off his shirt, he held it up to his nose.

"Good golly Miss Molly," he said as he pulled his head away from the shirt. "I think I'll give you a bath, too. This is sickening. No wonder Dave was in such a big hurry to leave."

He hung up his pants, but he threw the rest of his clothes on the floor. He was going to wash them in the bathtub after he had gotten a bath. He couldn't stop thinking about Dave.

"Davey boy, I hope I was wrong and that you are safe, and that this thing is over for you." he paused as he thought about himself. "But it's not over for me. Somebody set my grandmother on fire and I'm going to do something about it."

He remembered how Mammie had looked when she warned him about the witches. Tears of anger welled up in his eyes as he heard her words of warning.

"You're in danger. Only the crystal can save you," he could almost hear her say. "Gramma," Jason said looking up. "Whoever did this to you is the one in danger. I'm going to really hurt them. They are not the only ones who can play with fire."

Rage began to explode in him. Little did he know that in the next room with her ear up to the wall, Sibal was listening to every word. She moved quickly to the door that connected his to hers. She opened the door on her side and pushed a thin pry bar between the other door and the door frame.

Jason laid back in the hot bath water, soaking his tired and tensed muscles. He had calmed down and now he was beginning to dose. He rolled a towel and laid his head back on it as he relaxed and allowed himself to drift into sleep. He immediately began to dream. In his dream, he saw Laverne, a woman that he had been dating for a while. She and he were dancing to the rhythmic beat of a Reggae band. As the congas beat in his dream, the wood on the door that lead to the adjoining motel room was beginning to crack. Something was being force through it. In Jason's dream the beat and the dance became more and more frantic. The song and dance ended with a loud crash as the conga player raised his hand high above his head and slammed it down on the drum. Just at that same moment Sibal broke the door frame. The door was open. In Jason's dream, the band leader grabbed the microphone and began to introduce someone. The PA system had a slight ring in it, and it was difficult for Jason to hear what was being said. The band leader looked back and pointed. A figure began to walk forward. As the figure moved closer, the ringing sound from the PA grew louder. Jason could hear the steps as the person came to the front of the stage. Each step echoed in his ears. Each step louder than the last. In the room, the footsteps of the intruder moved over the carpeted floor toward the bathroom where Jason was. The footsteps of the intruder in Jason's motel room and the footsteps of the person moving to the front of the bandstand in Jason's dream landed simultaneously. In Jason's dream, he was now covering his ears because the ringing sound was now unbearable. He could now tell that the person coming forward was a woman with a hood over her head. As the bathroom door slowly swung open, the dream lady reached up and grabbed the sides of her hood. She pulled it back exposing a charred, black, badly, burned, head. It was Mammie. The intruder raised the Billy club over Jason's head. Mammie looked directly at Jason and screamed even louder than the now deafening ringing. "Danger!

Jason woke up, opened his eyes, and sat up with a start just as the club crashed down against the tub where his face had been. There standing over him was Sibal. Quickly she pulled her club back across her body. Now taking hold of it with her other hand also, she took a baseball swing at his face. He had no time to think. He hunched his hips forward and jerked his back and head down into the water as the club grazed his chin and hit the tile wall. Immediately, Sibal repositioned her hands on the club and push the club down through the water against Jason's neck. Jason had been able to get his hands up in time to partially brock her push. He had also been able to turn his head to the side before the club hit his neck. One second later and his Adams Apple would have been crush. Jason had no doubt that she intended to kill him.

"I told you that we would meet again," Sibal snarled. "Now, I'm going to send you to meet your Gram-ma. And yeah, I knew that was gasoline. I burned her up like a mangy dog, and now I'm gonna drown you like a filthy rat." There was a look of satisfaction on her face.

Jason could hear her even though his head was under the water. Her words infuriated him. He needed air, but he could not push the club off his neck. Then he remembered. He released the club with his right hand, reached down underneath the water in the tub beside his foot and grabbed his lug wrench. He had placed it in the bathtub in case of an emergency. He swung it up with every ounce of strength he had left. The metal rod hammered against her head catching her completely off guard. She almost lost consciousness. Jason swung again. This time she released her club and blocked the blow with her arms as she quickly fell to one knee. She was still dazed but she managed to get to her feet and reach for her gun. Jason scrambled to his feet just as she began to pull the revolver up. Jason swung down as she pulled the gun from the holster. The lug wrench slammed against her hand knocking the 38 to the floor.

Jason didn't waste any time. Now he had her club, too. He swung her club down at her head as he jumped out of the tub. She caught hold of his arms, as he drove her back out of the bathroom into the wall of the closest area. He hesitated, trying to decide what to do next. That moment of hesitation was all that Sibal needed. She went for his groins. He could see it coming but there was nothing that he could do to stop her. He clamped his legs together, dropped her club, and grabbed her hand so that she could not pull up. However, there was nothing he could do to keep her from squeezing, which she did.

"Ahhhhhhhhhhh," he screamed as he squeezed his legs on her hand as tight as he could.

"I've got you by the balls now, boy," Sibal snarled, "and I'm going to rip them off and shove them down your throat."

Jason knew that it was over for him. But if he had to go, he was going to do as much damage as he could.

"Please, please, Miss Sibal!" he said with tears running down his face. As they faced each other only inches apart, he saw no mercy in eyes.

"Beg!" Sibal shouted. "I said beg!"

Jason's head went back as cried out toward the ceiling. "I'm begging Y-O-U!" he yelled as he brought his head forward as fast as he could. He drove his forehead into her nose which broke immediately. Then he tried to stick the pointed end of the lug wrench into her face. She ducked her head and pushed his arm up. The lug wrench punched a hole in the wall. He pulled back for another try. She released his testicles, jerked her hand from between his legs and caught his wrist with her other hand. She now had both hands on his wrist. She pushed his hand back and twisted his arm causing him to drop the lug wrench. With his other hand still covering his aching testicles, he fell back, kicking her in the stomach.

She released his arm as he dove for the bathroom. He didn't make it. They both knew he was going for her gun which was just inside the door. Jason tried to crawl into the bathroom but Sibal caught his ankle and pulled. Jason grabbed the door frame. Sibal held his ankle with one hand and with the other she pulled up her pants leg exposing a small 32 revolver in an ankle holster. Jason pulled himself forward and lunged for the gun on the bathroom floor.

Sibal pulled him back as she bent over and grabbed the handle of the gun in the ankle holster. Then she heard a click. She froze. Then only moving her head and eyes, she looked up at Jason. He had both hands on the gun and it was aimed right between her eyes.

"Do it!" Jason said. "Let's just see how fast you are, butt breath."

Sibal moved her hand slowly away from the gun. "Of course, you know that they'll fry you for killing a police officer."

"You killed my grandmother," Jason said in a calm voice. "Now I'm going to kill you."

"It wasn't me. I didn't kill her. She was already as good as dead when we got there. I just put her out of her misery," Sibal explained.

"Well, who did it? Who set the house on fire?" Jason saw something in her expression.

"I don't know yet, but when I find out I'll let you know so that you can get your revenge. I can help," Sibal pleaded.

"Yes, I believe you can help me," Jason said. "Unstrap that ankle holster." Jason pulled the trigger of the revolver that was aimed at Sibal's head. "Now, my thumb is the only thing that is keeping this gun from blowing your head off. I hope it doesn't get tired and accidentally slip off the hammer."

Sibal hurriedly unstrapped the ankle holster and let it and the gun in it fall to the floor.

"Now kick it over here."

She did as he commanded. The gun slid across the floor and stopped against his knee. He did not take his eyes off her.

"Would you mind uncocking that gun?" she asked. "You are really making me nervous."

"First things first, hon," Jason said. "Is the key to your hand cuffs on that key ring." She nodded. "Toss them over here to me."

She unclipped the keys from her belt and tossed them to him.

"Now, take your handcuffs out, and cuff your right hand," he said.

"What?" she yelled wiping the blood from her nose.

"Either cuff your right hand or I'll shoot you in both your legs," he ordered.

She cuffed her arm. "Now what?" she said.

"Now, go in the bathroom, get down on your knees in front of the commode, put your arms around it and cuff your other hand," He said. "Then I'll uncock this gun. Then we can work something out."

She walked past him, got down on her knees, reached around the commode and cuffed her fist. The cuffs locked and she let it slide down over her hand. She was hoping that there would be enough room for her to squeeze her hand out.

Jason got up from the floor holding his aching testicles. He looked to see if her hands were cuffed. When he was sure, he closed the bathroom door. Sibal immediately began working the cuff over her hand. It was tighter than she thought. A drop of blood fell to the tile floor of the bathroom where Sibal was still trying to get the handcuff over her hand. The skin on her thumb joint was being scrapped off as she pulled the cuff as hard as she could. Sibal watched in anguish as more drops of blood fell to the floor.

"You'll pay for this blood with your life," she promised to herself.

Then the bathroom door opened. She looked up and saw Jason standing in the doorway. He was fully dressed now. He had her Billy club in his hands and her 38-revolver stuck down in his pants. The expression on his face was one of anger and revenge.

"I know you know who set my grandmother's house on fire," Jason said softly as he walked into the bathroom, stepped one leg over her and sat down slowly on her back.

"I told you. I don't know now but, I'll let you..." Sibal stopped talking when she felt him grab her hair roughly with both hands.

"I hate a liar," Jason snapped. He pushed her head down into the commode.

Sibal forgot about trying to pull the cuff off. She began pushing against the floor, trying to get her head out of the water. It was no use. She held her breath and hoped the he would let her head up soon. It was almost a whole minute before he pulled her head up. When he did, she began gasping for air.

"I want a name. Who did it?" Jason snarled.

"It was those boys from the bar," Sibal said.

"Wrong answer," he shouted.

Once again, he pushed her head down into the water, and held it there even longer. This time when he pulled her head up, she was coughing and spitting water. Jason let her take a couple of breaths. Then without saying anything, he began to slowly push her head forward.

"Dutchman did it!" she cried. "He's the one you want."

"Where is he now?" Jason said calmly. "Don't lie."

"He. He went after your friend," she said fearfully, "Parker."

"So, he went to kill Dave and you came to kill me. Is that right," he said.

"Yes!" she said. "Yes, that right but we are just following orders."

"So, you and this Dutchman are both witches, right?" Jason asked.

"Yes," she said hesitantly. "How did you," she stopped herself.

"Who sent you?" Jason yelled.

Again, Sibal began to try to work the cuff over her hand. Her plan was to keep talking until she got the cuff off. Then maybe she could take him by surprise.

"Tamera sent us," Sibal said. "We were sent to kill Pamela."

"But why?" Jason asked. "What did she do?"

"She didn't do anything. It's not what she did; it's who she is. She is Tamera's twin sister. That makes her an heir to the witches coven just like Tamera. There can only be one head witch."

"But why did Pamela have to die?" Jason asked.

"Was she really in the house when it burned down?" Sibal asked.

"Yeah, she was," Jason said sadly. "Before my grandmother died, she told me that Pam was inside when the house burned down. She's dead all right, but why was she killed?"

"I don't know everything," Sibal said, "but as long as Pamela was alive Tamera would only have half of her powers. And now, that Pamela is dead, Tamera is supposed to get all of her powers."

The revolver was beginning to annoy Jason, it was pinching his stomach.

"What kind of powers?" Jason asked taking Sibal's 38 from his pants and putting it on the top of the commode tank.

Sibal's eyes lit up when she saw the gun. She wanted to keep him interested until she got her hand free, so she continued to talk.

"She can hypnotize you and make you do what she wants you to do. She can move things without touching them. She can read minds, weak minds," Sibal explained.

"Did she hypnotize you? Is that why you're doing this?" Jason asked.

"No!" Sibal snapped. "I don't have a weak mind."

"Well, why are you doing all this?"

"Let me put it this way. Tamera is not the kind of person that you would want to disappoint. She doesn't handle disappointment well at all," Sibal replied. "You'd better pray that you never meet her. She's not nice like me."

Jason looked at her as if she had said the most ridiculous thing in the world. "Is that all she can do?" Jason asked.

"No, once I saw her go into her room. Then a black bird flew out of the room. When I went in the room she was gone. Then about an hour later the bird flew back into the room. Two minutes later she came out and the bird was gone."

"Are you saying she can turn into a bird?" Jason asked in amazement.

"She did something. You figure it out. But whatever she did it made her very weak."

The cuff finally slid over Sibal's thumb joint. She slid the cuff off her hand. She was free.

"Look," Sibal said. "My ribs are hurting, really bad. Your weight is crushing them. I'm telling you what you want to know. Would you mind getting off my back, please?"

"Yeah, well, all right, I guess I can do that," Jason said as he took the Billy club from his lap and stood up. He stepped back and was about to sit down on side of the tub when she made her move.

To his surprise, she quickly brought her arm around, swinging the handcuffs at his head. Jason tried to duck away but the cuffs hit the side of his head. She took the revolver from tank top and turned around and faced Jason who was backing toward the door.

"Get down on your knees, and beg me not to kill you," Sibal ordered aiming the gun at Jason.

"You wouldn't want to kill me before you've heard my proposition, would you?" Jason asked calmly.

"What could you possibly have to say that I would want to hear?" she said.

"I can give you what you want most," Jason said.

"And what's that?" she asked.

"You want to be the H.W.I.C." Jason said.

"I want to be what?" she asked as she frowned.

"You want to be the 'Head Witch in Charge', and the only way that you can do that is through me." Jason paused. "All I want you to do take me to this Tamera, I'll kill her, and you can become the head witch."

Sibal seemed very interested in his plan, however, she felt that there was no way that he could kill Tamera.

"What makes you think that you could kill Tamera," Sibal asked.

"If I can kill you, with no help, surely, I can kill her, with your help," Jason said calmly.

"But you didn't kill me," Sibal said.

"Not yet," Jason said calmly as he slowly reached behind his back and pulled Sibal's 32 revolver from his pants. Sibal reacted as soon as she saw the gun. She pulled the trigger four times before she realized that the gun was empty.

Jason aimed the gun at Sibal's liver. She quickly laid the revolver back on the top of the commode tank and raised her hands. Jason pulled back the hammer. She squinted her eyes and waited for the explosion. He didn't shoot.

"Lift that top up and let the gun slide down in the tank," Jason ordered. Sibal obeyed. The gun dropped into the water and she put the top back on the tank.

"Now, sit down on the tub," Jason ordered. Sibal obeyed. "Cuff your ankle," he said. Sibal obeyed. "I'm gonna give you a little time to think over my proposition," Jason said. "You just might change your mind. In fact, Tamera just might persuade you to help me, when she finds out what happened here tonight."

"What are you talking about?"

"You did say that she didn't like being disappointed, didn't you? Well, when she finds out that you failed to kill me and that you told me about her, she just may be a little upset with you," Jason said, pointing his finger at her.

Jason walked out of the bathroom and closed the door behind him. Sibal reached into her pocket. She pulled her hand out and opened it. There in her hand were five 38 caliber hollow point bullets. She laid them on the floor and began trying to quietly remove the tank top. She knew that she could not make any noise.

Sibal had tried several times to get the top off but each time there would be too much noise. She finally had an idea that might work. She lifted up one end of the top. Then she put her head underneath it and slowly lifted it with her head. She lowered the top down on the seat. Then she reached in the tank and pulled the gun from the water. Sibal quickly pushed the bullets into her 38.

"How dumb can you get," she said softly. "I can't believe he would leave my gun in here. Didn't he know that I would have extra bullets." She became suspicious as she thought about it. She wished that she had an extra key to her handcuffs.

"Maybe he could kill Tamera, if I got him a good opportunity," she said to herself. "Then I would make myself the head witch." She shook her head. "Now. I'm talking real dumb. That idiot couldn't' kill Tamera. I'd better kill him and get out of this town as soon as possible."

She placed the end of the barrow of the gun over the chain and pressed it against the floor. She covered it with a towel. She pulled back the hammer and turned her head away. There was a loud echoing bang, as the chain was cut in two. Sibal immediately got to her feet, ran to the door, opened it, and stuck the gun and her head out. She was totally surprised by what she saw. Sheriff Harris and a deputy were peeping through the front door of the room on both sides with the pistols pointing at her. Another deputy was peeping through the adjoining door. His pistol was also aimed at her.

"Lay the gun on the floor, officer Smith," Sheriff Harris said loudly. "Then step out of the bathroom and place your hands behind your head."

Chapter 18
Get Me to the Church on Time

Dave had not made any time. He had stopped to get gas and had fallen asleep in the car while the gas was pumping. He knew he couldn't drive as sleepy as he was, so he had pulled up to the front of the truck stop door and had taken a nap. He had slept for a couple of hours before the manager came out and told him to move. Now he was back on the road and behind schedule. Still, he felt that he would be home sometime after lunch time. He wondered what he would find when he got home.

He at his rearview mirror. He could have sworn that the car behind him was the same car that he had seen twenty minutes earlier when he left the truck stop. He thought about what Jason had said. Could it be that he was being followed? He had to find out. He looked at his speedometer. He was doing 65. He decided to slow down to 50 and see if the car would slow down, too. The car began to get closer. As it did Dave began to get more nervous. The car came up close behind Dave. It was a black sedan. There was a man driving. Dave did not get a good look at him because he was wearing dark glasses. It seemed as if he wanted to pass, so Dave turned on his blinker and slowed down even more. The car pulled around. As the car passed the two men faced each other. Even though the man had on dark glasses, Dave felt a coldness in his stare. The black sedan pulled in front of Dave's car and began to leave Dave behind. Within a couple of minutes, it was out of sight.

"I am freaking out. Nobody is following me," Dave said to himself. He increased his speed back to 65 again. He was right. Nobody was following him, not anymore. Dutchman was somewhere waiting up ahead.

Dave was so happy to be going home. He knew that he should be going to the conference, but he needed to touch Homeplate first. It might not be the happiest place in the world, but at least he didn't have to worry about being killed.

Dave saw a sign ahead 'Reduce Speed Dangerous Curve Ahead.' He slowed slightly and then heard a loud 'P-O-W'.

"Oh no! A blowout," Dave said aloud.

His steering wheel pulled sharply to the right. He jerked the wheel and hit the brakes as he slid toward the embankment. The closer he got to the edge the more he could see open sky.

"Stop! Stop!" he begged the car as it hit the reflector sign and went over the bank. The car almost stopped when it hit a bump as it started down the embankment. Dave could see the bottom of the ridge about 100 feet down. He knew that he had to jump out of the car now before the car picked up any more speed. He unhooked his seat beat and opened the door at the same time. Then he jumped. He landed on his feet, fell forward, rolled over, and the flew into the air. He landed into a thick bush of wild hedges. He was totally covered by them as he listened to the car as it tumbled to the bottom of the cliff.

"What next?" he said as he looked up at the sky. Then he caught sight of something at the top of the embankment. He could see him through the leaves of the hedges. It was a man. He was holding a rifle in one hand and what appeared to be a can of gasoline in the other.

"It was no blow out," Dave whispered. "It was a shootout. He shot my tire,"

Dave watched as the man began to climb down the embankment. Dave quietly worked himself loose from the bushes and crawled away toward the nearby trees. He kept out of sight of the man, but he kept the man in his sight. Dave worked his way up as the man worked his way down.

When the man reached the car, which was a smashed, upside down, pile of crumbled metal, he got down on his knees and looked inside. Then he got up holding the rifle out in front of him and looked all around. Dave knew that the man was looking for him.

"He must be one of them," Dave whispered. "Jason was right. I've got to get out of here," he said to himself. He started climbing faster. Just before he reached the crest of the hill, he heard an explosion. He raised up and looked back, he saw the car in flames. However, he didn't see the man.

'Where is he?' Dave thought leaning out a little further. Then dirt to Dave's right was knocked, up. A half second later Dave heard a gunshot. He had been seen. Dave ducked down as more dirt was knocked, up. This time it was above him. Dave was afraid to move. The man had him pinned down. Dave laid as flat as he could. Then he slid over and peeked to see if he could locate the man. He saw him he was running to get into position to get a clear shot at Dave. Dave had to make a run for it now. He jumped up and scrabbled up the hill. He heard three shots before he dove to safety. He was very relieved to know that he had escaped the immediate danger, however, he knew that it would only be a matter of minutes before the man reached the top of the hill. He had to do something. He looked down the highway and saw the black sedan. He immediately started running for it. When he reached it, he tried the door. It was locked. He looked inside. The keys were not in the ignition. He didn't have time to find anything to break the window with. He wouldn't have known what to do once he got in, anyhow. However, he knew that he had to even the odds.

He broke a little limb from a nearby bush. Then he broke it into four parts. Then he went around the car sticking them into the valve stems of each of the tires. Then down the road he ran, as fast as he could. There was a curve about 200 yards up ahead. He wanted to get there before the man reached the top of the hill. He didn't make it. He heard a gunshot and looked back. There at the top of the cliff was the man. He was aiming the rifle at Dave. Dave stopped and ducked down. He wanted to run into the woods but the hill next to the road was too steep. Then he started running again, however, this time he was moving very erratically. He would zig zag, then stop, then run, and then duck down. Each time he heard another shot he became more afraid. Then the shots stopped. He looked back and saw that the man was running to his car. Dave turned on the speed. Around the curve he went. Soon he found a place that was not too steep. He left the road and went into the woods.

When Dutchman reached the car, all four tires were flat. He balled up his fist and slammed it down on the roof of the car in anger. Then he got in, picked up his mobile phone and dialed.

Once again, Dave was in the one place, where he had sworn that he would never go again. He was in the woods, and once again, he was fearing for his life. He had left the road about ten minutes ago. After climbing almost to the top of a steep hill, he had gone straight into the trees on the hill and then started back parallel to the road, always keeping the road in sight. He figured that he needed to know if the man was following him. He back tracked until he could see his pursuer standing next to the black car. Then he found himself a good hiding place behind a bush. There he could see the road clearly, but he also had plenty of cover. From his location he could see that the man was talking on a mobile phone.

"Well, you said make it look like an accident," Dutchman paused. "How was I supposed to know that he was going to get out of the car before it reached the bottom of the cliff," Dutchman paused again.

"Where is he now?" a woman's voice said calmly.

"He's probably in the woods somewhere up ahead," Dutchman replied.

"I want you to walk down the highway slowly. Sweep the woods with your rifle scope as you go. Put your sights on wide focus. Keep the phone with you. I'll tell you what to do," she instructed.

As Dave watched, Dutchman began walking down the highway slowly sweeping the hill with his rifle sights as if he and his rifle were some sort of radar.

"What is he doing," Dave said to himself. "Does he really think he'll be able to spot me like that?"

Still Dave took no chances. He made sure he was completely behind the bush. He parted the branches and watched as the rifle pointed closer and closer to his position. When the rifle appeared to be aimed right at him it stopped. Dave watched as Dutchman talked for a few second on the mobile phone. Then Dave saw him adjust the sights on his scope. Dave began to wonder if the man could really see him. Dave released the bush and ducked lower to the ground. Just as he did, he heard shots. Pieces of the bush he was hiding behind were being cut off. Dave knew he had been spotted. He darted from behind the bush and ran behind a nearby tree. There was another shot. It hit the tree he was behind. Keeping the tree between him and the man below, Dave climbed to the crest of the hill. Over the hill he went as fast as he could. He was safe, at least for now. In the distance he saw a steeple with a cross on top. That would be his destination. Down the hill he went as fast as he could go while still being cautious.

Dave made his way through the trees and undergrowth. He tried as much as possible to keep moving in the direction of the steeple that he had seen from the hill. Soon he reached a gravel road. He was afraid to come out into the open at first. He listened and watched in both directions for several minutes before he came out onto the road.

"Which way?" he said aloud. "If I don't want to go wrong, I'd better go right," he said pointing to the right. He took a quick breath and blew it out. Then he started jogging down the road. It wasn't long before he saw it. Somehow, he had known it would turn out this way. He stopped in his tracks.

"Ain't this a lowdown dirty shame," he said looking at the highway. "Even when I go right, I go wrong. I can't win," he said sadly. "But I'd better get away from this highway or I won't be able to go wrong again."

The thought of being killed was motivation enough to start him moving again. He figured that if he could see the highway, someone passing by in a car would be able to see him. He quickly ran from the road and into the trees. He was now in the woods on the other side of the road. The under growth was not quite so thick on this side. He decided to stay under cover until he was out of sight of the road. Even though he could not go straight, he could weave his way around trees and bushes and still move speedily. Within five minutes he was across the road from where he had come out of the woods. Now he felt that it was safe to get back on the road. He was about to come out of trees when he heard noise from the other side of the road. He hid behind a tree and waited.

'Could it be the man with the rifle,' he thought. 'He couldn't have caught up with me this quickly.' His heart began to pound. He could hear himself breathing short quick breaths through his open mouth. His eyes became bigger and bigger as the noise grew louder. Then he saw something moving through the trees. It was low to the ground and it was moving swiftly.

'It couldn't be a man,' he thought. That made him feel a little safer, that is until it charged out onto the road. 'A wolf,' he thought ' a female.'

The she wolf was big, with black hair, red eyes, and long white fangs. She was making growling sounds as she moved. Dave watched as she moved down the road in the direction that Dave had gone when he had come out of the woods. In fact, she was following the exact same path that Dave had gone.

The wolf quickly ran down the road to where Dave had crossed the street. It crossed the street and ran into the woods just as Dave had done.

"It's tracking me," Dave said softly. "Why is this happening to me."

Dave ran out of the wood and down the road as fast as he could. He could only hope that this road would lead to the church. He looked back. He saw nothing. There was a curve in the road up ahead.

"Please, please let it be there!" he said aloud as he ran around the curve.

When the road straightened out, he saw the church. It was a beautiful sight for his eyes to see. It was a white wood frame building with a tall steeple. There was a sign out in front of the church.

"Gethsemane Church of Christ" the sign read, "Rev. L. W. Zackery, Pastor." That name seemed familiar to Dave. Dave didn't waste any time trying to remember. He was giving out of gas. His pace had slowed tremendously, and his lungs were burning. He could barely lift his legs to run. He looked back to see if the wolf was coming. He saw nothing.

"Just a little further," he said trying to encourage himself as he crossed a little bridge. "I can do it." He focused on the front door of the church.

'If I can just make it to the door, I'll be safe,' he thought. "Make it to the door?" said aloud. "I need to get inside. Suppose it's locked?' Suppose it locked! Who in their right mind would leave their door unlocked?"

He looked behind him again. He was glad the he had taken the time to pee when he was in the woods, because what he saw would have scared the pee out of him. The wolf was charging full speed at him. Her fiery red eyes were filled with hate, and her fangs were fully exposed. New strength came into Dave's legs as he ran toward the door which was only twenty feet away. He didn't want to, but he looked around anyway.

"Ahhhhhh," he yelled when he saw how close the wolf was. Now, the door was the only option. The woods were farther away from him than the church. He looked up toward the sky.

"God please! If you're there, please, let that door be open." He ran up the steps in two strides. When he reached the porch, he and turned and looked back. The wolf was coming up the steps. "Please!" Dave said as he grabbed the door and turned. It was not locked. He quickly pushed the door open just enough for him to slide in, which he did. He pushed the door to close it behind him. However, before he could close it completely, the wolf's head came through opening. The door slammed against her head, but she still, continued her attempt to force her way in. Dave pushed as hard as he could. Then he began kicking the growling and snapping wolf's mouth. Finally, the wolf pulled back out of the door.

Dave breathed a sigh of relief as he locked the door. He walked down the center isle to the communion table which was sitting in front of a raise pulpit. He looked up at the ceiling.

"I owe you one," he said.

The growling outside the front door suddenly stopped. Dave felt relieved. He hoped the wolf had gone. Dave's relief disappeared as quickly as it had come. Suddenly He heard a loud noise. Something or someone had crashed against the door. Dave became fearful again. Then there was another crash against the door. It was even harder than the first. Then, every few seconds there was another crash. Dave knew that the door could not take to many more hits like that. He began to look for somewhere to hide. The only thing he saw was the communion table with a large gold cross on it.

'Maybe he could get inside it,' he thought.

He ran up to it and grabbed the corner and pulled. It did not bulge. He crawled on the table and using his legs he pushed against the podium on the pulpit and was able to tilt the top of the table away from the front wall of the pulpit. The large cross slid off the table and hit the floor. The table was so heavy that he couldn't keep it away from the pulpit wall long enough so he could get in. The reflection of the cross hit his eyes. Instantly, he knew what to do. He got the cross, tilted the table out, and placed the cross between the pulpit wall and the top edge of the communion table. This held the table in place far enough back so he could climb inside. Once inside, he slid the communion trays out of the way, braced his back against the communion table and then with his feet he pushed against the pulpit wall. He removed the cross and let the table back down slowly.

'Nobody would think to look for him here,' he hoped. He made himself as comfortable as possible. Then he heard a terrifyingly loud crash. He knew what it was. The doors had been knocked open. It, whatever it was, was in. Dave listened carefully. He could hear low growling sounds of something that was coming toward him.

Dave couldn't see it. He could only hear the growling. It was a very large female grizzly bear. She walked down the aisle on her four paws until she reached the front pews. Then she froze. She looked around carefully moving only her eyes. Then she stood up on her hind legs and sniffed the air.

Dave was straining to hear but could hear nothing. He moved his head so that his ear was closer to the top on the table. However, when he moved, his foot kicked a communion plate and knocked it off the shelf. It made a loud noise when it hit the bottom inside of the communion table.

Instantly, the bear's head moved forward as she looked at the communion table. She moved up to the communion table, leaned down and grabbed it on both side and snatched it off the floor.

Tears welled up in Dave's eyes. He positioned himself and was about to jump out of the communion table and make a run for it, then he heard a horrible scream of anguish.

"Ahhhhhhh!"

The communion table with Dave inside was thrown back to the floor where it had been before. When Dave regained his bearings, he heard something running out of the church. Everything became quiet. He thought about getting out of the communion table, but he couldn't think of anywhere else to go. So, he made himself as comfortable as possible and he rested. He was very tired. He closed his eyes and in minutes he was asleep.

A few miles away Dutchman was paying a tire road serviceman for pumping up the tires on his car. As the truck pulled off, his mobile phone rang. It was Sibal.

"Dutchman? Is that you?" she said.

"Yeah, did you get him?"

"No! But it gets worse. I'm in jail," she said dejectedly.

"I didn't do any good either. I had to call the boss."

"What did she say?" Sibal asked.

"She wasn't happy. She said she would come out here and handle it herself. I'm just waiting for her to get here."

"Can you come and get me out of jail?" she said.

"I'll get there as soon as I can, but I don't know when that's going to be. You know how much of a pain she be." As he spoke, he saw the reflection of something very large in the window of the car. Dutchman sensing that something was wrong, turned his head and saw the open mouth of a large grizzly bear. He only had time to scream before the bear caught his head with its paw and pinned him to the car. The phone dropped from his hand to the highway and broke.

Sibal who had heard his scream, now, she could only hear static. She didn't say anything. She just quietly hung up the phone and walked with the guard back to her cell.

Chapter 19
The Preacher

A short stout black man walked into the sanctuary of the church. He was dressed in coveralls and he had a white towel in his hand. The morning light shining through the window bounced off his scalp making the top of his head glow through his thinning hair. It was as if he had a halo. He slowly crept up the steps of the pulpit. His short steps revealed his seventy-two years, forty of which were spent as pastor of this church. He began dusting the pulpit furniture.

"Lord," he began to pray softly, "I just want to thank You, for waking me up this morning." He continued to dust as be began to get into a rhythm. "I want to thank You, Lord, mmmm hmmm, for starting me on my way. Oh-o-o yeah. And Lord Lord, I want to thank You, for food on my table, and clothes on my back. Yeah!" He continued dusting the chairs in the pulpit. His voice began to get louder.

"I know Lord, that You didn't have to do it. Mmmm Hmmm. You didn't have to wake me up. You didn't have to provide food for me to eat. You didn't have to give me strength. But because You love me so much, You, let the fire keep on burning just a little while longer. And Lord, I thank You. Now Lord, I just want You to use me. Use me for Your glory. Use me like You never used me before. Just tell me what You want me to do, Lord. If You need somebody, here am I. Use me."

He finished dusting the pulpit furniture and he walked down the steps toward the communion table. He began to get more emotional, and his pitch increased.

"Use me in a mighty way. Give me power! Power to lay hands on the sick and have them recover. Give me power! Power to cast out demons in Your name."

He walked out in front of the table with his arms and head pointed toward heaven.

"Reveal Your will to me Lord. Just show me what You want me to do. I'll go through the storm, and I'll go through the rain. I'll go through the valley, yes I will, of the shadow of death."

He turned around to dust the communion table.

"I'll even go to the gates of," he abruptly stopped when he saw the burned handprints on the table, "hell," he said softly.

He stepped back from the communion table.

"Good Lord! What in the name of God happened to my, I mean, Your table, Lord." He walked up a little closer.

"Are You trying to tell me something, Lord? Is there something You want me to do for You? Is this a sign, Lord?"

He walked right up to the table began to examine the burns closely.

"This had to be done by hands, red hot hands, Lord. But that's impossible!"

He laid the towel down and placed his hands onto the burned handprints. His fingers went down into handprints. The wood had been burned deep.

"Lord, these were hands. Is this some kind of sign, Lord?" Suddenly his hands began to get very cold.

"Ahhh," He said pulling both hands away. "That table is freezing. This is getting pretty weird."

He touched the end of the table. The temperature was normal. Then he put both hands on the table again. Each of his hands were on the outside of the two burnt handprints. Still, the temperature was normal. He quickly moved his hands into the burnt handprints. Instantly, his hands began to get cold.

"Good God Almighty," he said smiling. "This is freezing cold." And it was freezing cold. When he tried to pull his hands away, he couldn't. They were stuck.

"Okay, Lord, I get the message," he said snatching his hands away. He put his hands under his armpits, then he started rubbing them together and blowing on them.

"Lord, okay. I know it's a sign, but a sign of what?" He laughed. "A sign that I need to get a new communion table." Then he looked up. "Just a little joke, Lord." He walked over to the first pew, sat down, and bowed his head.

"Now Lord, you know that I'm not one of Your brightest preachers," he said seriously. "In fact, I'm kinda slow, but once I get to going, I steady as a rock, though. However, this is a bit much for me to figure out. You got to make this thing plain. You got to speak to me in words that I can understand." He looked up. "Please Lord. I'm asking You in the name of Jesus. Speak to me." At that moment he heard a voice.

"Excuse me sir," the voice said, "could you help me get out of here?"

Rev. Zackery jumped to his feet, and his mouth dropped open. He looked around to try to determine where the voice was coming from. Then he began to wonder if he had really heard anything at all. He had almost convinced himself that it was his imagination when he heard it again.

"Sir? Could you give me a hand, please?" the voice said.

He was sure that the voice was coming from the communion table. He looked at his hands and then looked at the burnt handprints on the table.

"Not likely," Rev. Zackery said. "You best forget about the hand for the time being. Anyway, who are you and what do you want?"

"My name is Dave Parker, and I really would appreciate it if you would help me move this table so I can get out of here."

Dave stuck his fingers up from behind the table so that the Reverend could see them.

"Praise the Lord," the Reverend shouted. "You're real," Rev. Zackery said as he walked up to the side of the communion table.

"Yes sir," Dave replied, "real stuck."

Rev. Zackery walked up to the side of the communion table and peeped over and saw Dave's white face.

"What are you doing in my communion table."

"Sir, I don't know if you'll believe me, but something was after me yesterday. It looked like a big wolf."

Rev. Zackery leaned against the communion table and slid it away from the wall of the pulpit.

"A big wolf chase you in the communion table."

Dave crawled out onto the floor knocking the communion serving trays out onto the floor with a loud noise.

"When it chased me in the church it was a wolf. I ran in the door and locked it. But then whatever it was tried to open the door. I saw the nob move. Then it started beating against the door. So, I looked for somewhere to hide. The communion table was the only place I saw. And I knew that it was," Dave paused, "holy." Dave put the trays back inside the communion table and stood up.

"Is that it?"

"No. I tilted the communion table back from the wall, got inside and let it fall back in place. I was as quiet and as still as I could be. I listened and waited," Daved stopped.

"Well, what happened then?"

"I heard this loud noise. Well, actually it was several noises. I knew that the first noise was something knocking the door open. The second noise was the door hitting against the wall. I knew whatever it was, it was inside the church. I could hear footsteps moving down the aisle toward me. It knew where I was. It came right up to the table and grabbed it. The table was lifted off the floor."

"What, this heavy thing," Rev. Zackery said in astonishment.

"I swear to God," Dave said, "this high." Dave held his hand up to his chest.

"Don't swear," Rev. Zackery said scolding. "You should not take the Lord's name in vain."

"Sorry," Dave said. "Anyway, then I heard it scream in pain, and the table fell to the floor. I heard it run down the aisle, and then I heard the door slam shut. I was too afraid to move. Anyway, I felt like I was in the safest place in the world."

"I think you were right," Rev. Zackery said. "Oh, I didn't introduce myself. I'm Rev. Zackery, the pastor of this church."

"I very glad to meet you," Dave said reaching out his hand. The Reverend grabbed it firmly and shook it.

"I guess you're glad I have an open-door policy," Rev. Zackery said.

"Yes, sir. Yesterday was the first time that I have prayed since I was a little boy." Dave said.

"Really now."

"Yes, sir. That wolf would have killed me on the porch of this church if the door had been locked. I remember saying 'Oh God, please let it be open.' It was open."

"Did you tell God, 'thank you.'"

"Now that you mention it, I guess I didn't," Dave said.

"Well, He's still waiting."

Dave looked up. "Thank you, God. Amen," Dave said.

"You believe in getting right to the point, I see," Rev. Zackery said.

Dave smiled. "I'm a little out of practice. But I think it's about time to catch up." Dave looked up at the cross on the back wall of the church. "In the last few days, I've learned a lot about the existence of evil, and yesterday I learned about the power of good."

"There's a lot more to learn, but you came to the right place," Rev. Zackery said. "I'm not sure about this, but I think the Lord wants to use you."

"Use me!"

"I think the Lord has chosen you to do a work for Him," Rev. Zackery said. "Have you ever heard the Lord speak to you. Not like He spoke to Noah or Moses, but in a still small voice. Have you ever had a thought so strong that you could almost hear it?"

"Yeah, just a couple of days ago, when I saw my wife having sex with another man, I had this very strong thought, 'I'm gone kill you'," Dave said angrily.

"Now, let me get this straight. A couple of days ago you saw your wife having sex with another man, last night a wolf chased you into my communion table. Is there anything else?"

"Yes sir," Dave said. "Three times, this man tried to kill me and my friend. He shot me in my leg, killed a clerk and two policemen. Then these hillbillies attacked us, and they killed my friend and her aunt. They burned her house down with her and them in it. The hillbillies, my friend, and her aunt, they all got burned up. Then another man tried to make me have an accident by shooting out my tire. When that didn't work, he tried to shoot me. Oh yeah, last, but not least, I got trapped inside a crystal ball at the fortune teller's house."

They stared at each other for a minute. Dave was waiting for him to respond. Finally, Rev. Zackery looked up, began moving his head up and down as if saying yes to the Lord, and then he spoke.

"Finally, my brethren, be strong in the Lord and in the power of his might. Put on the whole armor of God, that you may be able to stand against the wiles of the devil. For we wrestle not against flesh and blood, but against principalities, against powers, against the rulers of the darkness of this world, against spiritual wickedness in high places: Ephesians five, eleven and twelve." Rev. Zackery gave a look of concern. "It looks like you are under spiritual attack, son."

"Spiritual attack?" Dave said, questioningly. "No sir. I just accidentally got caught up in somebody else's problems."

"It may seem that way, but these things were no accidents," Rev. Zackery said shaking his head. "God brought you here to me because He wants us to do something. I don't know everything, but I know that He wants you to put on the armor of God. You won't make it through this if you don't."

"What is this armor you're talking about?"

Well, there is the girt of truth, the breastplate of righteousness, the shoes of the gospel of peace, the shield of faith, the helmet of salvation, and the sword of the spirit, which is the word of God."

"Reverend," Dave said interrupting. "I don't mean any harm, but I just need to call the police, report what happened to my rental car, and get back home. Then all this will be over. I promise you, as soon as I get home, I'm going to find a church, and start putting on all this armor."

"You know, you could probably get by with just the shield of faith and the sword, for right now," Rev. Zackery said. "Oh yeah, you've got to have the helmet of salvation. Are you saved, son?"

"Rev. Zackery, can I use your phone?" Dave pleaded.

"Why don't you come with me? We'll eat a little breakfast and talk a while. Maybe we'll both discover what it is that the Lord wants us to do."

Rev. Zackery took Dave by his arm and the two men walked out of a back door of the sanctuary.

CHAPTER 20
SAVED

Several miles away, Jason sat in Mammie's car which was parked on the road in front of the charred remains of Mammie's house. Tears rolled down his face as he remembered what Mammie had said to him. He was going to have to use the crystal to fight the witches. He had no idea how he was going to do it, but he was sure that he would be able to figure something out. If nothing else, he could keep an eye on them. But first things first, he had to find it, then he would start to plan his revenge. He would repay them for killing his grandmother and Pam too. His eyes began to steam as hate began to burn in him. First, he was going to locate their leader, then he was going to kill her and the one who killed his grandmother. Rage began to build in him. He could hardly wait, but he had to wait, and he had to be calm so he could think clearly.

His mind began to roam through the recent past. He saw Pam in his mind the first time he had seen her. She was so exciting and attractive. If they had met in different circumstances, he would have made a play for her. She was so fine. Even though they had not spoken very much, he felt that they had established a closeness like the closeness that brothers and sisters who grew up in different household have when they finally meet. Suddenly, he felt sorrow realizing that he had been robbed of the opportunity and joy of getting to know her better.

Though the sun had been up for a while, it's light was just now reaching the edge of Mammie's yard. When the sun pushed the shadow of a nearby mountain past the remains of the house, Jason got out of the car to begin his search.

"Now, where was that crystal room," Jason said as he worked his way slowly and carefully through the rubble. Portions of the hardwood floor were still intact, and other areas were totally, destroyed. He could not tell what was good or bad until he stepped down. Therefore, he tested each step to make sure he wouldn't fall through. When he reached the place where the crystal room had been, he began he began to pick up the burned planks and throw them out into the front yard. He cleaned out enough of the woods to see that the crystal was not there. At least it is not here now, he thought. 'Maybe they beat me to the punch. Maybe they have it,' he thought.

He looked at all the debris left to look through. It was too much, plus it should have been where he had searched. He decided it was pointless to look anymore. As he made his way out of the rubble, an image appeared in his mind. He saw Mammie's burned body. He could hear her say, 'Only the crystal can save you.' He stopped.

"She never would have told me that if they had the crystal," he said aloud. "It's got to be here, and I've got to find it."

He turned around and surveyed the area. He would begin in Mammie room. He was about to step over a beam when he heard something. Immediately, he ducked down into the burned wood. He made a three-hundred-sixty-degree sweep of the area. Then he made another sweep. He could see nothing. He could have sworn that he had heard something. He stood still and listened. Nothing. He moved toward Mammie's room. He heard it again. The sound had come from his left, the area of the house where Dave had been sleeping. There it was again. It was very faint, but it sounded like somebody saying 'help.' Jason was moving toward the sound when his foot hit something that rolled under his foot causing him to lose his balance and fall back into the rubble.

"What the ..." He didn't finish his sentence because he knew what it was that had caused him to fall. He reached down and pulled the crystal from the rubble. He quickly placed it in his pocket and continued toward the spot where the sound was emanating. He could hear it better now. It was a voice calling out for help. Jason moved closer. Suddenly a thought occurred to him.

"This could be a trap," he said reaching inside his coat and pulling the jack handle from his belt. He moved forward again until he reached a spot where the burned wood had fallen into a hole.

"Is anybody down there," he said yelled.

"Jason! Is that you! Get me out of here," the voice said.

"Pam?" Jason shouted.

"Yeah," the voice said. "I'm penned down and I can't move. Be careful," she said, her voice getting weaker.

"Well, if you are Pam, what did I have on when you first saw me?"

"I don't give a damn what you had on! Jason! You get me the hell out of this hole."

"Pam!" Jason smiled. "I'll have you out of there in a few minutes. Are you hurt?"

"I don't know. My legs are numb."

"Just hold on," he said worriedly, "I'm coming." He cleared away the debris as quickly as he could and then went down the ladder. When he reached the bottom, he moved two large beams that was lying on the blankets she was under. Then he dropped to his knees in front of her, grabbed her tightly, but tenderly. She responded by holding him and kissing him on the cheek.

"I thought you were dead," Jason said as he pulled back to look into her eyes.

"What about Auntie? Did she get out?"

Jason's joyous expression turned to sorry as he shook his head 'no.'

"What?" Pam yelled.

"She didn't make it, she's dead," Jason said. She was caught in the fire."

"I'm so sorry, Jason," she rubbed the back of his head as he sobbed on her shoulder. "When I woke up the house was burning. I wanted to find her, but when I opened the door flames were everywhere. There were even flames outside my window. I only had time to get down here. No, no, Auntie," she moaned. Tears began to fall from her eyes. "What happened? How did the house catch on fire?"

"It was set on fire. The police believe it was those guys, you and Dave had a fight with."

"How was that possible? They didn't know that we were coming here."

"That's my fault," Jason said. "Last night, me and Dave had an altercation with them. They jumped me and I told them that I was Miss Mammie's grandson. Remember, Gramma told me to tell that, to anyone who bothered me."

"So, they came and killed Auntie because of you?" Pam asked. "You are the reason Auntie is dead."

"Partially, I am," Jason said. "I'm the reason the they found out where gramma lived, but they came to gramma's house, looking for you and they killed gramma."

"Why would those guys want to kill Auntie," Pam screamed. "That doesn't' make any sense."

"The guys didn't kill her. They died in the fire, too. It was the witches."

"Witches?" Pam said dejectedly.

"They didn't know that you were in the house. They searched the house. They thought you had gotten away," Jason said softly.

"If they searched the house, they should have found me. I was in the guest bedroom, asleep," Pam explained "She must have used the crystal to hide me."

"They tied Gramma to a chair with coat hangers and set her on fire, trying to get her to tell them where you were. But she never did. They burned her up, alive."

"No, no, no," Pam cried. "It's all my fault. Auntie, I'm so sorry." Pam moaned, as the tears flowed.

"It's not your fault. They would have killed her anyway. They thought you got away. I know because they tried to kill me last night."

"What?"

"It was a deputy sheriff. She broke in my room to see if I knew where you were and to kill me. I stopped her and turned her in, to the sheriff. I found out, they sent someone to kill Dave, too. He may already be dead."

"How did you know to come looking for me?" Pam asked. "Did Dave tell you about the well?"

"I didn't come here looking for you. I came looking for the crystal ball," Jason explained. "Gramma told me that I would need it to fight the witches. I'm going after the ones that killed gramma."

"Auntie told you?" Pam said confused. "I thought she died in the fire?"

"I'll tell you everything later, let's get you out of here and taken care of, first."

Minutes later, Jason had Pam draped over his back as he moved through the debris toward the front yard. He carried her to his car and put her in the back seat.

"Get out of those wet clothes," he said handing her his coat.

He walked around the car, got in, started the engine, and the heater fan began to blow. He reached down to feel the air. It was cold, so he turned the heater off.

" The engine will be hot in a min...", his words stopped when he looked around and saw her half naked body. She didn't try to cover up.

"Sorry," he said looking away. A picture of her breast locked in his mind. He turned the heater on again.

"Can you give me a hand with these pants," Pam signed, as she struggled to get her pants off. Jason turned quickly and looked at her. She had his coat on now.

"Yeah," he said reaching over the seat and grabbing hold to her pants just below the hips. "I'm real good at this."

He lifted her, gave a little pull and the pants came off her hips. He lowered her and three seconds later the pants came off, leaving her legs and feet pointed toward the sky.

"You are good at this," she said as her numb legs fell against the back window. Within seconds he was on the back seat with her legs in his lap messaging them. He started at her feet; one hand on each foot. Then he worked his way up. When he reached her thighs, his hands began to sweat.

"What's this?" she said. He looked up and she was pulling the crystal out of his coat pocket. "We can use this to see Dave."

'I just saved your life and all you can think about is Dave,' Jason thought. "Yeah, we need to warn him, that deputy bitch said that the guy who killed Gramma was going to try to kill him," Jason said as he took the crystal from Pam and sat it in the back window. He rubbed it and thought. Immediately the crystal disappeared as an image began to appear. Pam could not tell what it was.

"What is that!" she said looking at Jason. His mouth was open as he looked at the image and then looked down. Then Pam looked down and she knew. She put her hand over her panties and wiggled her fingers. She could see her fingers wiggling in the crystal ball image. She looked at Jason with a questioning look.

"Well, I thought I was thinking about Dave," he said taking her wet T-shirt from the floor and covering the crystal. The image disappeared. "You do it."

"What's on your mind?" she said as she rubbed the crystal. Instantly, an image appeared. "He's alive!" she shouted.

In the image Dave and this older black man were eating breakfast.

"This is so good. It doesn't look like it's supposed to be good, but it is," Dave said in the image.

"You better slow down, son. You're gonna hurt yourself eating so fast," the old man said.

"What is this anyway," Dave said as he crammed two big forkfuls into his mouth.

"Aw, this ain't nothing but some grits and brains."

The food in Dave's mouth exploded back onto his plate. "Brains!" Dave shouted. "Pig brains?"

"Oh, I'm sorry son, I didn't know that didn't eat pork."

"That's okay reverend. It hasn't been that long since I stopped."

"Dave is such a snob," Pam said to Jason. "He knew those brains were tasting good."

"Okay," Jason said. "He's alive, now, but he may not stay that way if we don't find him before they do. You keep watching. Maybe, he'll say something that will help us locate him." Jason started massaging her feet again as Pam watched the image.

"So, what did the police say? Rev. Zackery asked.

"They said they would send a car to the scene of the accident, and I would have to come in and fill out a report. I don't think they believed me, especially when I told them about the witches."

"Witches," Rev. Zackery shouted. "What witches?"

"Oh, I didn't tell you about the witches that are after me?"

"No! I'm sure you didn't," Rev. Zackery said and then looked up. "Howbeit this kind goeth not out but by prayer and fasting, St. Matthew 17:21."

"I didn't tell you because I didn't think you would believe it. I really don't believe it myself.

"There has been some talk about witchcraft ceremonies in these woods a few years ago."

"You don't believe in that witchcraft stuff, do you?" Dave asked.

"Of course, I do. You see, there are two kinds of witches. There are the ones that do spells, read fortunes, and you know, put roots on people. They are not so bad. They can change, repent, and be saved. Then, there are the really, evil ones who have made a vow to satin. They have sold their souls to the devil. They can't be saved." Rev. Zackery began shaking his head. "Yes. Witches are real, demons, too. If the evil witches are after you, we better start fasting and praying. Jesus is the only one who can save you from them. Before you do anything else, you need to accept Jesus as your Lord and Savior."

"Rev. Zackery! I told you I would find me a church when I got back home. I really don't know much about Jesus," Dave said anxiously.

"Look! I'll make this short, and straight to the point." He paused. "God, the father and creator of us all, sent His only son, Jesus, into the world to die on a cross to pay for the sins of all mankind. So, now all a person has to do is confess that Jesus is the son of God, believe that God raised Jesus from the dead, and accept Jesus as their lord and savior and they shall be saved. Can you do that? Now!"

"Okay, I guess so," Dave said slowly.

"Okay. Bow your head and repeat after me, this prayer to God."

"All right," Dave said bowing his head and closing his eyes.

"Lord God, I know that I don't know you," Rev. Zackery said. As he spoke, Dave repeated his words. "But I come to you in faith. I confess that Jesus is Your only begotten son, that Jesus died for my sins, and that You raised Jesus from the dead. Now Jesus, come into my heart. I believe, but help my unbelief, save me now, in Jesus name I pray, amen."

They both opened their eyes and Rev. Zackery hugged Dave tightly. There was silence for a minute as the two men looked at each other. Dave thought that he would feel changed, but he didn't feel any different.

"Is that it?" Dave asked.

"That's just the beginning, but you are saved." Rev. Zackery hugged him again.

"I thought that I was going to feel something."

Rev. Zackery hit Dave hard on his forehead with the palm of his hand and yelled. "You're saved." Dave fell back two steps. When he had regained his balance, Rev. Zackery said quietly, "Did you feel something?"

Dave rubbed his forehead, while blinking away the water forming in his eyes, and then he spoke. "Rev. Zackery, would it be possible for you to take me to rent a car?"

"Certainly, son. However, I need to fix the door of the church. It's okay for it to be unlocked, but at the least, it needs to be able to close securely," Rev. Zackery said as brought a bible over to Dave. "While I do that, I want you to read the first fifteen chapters of Saint John."

"All right," Pam shouted. "I've heard that name before."

"What name?"

"Rev. Zackery," she said slowly "in Tipton."

"You saw something?"

"If anything happens to me go see Rev. Zackery in Tipton. That's what Auntie said the night she was killed."

"Okay! Let's go find a phone book and call the righteous Rev. Zackery then we'll get you some clothes, and then we need to get some food. I'm starving. I could even eat a plate of those grits and brain right about now."

Minutes later, they were driving down the highway, Jason and Pam on the inside, Dave, sitting at the kitchen table reading the bible, where the back window of the car should have been.

A car approached them. The driver was a young man in his early twenties. He had a cigarette hanging precariously from his mouth. When he passed by Jason's car his eyes became glued to the back of the car where the image of Dave, sitting at a table, was. The cigarette dropped from his mouth into his lap. Jason looked into the sideview mirror as the young man's car fishtailed and then went into a spin. It ended up in the ditch beside the road.

"I think you better cover up that crystal," Jason said.

"Yeah, right," said Pam. She had seen the car too. "I hope he's all right," she said with a guilty expression. Neither of them said anything for several miles.

Chapter 21
The Release

Dutchman walked into the sheriff's office. The deputy at the desk looked him over suspiciously.

"May I help you?" he asked.

"I'm attorney John Peters. I understand the you have my client locked up," Dutchman said.

"What is your client's name?"

"Sibal Smith," Dutchman replied.

"That's right. She's in lock up. But if you have come to bail her out you can forget it. Bail won't be set until one o'clock, this afternoon. That's when her arraignment is scheduled. Come back after three, you should be able to get her then," the deputy said.

"Well," Dutchman said wondering if he should push the deputy into releasing Sibal. He decided against it. "Would it be possible for me to see her."

The deputy opened a draw in his desk, pulled out an empty box, and put it on the desk. "Empty all of your pockets and put everything in here," the deputy said.

Dutchman began taking everything out of his pockets. "By the way, what are the charges against her."

The deputy type on his computer and began to read. "Breaking and entering, one count; simple assault and battery, two counts; assault with a deadly weapon; two counts; destruction of private property, one count;

attempted murder, two counts; and conduct unbecoming an officer, eight counts." The deputy looked up at Dutchman. "If your client is convicted, she'll be in jail for five years minimum."

"May I see her now?"

"Yeah, just step through the metal detector and follow me," the deputy said as he walked toward a door on the side of the room.

When they entered the next room, Dutchman could see her about three cells down on the right.

"There she is," the deputy said. "You got ten minutes."

"Thank you," Dutchman said as he continued to walk toward Sibal.

"Man, I am so glad to see you. I thought you were dead. What happened to you when I called you earlier? Why did you scream?"

"It was Tamera. She was a bear. She came up behind me while I was talking to you and pinned me against the car. I thought she was going to bite my head off," he said.

"Back up a minute! What are you talking about? What is this bear stuff?"

"While I was talking to you on the phone this grizzly bear came up behind me. That's what made me scream. It pushed my face against the car with one of its paws. Then, it, the paw, began to change."

"Change?"

"Yeah. It changed into a hand, Tamera hand," Dutchman paused and waited for a response.

"I knew it. I knew she could change herself into other animals?"

"Well, I wish you had told me, because she almost made me pee on myself."

"So, what happened when she changed?" Sibal asked.

"I turned around and grabbed her. She was in daze. Her eyes had rolled to the back of her head and she was naked as a Jay bird."

"How long was she in this daze?" Sibal asked.

201

"Oh, about three or four seconds."

"That's plenty of time," she said.

"Plenty of time for what?"

"Nothing."

"Anyway, something had happened to her while she was a bear. Both of her paws, I mean her hands were burned. I mean, when she was a bear her paws were burned and then when she changed back into herself, her hands were still burned. And she did not kill Parker. He must have gotten away, and she was mad. I'm supposed to go to his home tomorrow and kill him."

"He got away from her." Sibal whispered.

"Yeah. But let me tell you this. When the dude got away from me, he hid in the woods. So, I called her on my mobile phone. She told me to look through my scope and sweep the woods. Then she told me where aim my rifle and when to shot. Somehow, she saw Parker though my eyes, cause when I shot where she said, he jumped up and ran over the hill. Then she told me to wait there for her. She said that she would take care of him."

A door opened and the deputy stuck his head inside. "Okay buddy, times up."

"Five minutes?" Dutchman pushed the thought at him.

"You can hear, can't you? You got five minutes!" He walked out.

"You are getting me out, aren't you?" Sibal asked.

"No, I can't do anything until after your arraignment. That's when bail will be set."

"So, I've got to sit in here till after they set bail?" Sibal growled.

"Maybe longer."

"What do you mean?"

"You have been charged with attempted murder and a million other crimes. The judge may not allow bail, or it may be so high that I won't be able to pay it."

"You can't just leave me in here," Sibal pleaded.

"When you go to court, I'll try to push the judge into dropping the charges," Dutchman said. "I can't make any promises, I may not be able to get close enough to project any thoughts into his head."

"Just do your best. I know you'll think of something."

"How did you get yourself into this mess, anyway," Dutchman said disgustedly.

"You didn't do so good yourself, you know."

"Well, at least I didn't get myself locked up."

"I don't know," Sibal said. "I guess I just underestimated him. I didn't know that he had this force working in him."

"Force? What force!"

"Revenge," Sibal replied. "He wants revenge for his grandmother's death."

"He's going to try to kill me?"

"No, he's going to try to kill Tamera."

"Tamera!" Dutchman shouted. "How does he know about her."

"He was going to drown me."

"He was going to drown YOU! Why didn't he?"

"He wants me to take him to Tamera," she said softly. "He's sure he can kill her."

"What?" Dutchman shouted again. "You're going to take him to her, aren't you?" Sibal said nothing. "You have gone completely crazy!"

"I don't know. Maybe he can kill her," she said. "Anyway, what do we have to lose?"

"Didn't you hear me? I just said she could see through my eyes. Maybe she can hear through my ears as well. Maybe, she's listening right now. I'm out of here," Dutchman turned and began walking away. "I'll see you in court. They should be coming to get you soon."

"How many times is she going to allow you to fail before she decides to replace you?"

Dutchman didn't look around, but he heard her. He knew that Tamera would probably kill him if he failed her again. He had a big problem.

He walked over to the courthouse and panic struck his heart. There she was. Tamera was waiting for him. He wondered how she knew about Sibal. He walked up to him. She whispered something in his ear and then he walked out.

Tamera was waiting in the hall of the courthouse when Sheriff Harris and his two deputies escorted Sibal down the hall to the courtroom. When they were about to pass her, she called to him.

"Sheriff Harris!"

"Yes Ma'am," he said looking her way. "What can I do for you?"

"I have some important information for you concerning the death of Mammie Scott," she said beckoning him closer.

"Take her in the court," he said to his deputies. "I'll be there in a minute." Sibal's eyes grew big as she looked at Tamera.

When the sheriff walked over to her, she cupped her hand next to her mouth and leaned over to whisper in his ear.

"I was told to warn you that if you didn't drop the charges against Sibal Smith something bad was going to your johnson." While she had been talking, she had rubbed a white powder in his hair above his ear.

"My johnson? What are you talking about?" he said backing away.

"I'm talking about your johnson, you know, little Willie," she said looking down at his crotch. When he looked down, she raised her balled up fist of her other hand to her mouth and quickly blew through it. A fine mist of white dust encircled his face. When he raised his head, he inhaled some of the dust.

"Look here woman," he said coughing, "I don't know you think you are, but I could put you in jail for saying that to me."

Tamera took a little medicine bottle from her bag and put it on the water fountain.

"I was told that you should drink this on after you drop, what you're supposed to drop." Tamera was backing away now. "You really should go to the rest room before you go to court." She turned and walked into the courtroom.

Sheriff Harris was about to follow Tamera into the courtroom when he felt a severe itch in his crotch. He began scratching vigorously before he reached the rest room. He was pulling down his pants as he walked into the stall. He leaned back against the stall door as he pulled down his shorts. His mouth dropped open as his head lowered so he could see better.

"What in the hell is that," he gasped holding his penis. It was covered with big red bumps that were itching like hell. He quickly pulled up his clothes and rushed out to the water fountain. There it was. The medicine bottle was just where she had left it. He grabbed it and put it in his pocket. He then walked down the hall and into the courtroom.

"Glad you could make sheriff," said the short-haired female judge behind the bench.

"Sorry your Honor. I received some new information on this case just a few minutes ago," he said as he spotted Tamera sitting in the courtroom. "Because of this information," the itch was making him squirm, " I feel that officer Smith acted appropriately and I am dropping all charges against her."

"In that case, officer Smith, you're free to go," the judge said striking her gavel on her desk.

Sheriff Harris rushed from the courtroom as Sibal walked up to Tamera.

"Thanks for getting me out of this," Sibal said cautiously. "I thought Dutchman was coming."

"I sent him to get some supplies. He's going to meet us in Tipton, we're going to church." Tamera gave Sibal a cold stare.

"Okay," Sibal said as fear began to build in her.

She wondered if Dutchman had told her what she had said. They walked out of the courtroom down the hall and past the men's rest room.

Inside the rest room, Sheriff Harris was pacing back and forth, waiting for one of his deputies to come out of one of the stalls. When the deputy opened the stall to come out, Sheriff Harris pushed him back in and locked the door.

"What going on, Sheriff?" the deputy said loudly. The sheriff began to unzip his pants. "Hey man! What the hell are you doing?" the deputy shouted as he tried to push his way out of the stall. The sheriff blocked the door as he pulled out his penis. The deputy backed away pulled his pistol and aimed it at the sheriff's penis.

"You better put it back in there before I blow it off," the deputy yelled.

"Do you see any bumps?" the sheriff pleaded, afraid to look himself.

"Bumps?"

"Yeah, big red bumps," The sheriff said.

The deputy stuck his gun in the sheriff's chest and pulled the hammer back. "If you move, I swear, I'll kill you. Do you hear me, Sheriff?" Sheriff Harris nodded as the deputy lowered his head and looked a little closer.

"No! I don't see no bumps."

The sheriff looked down and relief filled his heart. "Oh Lord, thank you! Thank you! Oh Lord, thank you, thank you, thank you!"

"Okay Sheriff, now let me outta here," the deputy demanded.

The two men walked out of the stall as the sheriff zipped up his pants. There were several men in the rest room now. When they saw the Sheriff, they began to whisper and smile. However, when they saw the cocked thirty-eight revolver in the sheriff's back, they and their smiles quickly left the room.

Chapter 22
Showdown at the Church

Jason and Pam were driving down the highway looking for the turnoff that the service station attendant had told them about. Pam had on a pair of loose-fitting jeans and a sweatshirt that Jason had bought her. They were both were eating hamburgers and fries.

"Hey, that looks like it up there," Pam said. Jason slowed down. There was a small old faded sign that had the word, "Church" painted on it. Below the word, there was an arrow pointing down the gravel road. Jason turn off the road and slowly drove down the road.

"You'd better keep your eyes peeled," Jason glanced at Pam.

"Yeah, we need to get in here, get him, and get out of here as quick as we can."

They went around a curve and saw the white church. They crossed over a little bridge, and then saw a house about two hundred feet back and to the left of the church. There was no grass for about twenty feet in front of the house. It was just sandy dirt that looked as if it had been swept with a broom. They drove up toward the front of the house, stopping before they reached the swept area.

"We'd better check the crystal out," Jason said to Pam as he reached into his coat pocket a pulled out the crystal.

"Yeah, I'll do it," she said taking it from Jason. "We already know what's on your mind." She rubbed it and an image appeared. Dave and Rev. Zackery were playing a game of checkers. Pam covered the crystal with her T-shirt and put it in the glovebox. "Okay, looks like the coast is clear. Let's go."

They got out of the car and walked up on the porch to the door like two police detectives. Jason knocked. A few moments later a frowning Rev. Zackery opened to the door just enough to see out.

"May I help you?" Rev. Zackery said.

"Yes sir, you may. We're looking for Dave Parker. He's a friend of ours," Pam said politely.

"Your face look familiar, Miss," Rev. Zackery said, "what is your name?" "Pamela Williamson," Pam said.

"Little Pam? Mammie's god niece?", he said excitedly.

"Yes sir. Do you know me?"

"Lord have mercy! Yes, I do and your god aunt too!" Rev. Zackery said smiling from ear to ear. "How is that old girl doing?"

"She's dead," Pam and Jason said at the same time.

"She told me if anything happened to her, I mean if she died, she said to contact you."

Yes, we talked a few weeks ago about her funeral plans." He said as his expression saddened. "What happened to her?"

"She was killed yesterday," Jason said angrily.

"Who are you son?"

"Mammie Scott was my grandmother, I'm Jason Scott."

"Won't you come in?" Rev. Zackery said opening the door. "Dave! You've got some company."

When they walked in, they saw a long-barreled pistol in the reverend's hand. The door of a back room opened, and Dave stood in the doorway motionless for a moment as he looked at Pam.

"We thought you were dead," Dave said as a smile exploded on his face. He ran to her and hugged her tightly. "Where were you? We thought the you had been killed in the fire with Mammie."

"I was in the house when it was set on fire, but I went down in the pit to get away from the fire. I was trapped down there until Jason came and found me."

"How did you know where she was?" Dave said turning to Jason.

"I was looking for the crystal and I heard her calling for help," Jason said impatiently. "But we don't have time for this. Those witches are after us. That woman deputy is one of them. She tried to kill me, and she said that the one who killed my gramma was sent to kill you. So, we need to get out of here, now!"

"Somebody did," Dave shouted.

"Did what?" Pam asked.

"Somebody shot my tire out as I was going around a mountain curve and caused me to drive off a cliff," Dave said and stopped.

"Then, what happened?" Pam said anxiously.

Dave told them everything that happened from the time he drove off the cliff till he met Rev. Zackery. Everyone remained quiet for a few minutes when he had finished.

"Look!" Jason said as a frown appeared on his face. "You can either run or fight. I know that I'm going to kill those witches that killed my grandmother."

"I hate to interrupt your homicidal plans," Rev. Zackery interrupted, "but, what about the funeral arrangements."

"How long will that take?" Jason asked impatiently.

"We could be through in thirty minutes," Rev. Zackery said. "Just let me get my funeral book."

"Okay, but the sooner we leave, the better it will be for us and you, Rev. Zackery."

Rev. Zackery walked out of the room and closed the door. As soon as the door closed, Jason started talking. "This is what I was able to find out from the deputy witch-bitch," Jason whispered." Pam has a twin sister, who is the head witch of this coven. Somehow her powers are reduced because of Pam. That's why she wants Pam dead. And, I guess they are killing anybody who knows about them. So, they want us dead, too."

"Does that mean they are going to keep coming until they kill us?" Dave asked.

"Or until we kill them," Jason said angrily.

"And just how are you planning on doing that?" Dave said.

"I going to choose where I want her to catch up with me, trap her, and then I'll blow her witch-bitch, brains out. It's as simple as that," Jason said.

"I'm in," Pam said.

"Do you call that a plan? Let the police handle it," Dave pleaded.

"Have you forgotten that Officer Smith is a police officer. We don't know how many..." Jason words were interrupted when the window was broken by a stick of dynamite which landed in the middle of the floor. Jason started toward the dynamite. His plan was to pull out the fuse. However, as soon as he stood up two more sticks came in through two other windows. Just then Rev. Zackery opened the door from the back room. He saw the dynamite on the floor in front of him and he quickly closed the door again. Pam ran for the front door with Dave right behind her. Jason picked up a chair and rammed it through a nearby window. Then he dived through the window. The dynamite exploded. The force of the blast propelled them forward and down into the dirt twenty feet away. Debris and dust rained down on them. The house was instantly transformed into flying kindling. The wood rained down on them for almost fifteen second which to them seemed like an eternity. They each covered up their heads as best they could as their bodies were bombarded from the sky.

"Aaaaaah," Dave yelled as a large plank hit his leg.

"Oh, aah, sheeee," Jason moaned as he was hit three times in three seconds. The first two on his legs, but the third hit was to his ribs on his right side. The pain shot throughout his body. He instantly grabbed his side and began feeling for protruding bones. He breathed a sigh of relief when he didn't feel any. Eventually, the pain diminished as the last few bits of wood hit the ground.

"Pam? Are you okay?" Jason said.

"Yeah," she said as she pushed a part of the front door off her. It had landed near her and she had crawled under it for protection.

"What about you Dave, are you okay?" Jason said.

"I just hope this is sweat on my leg," Dave said feeling his leg. It was not sweat. He had been cut but it was not deep. Then he remembered. "Rev. Zackery!" They all looked back to see a pile of rubble where the house had once stood. The same thought came to each of their minds. 'No way he could have made it.'

"Let's get to the car before the dust settles," Jason said.

"What car?" Dave replied, "I don't see a car." They all strained to see through the dust.

"There it is! Over there to the left!" Pam said.

The explosion had blown them farther than they had thought possible. The car was behind them to the left. They hurried to the car which was covered wood and broken glass. They open the doors on the left side. Pam and Dave got in the back moving wood and throwing it out the windows as soon as they could. Before Jason could get in, he had to move a long two-by-four that had probably taken out the whole front missing windshield.

The dust was beginning to clear as Jason started the car. He turned the wheel and stomped the accelerator. The car spun around and moved swiftly past the church toward the little bridge. Pam was peeping over the back seat while Dave lay on the floor behind Jason.

"Get down!" Dave shouted as he pulled Pam's arm. Pam would not move. She saw something on the bridge.

"Stop!" Pam said as she reached over the seat and grabbed the wheel and pushed up. "There's dynamite on the bridge."

Jason hit the brakes and the car immediately began to spin around to the left just before they had reached the bridge. Then the bridge exploded, and the car left the road. It rolled over and came to rest upside down in the ditch near the road where the bridge had been. The occupants wasted no time vacating the car. They quickly climbed through the opening where the front windshield had been.

"Stay in the ditch and follow me," Jason whispered, "and stay low. When we get up to the bend, we'll have to make a run for the church."

As they crawled down in the ditch a gunshot was fired. It hit the gas tank and the car exploded. They stopped for a second ducking down, but when they started again, they were moving twice as fast. When they reached the bend where the ditch turned right away from the church, they stopped.

"Okay now," Jason said, "when I say go, run as fast as you can for the church. Spread out and don't run in a straight line, zig zag a little. Don't give them an easy shot." Jason looked at them both. "We can make it. You ready? Go!"

They did just as he had instructed. As they ran toward the church Jason took an early lead that increased with every step. They did not hear a single shot. Jason was the first to reach the steps of the church. Somehow Jason knew that the shooter was waiting for his best shot, a shot at the door. That's what he would do. Jason took the steps three at a time. He visualized that he was the shooter and that he had the cross hairs aimed at the door. When Jason reached the top of the stairs, instead of going toward the door he ducked and went to the right. A hole appeared in the door. As Jason hid behind the right column of the church porch, he heard the shot catch up with the bullet. Pan was coming up the steps by this time. Jason dashed back across the porch opening the door as he went by. Another hole appeared in the door this time knocking it partially open. Pan ducked, and dived through the opening, sliding on the floor. Dave came up the steps finally, he was moving so slowly that Jason knew the shooter would not miss. Tears welled up in his eyes as he anticipated the explosion in Dave's chest as his lungs were being blown out. Then Jason did the unthinkable. He put his life on the line for a man he barely knew, a white one at that. He stepped out from behind the column facing in the direction of the shooter and raised his bird finger as he pushed the door completely open. By this time, Dave was almost at the top of the steps. Jason surprised that he wasn't dead by now, dived to the floor and kicked out his leg tripping Dave who fell flat on his face. Another hole appeared. This time it was where Jason had been. Jason scrambled to get behind the column again, as Dave crawled on his hands and knees through the doorway of the church. Once inside turned to the right and was almost completely out of sight when flesh from the back of his thigh was ripped apart by a bullet.

"Oh, God! I'm hit," Dave screamed as he fell forward. "He got me, he got me."

Dave's foot was of view of the rifle sights, and shooter stabilized the crosshairs on it and began to squeeze.

"Let me take a look," Pam said dragging him toward her. A shot rang out. Pam had pulled his foot out of view just before the shot was fire.

"Is Dave all right," Jason yelled.

"No! Dave is not all right. Dave has been shot," Dave yelled back.

"He'll live," Pam said shaking her head. "He just lost a little meat in his thigh." It was the same leg that had been cut during the explosion, and the same leg that had been shot. "One thing is sure," Pam said softly.

"What?" Dave snapped, his expression showing his discomfort.

"This is not your lucky leg," she said smiling.

"You're so funny. Next time I'm shot remind me to laugh at your jokes."

"Sorry," she said apologetically, "but you need to get up cause we've got help Jason get inside.

Jason, who was now stranded, had no idea how he was going to get inside. He would just have to go for it. Either he would make it, or he wouldn't. He was just about to make a dash for it when he heard this noise from inside the church. He looked and saw one of the church pews sliding out the door toward the column. Dave and Pam slid the pew all the way out past the front of the column. Jason had plenty of room to hide. He could crawl on the pew into the church. Jason waited for a few minutes then he shook the pew with his foot so that pew rocked.

Instantly, three shots rang out, three seconds apart. The pew had been hit three times in three different places, leaving three big holes. Then the pew was pulled back into the church and the door closed.

The shooter, Dutchman lower the cross hairs and turn to face very angry Tamera. Sibal look anxiously not knowing what to expect. He had failed her. Was she going to kill him here and now?

"You take the side door on the right," Tamera said to Dutchman, "and you take the one on the left," she said to Sibal. "I'll take the front. Kill anything and everything that moves. Don't fail me. Nobody gets out."

They were all still looking at the church when suddenly to their surprise they saw Jason walk casually from behind the column, open the door and walk into the church.

"I'm going to enjoy killing him," Tamera growled. "Now let's go.

Inside the church, while Dave was leaning against the communion table with his pants down to his ankles wrapping his wounds with white cloth, he had taken from inside the communion table, Jason and Pam were piling the pews up against the door. As they were both lifting one end of a pew, Dave broke the communication silence.

"I guess you need to make a few changes in your plan. Huh. Let me see. What was it? Oh yeah! I'll choose where I want her to catch up with me and then I'll blow her brains out."

They pushed the pew and it fell like a tree against the pile of pews which was beginning to look more like wood stacked for a campfire.

"Yeah, you're right, Dave. We need a plan and, we, need one now. We're safe for a minute, but this barricade is not going to keep them out for long," Jason warned.

Suddenly Dave remembered. "No! We aren't safe, there are two more doors in the back, one on each side."

Jason immediately started running. "I check the one on this side. Pam, you check the one on that side. Block the door with whatever you can find."

He stopped at the door leading to the back of the church. "Holler if you need me."

"Will do," she yelled back.

Jason walked swiftly but as quietly as possible down the hall on the right side of the church. When he reached the door, he listened. He opened the door slightly and peeped through the crack. He wished that he had something that could be used as a weapon. He pushed the door and let it swing open as he positioned himself outside against the wall. He raised the only weapon that he had, his fist. He quickly stuck his head in and back out the door. He had not seen anybody, but felt like he had seen something, because adrenalin was flowing through his veins. He looked back into the room. 'What was it,' he thought. The door to the outside was straight ahead, and now he knew what it was that he had seen. The doorknob was moving ever so slightly.

On the other side of the church, Pam had reached the first and only door in the hallway. When she turned the knob, she had no idea what was waiting for her on the other side of the door. If she had, she never would have rushed right in. Inside the room, standing against the wall beside the doorway, Sibal waited with her nightstick drawn back. When Pam opened the door and took one step inside, Sibal swung the nightstick with all her might. When Pam saw the stick coming toward her, she only had a second to react. As she jerked her head back and raised her arm, her feet slid out from underneath her. She had not moved fast enough. Sibal's swing was so powerful that the stick knocked Pam's arm back, glanced off the top of her head, and slammed into the door frame, cracking the wood. Pam went down hard against the floor. She could see only stars and blackness. A second later, when Pam's sight returned, she saw this woman in a policeman's uniform standing beside her with the nightstick raised above her head. She knew that this must be the one that Jason and Dave had been talking about.

Sibal's expression told her that Sibal intended to do her serious harm. As the nightstick came down toward her, she quickly rolled toward Sibal, raised her leg, and kicked toward Sibal's knee. She also raised her arm in an attempt to block the stick. Then she held her breath in anticipation of the blow and pain that was sure to come. As her foot hit the side of Sibal's knee, the stick struck the rib cage of her back. The two women moaned in harmony to the sounds of a drumbeat and cracking bones. Pam was sure that her ribs were fractured, but she knew that Sibal's knee was also severely damaged.

When Sibal's knee gave, she fell forward. Pam tried to roll away from her but Sibal came down on top of her. They both struggled for control of the nightstick. It ended up between them. Sibal was holding it with both hands trying to push it down into Pam's throat. Pam was using both hand holding the stick to prevent Sibal from succeeding. Pam was able to match Sibal's strength for the moment, but she wasn't sure how long she could hold out.

On the other side of the church, Jason was standing next to the door holding a chair ready to swing it and hit whoever or whatever came through the door. He had been standing there for a few minutes and his arms were getting tired. There was a dead bolt lock on the door, and it was evidently locked. Jason looked around the room for anything that could be used as a weapon. He saw some pins in one coffee mug and some sharpened pencils in another coffee mug on a desk, so he grabbed some of the pencils and put them in his back pocket.

Then without warning, there was a hard kick against the door. Jason raised the chair again and got ready to swing it. There was another kick and this time the frame around the door cracked. Then there was a final kick and the door flew open. Jason swung the chair as the foot that had kicked in the door and a rifle barrel came through the doorway. Even though Jason could not see the person, he swung the chair through the doorway just above the barrel of the rifle. The chair found its mark. The legs of the chair hit Dutchman in the chest and face. He dropped his rifle and fell back against the rail of the small porch outside the door. The rifle slide down the steps, as Jason charged forward. Jason swung as hard as he could at Dutchman's head. It would have been a knockout punch if it had only hit its target. However, Dutchman recovered in time to duck to the right. The force of the swing took Jason all the way around. With Jason's back to him, Dutchman took aim at Jason's kidney. As Dutchman drove his fist forward, Jason continued to spin.

His left elbow caught Dutchman flush in the nose. Dutchman's fist lost all its power. He fell underneath the rail onto the ground. His nose was bleeding profusely. Dutchman was about to get up when Jason, holding on to the rail, swung himself feet first toward Dutchman's head. Dutchman quickly knocked Jason's legs up with his arm and rolled away. Jason hit the ground on his back with a jolt. In seconds, the two men were in fight stances facing each other.

Dutchman wiped away the blood from his mouth and chin and flung it to the ground in anger. "I'm going to take you to school now, Sambo," Dutchman said.

"You're going to think it's Rambo before you finish your lesson, Dumbo."

Dutchman attacked. He struck Jason with a glancing blow to the head, and a kick to the side that Jason partially blocked. Jason backed away retaliating with two quick defense kicks, one to the chest and the other to the already broken nose. The kick to the nose didn't hit very hard but it was enough to send a sharp pain through Dutchman head and start a fresh flow of blood.

Pam and Sibal were still struggling with the nightstick. Pam was giving out of strength and Sibal could tell. Pam had to do something. Sibal had shifted her body so that she could put more of her weight against the stick and it was getting closer to Pam's throat. With her last bit of energy, Pam tried to push the stick back, but it didn't budge.

Sibal knew that she had her now. She could see the fear in Pam's expression, so she lowered her face down toward Pam's and spoke softly. "I don't know how you beat Jake, but I'm gonna smoke your butt now. Say good night, Gracie." With that said Sibal prepare for one final push.

Then as Sibal was looking into Pam's eyes, Pam's expression changed. The fear disappeared.

"Thanks for reminding me," Pam said confidently. "Good night George."

Sibal push and the stick went down, however Pam turned her head to the left so that it went down on her side neck muscle instead of her throat. Then

Pam released her grip on the stick with her right hand, and using it as a claw, she racked her nails down Sibal's face. Sibal screamed. Forgetting the nightstick, she rolled off Pam holding her face with one hand and reaching for her pistol with the other.

Pam jumped up with the nightstick in her hand. She threw it as Sibal took aim at her. Sibal only had time to duck her head into her shoulders as the nightstick struck her. She fired the gun as she ducked. She missed. Pam ran out of the room. Sibal fired four more shots through the wall until her weapon was empty. While she was firing, she was limping as fast as she could toward the outside door. When she reached, it she was gone.

By this time Pam was at the door going into the sanctuary of the church. She busted through the door, frightening Dave half to death.

"Give me a heart attack, why don't you?" Dave said holding his heart with both hands. "What took you so long?"

"We've got to block this door. She's coming."

"Who's coming?" Dave said.

"That policewoman." Dave immediately ran over and helped her slide a pew against the door.

When Dutchman heard the shots, he knew that Tamera would be expecting him to be inside. He had to finish Jason off now.

"You do know that I'm the one who killed your grandmother, don't you?" Dutchman said nastily.

Jason remained calm. "I was told you were just following orders. So, you're just a flunky, doing somebody else's dirty work."

"I enjoyed every minute of it. I pour high test all over her. I even made her drink some. Amoco Gold, that's the only brand she drank. Did you know that?" Dutchman snickered.

When Dutchman saw that Jason was angry, he pushed a thought at him. "Snake." Jason looked down and thought he saw a snake between his legs. Jason jumped to the side. Dutchman spun and kicked the side of Jason's head knocking him to the ground. Quickly, Dutchman pulled a knife from his pocket, snapped it open, and lunged toward Jason. Jason grabbed a handful of dirt and threw it into Dutchman's eyes and rolled as fast as he could away from the knife. Even though Dutchman was momentarily blinded he could see Jason's image. He reached out, bringing the knife down full force. Jason jerked his upper body away from the blade just in the nick of time. He knocked Dutchman's arm away as the blade dug deep into the ground. Dutchman was fully extended on his stomach, and Jason wasted no time. He clamped Dutchman's hand down and spun around on top of him. He quickly pulled the pencils from his back pocket and drove them deep into Dutchman's neck. A puddle of blood began to grow below Dutchman's neck. Then he broke the pencil off so that Dutchman would not be able to pull them out.

Pam and Dave were still waiting near the door expecting Sibal to try to enter. Nothing happened.

"Where's Jason?" Pam asked worriedly.

"He never came back."

"Well, let's go and look for him," she scolded.

As they walked swiftly across the pulpit toward the door to the hall on the other side, they heard something hit the front porch of the church. They both stopped and looked back at the front door in time to see it explode. They both dove to the floor behind the rostrum. When Pam and Dave peeped up from behind the rostrum, they saw a large opening at the front of the church. The pile of pews that had once blocked the door were broken and scattered throughout the sanctuary making it appear like an abstract work of art. Then without warning, a figure in a black hooded robe was in the doorway.

When Jason heard the explosion, he got up off Dutchman. He stood over him for a second. Dutchman didn't move. He started running toward the rifle near the side porch. However, before he reached the side porch, he caught something out of the corner of his eye. He turned and was shocked to see Dutchman running toward him with the knife raised over his head. Jason turned, picked up the rifle and then turned back toward Dutchman. Firing from the hip, the bullet hit Dutchman in the gut. Dutchman stopped for a second and then kept coming. Jason quickly pulled back the bolt, ejecting the shell, and pushed it forward again chambering the next round in the rifle. Dutchman was almost on him.

"I don't care if you don't die," Jason said. "This is for my grandmother."

Jason aimed the rifle at Dutchman's knee and fired. The kneecap exploded and he collapsed to the ground at Jason's feet, dropping the knife beside him. Dutchman was in terrible pain. Jason pulled the bolt back and another empty shell flu out. Then he pushed the bolt forward.

"I wouldn't even let a dog suffer like this," Jason said putting the rifle barrel to Dutchman's head. He pulled the trigger and there was a loud click. The rifle was empty. "This is definitely not your day."

Jason started up the steps but then stopped. He ran back down the steps. He tossed the rifle down as he ran into the woods.

The figure walked down the aisle, which was mysteriously clear of any obstructions. Pam and Dave were still peeping from behind the pulpit rostrum. They watched as the hood moved back, seemingly by its own power, exposing the head of a woman. She had feature like Pam. However, her eyes were extremely cold. It was Tamera. When she saw Pam and Dave she stopped. She raised her fist, pulled it back, and then drove it forward toward Pam and Dave. Something seemed to come from her fist. It was like a big ball of distortion. It was clear but everything seen through it was distorted. Pam and Dave could see it moving quickly toward them. "Move!" Pam shouted as she gave Dave a hard push.

They both dove from behind rostrum Just as the force hit it. The rostrum was knocked up and back into the air. It crashed into the choir stand. Pam and Dave were left exposed, lying on the pulpit floor. Dave scrambled off the pulpit pushed one end the communion table away from the pulpit wall and got behind it. As he pushed the other end out, he yelled to Pam.

"Pam! Come and get behind the communion table it won't he won't be able to get you."

Pam didn't move. She laid there in a trace as she realized that the person standing in front of her was her sister.

"Pam! Come on! Hurry up!

Pam's trace was broken, however, before Pam could move Tamera drove her fist forward again, this time at the communion table. The force moved through the air and when it hit the table, Dave ducked down. The force dissipated. Tamera was surprised and a little fearful. As Pam got off the pulpit and ducked behind the communion table. Tamera reached into her robe pocket, and pulled out a stick of dynamite. She lit the short fuse as Dave and Pam watched and tossed it up to the front of the communion table. They all ran for cover. Tamera ducked into the pews. Pam jumped over the first two pews and laid down on a pew on the third row. Dave crawled underneath the pews on the other side of the church and was still crawling when the dynamite exploded. The communion table is blown to pieces.

Tamera stood up. She looked at her handy work. The communion table was history. Tamera walked down the aisle. On one side of the church, Dave was lying motionless on the floor. On the other side, Pam was sandwiched between two pews. Tamera moved the pew that had Pam pent, then she walked up to her.

"Sister dear," Tamera said. "Finally, we meet."

"Are you really my sister?" Pam murmured.

"For as long as you live, baby sister," Tamera smiled grabbing Pam's shoulders and standing her up. "Unfortunately, our sweet little family is about to end. I'm going to have to kill you."

"Why?" Pam asked. "I'm your sister. Why is necessary for you to kill me. I'm not a threat to you in any way. Plus, I've always wanted a sister, someone just to talk to, someone that I knew, would always be there for me, my blood. Don't you want a sister?"

Tamera thought for a moment, "Come to think of it, it would have been nice to have had a sister to play with while I was growing up. We could have shared secrets, and we could have done all kinds of neat things together."

"We still can," Pam pleaded. "We're still sisters."

"Sorry sis," Tamera said coldly. "Your draining my power, so you've got to die."

Pam brought her arms up between Tamera's knocking them away. Then she pushed Tamera back roughly. "Not without a fight," Pam said raising her arm to fight. The softness that had been in her eyes was replaced with fiery rage.

"You're my sister all right," Tamera seemed please that Pam, her sister, had pride enough to fight. Tamera looked at her and began to concentrate. As she did Pam right arm went down and was clamped to her side by some invisible force. Then the left arm became clamped to her other side. Tamera walked slowly up to Pam and placed her hands around Pam's throat and began to squeeze. "I can already feel my power increasing." Tamera began taking deep breaths as she closed her eyes. Pam's eyes rolled to the back of her head as she lost consciousness and became limp in Tamera's grip.

"Don't die just yet," Tamera said, loosening her grip to allow a little blood to go to Pam's brain. "This feels so good, so good." She tightened her grip for one final squeeze, when she felt this terrible pain in the back of her head. Sparks were flying and there was a burning sensation. She dropped Pam to the floor, grabbed the back of her head and turned to see what had happened. Dave was standing in front of her with a piece of wood in his hand, and her hair was on fire. While was she was rubbing the fire out with hand, Dave looked at the piece of wood and realized that it had caused the fire. It was a piece of the communion table. He quickly moved forward and pressed the wood against the side of Tamera's face. Immediately, her skin began to burn. She screamed as she knocked his arm away. He had heard that scream before when he was in the communion table. Tamera grabbed his arms and pushed him back. Her face was one of pain, fear and rage. When they were in the aisle and some of the pain had subsided, she stretched his arms out and put her face close to his.

"I'm going to rip your head off," Tamera snarled. That's exactly what she would have done if Dave hadn't worked the wood to the end of his fingers. Just as she released his empty hand and caught hold of his jaw, Dave was able to touch her hand with the wood.

"Aaaa," she yelled releasing him and jumping back. Dave wasted no time. He came after her holding the wood out in front of him. She turned to run but Dave stepped on her robe and stopped her. Dave knew, this time he had to hold the wood to her head until she was dead. He was about to push the wood to the back of her head when suddenly the robe dropped to the floor. It was as if she had disintegrated.

Dave looked at the piece of wood in his hand again and smiled. "Praise God," he said thinking of Rev. Zackery. "I guess that makes me the hero," he said aloud to himself. "But who did I save?" He remembered Pam. "Pam!" he shouted. He was about to turn when he saw the robe on the floor move. Something was moving under the robe. "What the" he said. He grabbed the end of the robe and quickly pulled it toward him.

There on the floor in front of him coiled and ready to strike was a black snake. Its fangs dripping with venom. It struck. Dave had no time to move out of its way. He could only throw the robe up between him and the snake. The fangs of the snake hit the robe as Dave ran back and jumped up on the seat of the pew behind him. He watched in amazement as the snake shook itself free from the robe and slithered under the pews on the same side of the church that he was on.

He looked between the pew he was standing on and the one behind it. Then he looked in the aisle. He had to make sure the snake didn't get any closer. Dave became frantic. He kept watching, the aisle, in between the pews, and back again. Dave didn't know, at the end of the pew he was on, a set of little snake eyes were watching him.

Sibal limped toward the side of the church unrolling wire as she went. She had put a splint on her leg, but she still couldn't move very fast. She had already put dynamite at the back of the church and rolled a line to the detonator which was in the woods behind a big rock. Now she was rolling a line of wire from the detonator to the dynamite she had placed at the front of the church. She knew this was her best opportunity to become leader of the coven. She could kill all of them, Tamera and Dutchman included. As for as she knew they all was inside the church. However, while she was rolling her wire to the front of the church, someone else was taking the dynamite she had placed at the back of the church and placing it in the woods near the detonator. While Sibal was connecting the wire to the dynamite in the front of the church, someone else was cutting that same wire. Sibal hurried back to the detonator as fast as she could. She carefully raised the plunger on the detonator, connected the wires to the two terminals, and then grabbed the plunger. She was about to push the plunger down, when she saw someone walking toward the front of the church. Sibal recognized him. It was the preacher. He had a long-barreled pistol in his hand.

"Preacher, I don't know how you made it out of that house, but I do know, you are not having a good day. In fact, it is going to be your worst day, your last day," she whispered to herself.

She waited because she wanted him to get closer before she detonated the dynamite. When got to the front of the church, he stopped and looked down as if he had seen the dynamite, and then he looked in her direction. He made the sign of the cross on his chest and walked up the steps.

"The cross won't help you now, Preacher. There a new head-witch running things now," she said as she pushed down. There was an explosion in the woods behind the big rock near the detonator.

When Dave heard the explosion, he looked in the direction of the sound. Then he got down on his knees on the pew, ducting his head down so he could see beneath it. When he did the snake slid over the arm of the pew Dave was on and started moving toward him. Dave knew he had to locate the snake. He slowly lowered his head down looking cautiously for the snake. Eventually his whole head was below the seat, but he couldn't see the snake anywhere. Then a scary thought occurred to him. The snake may be right behind his head, right now, ready to strike. He didn't want to, but he had to look. He rotated his head back toward the front of the church. First, looking straight down, then more and more to the front until he could see Pam's body lying on the floor. He raised up breathing a sigh of relief. His relief turned to shock, because on the bench directly behind him was the snake. It was ready to strike. When he saw it, he jumped back, but it was too late. The snake spring forward with fangs pointed. The snake hit Dave's leg as he fell back over the arm of the pew. The fangs were deeply imbedded in Dave's thigh. He fell back to the floor. Still holding the piece of wood from the communion table, he tried to hit the snake with it. The snake saw it coming. It quickly withdrew its fangs, crawled down the aisle and into the robe that was lying on the floor.

Moments later the robe began to fill up. It was Tamera again. She laid there for a few seconds with the robe covering only to top half of her body. Then she sat up, adjusted her robe, and then stuck her head and arms out. The side of her face where she had been burned was running. The pain caused her whole face to twist to that side. She got up and walked up to Dave who was lying in the fetal position with the wood against the snakebite.

"They say that the bite of the black Mamba is deadly in 20 minutes," Tamera smirked. "You've got fifteen minutes left." She stepped around him keeping far away from the wood he was holding. Dave was getting very weak. His leg seemed numb. She walked over to Pam.

"Now, where was I?" Tamera said. "Oh yeah, I was in the middle of killing you, sister dear." She stood Pam up. "I going to make this quick and painless, cause you're my sister, and I love you." She put one hand on the back of Pam's head and one on her chin. Pam was too weak to fight.

A shot rang out. It hit the chair in the pulpit. Tamera release Pam and ducked down below the pew. Pam fell back on the pew, while Tamera worked her way to the end of the pew. She peeped out and saw Rev. Zackery. He was walking down the aisle aiming the long barreled gun in her direction ready to fire another shot.

Tamera stood up quickly and pointed her finger at him. He aimed the pistol at her heart. Tamera rotated her hand while still pointing at him. His elbow began to bend and even though he was trying not to, he placed the barrel of the pistol under chin and began to squeeze the trigger.

"Lord help me Jesus," Rev. Zackery whispered. Suddenly through no effort of his own, the gun pulled away and fired two times up into the ceiling.

Tamera looked confused. She raised her other hand. Now she was pointing both hands at him. She rotated both her hand and once again Rev. Zackery was holding the pistol under his chin.

"Lord! You delivered Daniel from the lion's den," Rev. Zackery said loudly. "I know you can deliver me."

Tamera squinted her eyes expecting the gun to be fired, but it didn't, at least now then. A second later, the gun pulled away and fire two more shots into the ceiling. Tamera quickly turned her head toward Pam. There she was sitting on the pew with both her hand pointed at Rev. Zackery. Pam looked at Tamera.

"You bitch." Tamera said, turn her hands toward Pam.

"You witch." Pam replied angrily turning her hands toward Tamera.

Rev. Zackery had control of his body again. He aimed the gun at Tamera, while they were facing each other. His aim was very unsteady.

Tamera rotated her wrists quickly and Pam balled up her left hand into a fist, turned it toward her face, and then Pam hit herself hard in the jaw. Pam fell back on the pew. She was out cold.

"Keep my hand steady Lord, please!" Rev. Zackery said as he fired the pistol. It found its mark. The bullet hit Tamera, but it did not hit any vital organs. It passed completely though the muscle in her arm. It didn't hit the bone. Tamera grabbed her arm and turned toward Rev. Zackery. Then she pointed at him. She was enraged.

"Lord? You remember the Hebrew boys, don't You?" Rev. Zackery became afraid when the pistol was under his chin again.

"Why don't you pick on somebody your own size."

Tamera turned her head and saw Jason standing on the right side of the pulpit.

"You're always picking on old people," Jason said. "Come and get some of this."

Tamera quickly turned her head back toward Rev. Zackery, rotated her wrist, and he pulled the trigger of the pistol. There was a loud click. It was out of bullets. Tamera brought her hand up and Rev. Zackery slapped himself in the face with the pistol and he went down. Then she turned back toward Jason.

"Now, what did you say, boy?" Tamera snarled. "Come and get some of what?" Tamera drove her fist out a force shot out toward Jason. Jason ducked and the force hit the wall behind him, cracking the plaster. She tried again. This time Jason did not duck. He stood boldly and defiantly against the force. It passed right through him and hit the wall again. More plaster fell from the wall exposing the wood beams.

"You can't use that witch mess on me. I have a force working in me that's stronger than yours," Jason said.

"What is it, the love of Jesus?" she said sarcastically.

"No! If it was that, then I'd have to try to save your soul. I don't want to save your soul. I want to send it and you straight to hell. My force is revenge. You had your little flunkies kill my grandmother. Now, you are going to have to answer to me. You're going to have to kill me with your bare hands, that is unless you're a chicken witch."

Tamera raised and lowered the arm that had been shot. There was pain but it was very functional. Jason folded his arms.

"Well, Scarface, let's get it on," he shouted.

Tamera charged forward so fast that she was on him before he had time to react. With one hand, her fingered encompassed his neck and with the other she came down with all her power on his head with a piece of pew wood she had grabbed as she was moving forward. Then it happened. The image disappeared, and all that was left was the crystal ball sitting on a short column at the end of the pulpit. Jason opened the hallway door, and he walked into the sanctuary and looked at the crystal. There trapped inside was Tamera.

Jason started walking looking for his friends. He saw Dave lying in the aisle first. He went to him.

"How are you doing, man?" Jason asked.

"I think this wood from the communion table is healing me," Dave said assuredly, looking down at the wood he was still holding to his snakebite. "Well, keep it right there, then." Jason as he walked toward Pam. He revived her. When she saw him, she hugged him and gave him a tender smack on the lips.

"Are you okay?"

"Yeah, my neck and my side hurts, but other than that I'm fine," she said.

"What happened to..."

"I'll fill you in later. Let me check on Rev Zackery."

By the time Pam and Jason reached the aisle, Dave was standing. Pam hugged him tenderly for several seconds. Then she said without looking up, "thank you."

Dave just smiled. They all gathered around Rev. Zackery. Jason shook him. When he became conscious and saw them, he smiled from ear to ear.

"If it ain't the three Hebrew boys. Lord, I knew you remembered them."

"Are you okay?" Jason asked.

"How did you get out of that house?" Dave said.

"I went down in my shelter. It has been very, useful for storms and the Klan. I never thought I'd need it for witches and dynamite," Rev. Zackery said.

"We thought you were dead. It's so good to see you," Pam added.

"Yeah man, we couldn't have done it without you. Thanks," Jason said.

"Thank the Lord, son. He did it all," Rev. Zackery said standing up.

They all gathered around the crystal ball, afraid to touch it.

"Did we get all of them," Pam asked worriedly.

"I think there were three," Jason said. "I killed the one who killed gramma. We got her," he said pointing to the crystal. "But what about Sibal."

"I hurt her, but she got away," Pam said disappointedly.

"No, she didn't get away," Rev. Zackery said. "That explosion you heard, was her, blowing herself up. She was going to blow up my church, but I moved the dynamite and put it by the plunger."

"It couldn't have happened to a more deserving person," Pam added.

"Reverend, do you have anything we can put this in?" Jason asked.

He didn't answer right away. He just kept staring at the miniature Tamera who seemed to be trying to break out of the crystal.

"Yeah, I have a safe box in my office," Rev. Zackery said finally. I'll call Sheriff Harris while I'm in there." He immediately walked out.

When he returned, they wrapped the crystal in a towel, and placed it in the small safe box.

"Okay, you have got to tell us how you did it," Pam said. "How did you trap her."

"After I killed the witch that killed gramma, I thought about what she said.

"What did Auntie say," Pam asked.

"She said, 'only the crystal can save you.' So, I went and got the crystal out of the car and brought it back here. I rubbed the crystal, thought about myself, and put it on the column. The image of me appeared. Tamera thought it was me. When she charged, the image sucked her in, and she was trapped."

They didn't have time to question Jason further, because they heard the sirens and looked through the hole in the front of the church to see two sheriff cars come down the road. The cars stopped where the bridge had been. Four officers jumped the ditch and ran to the church. After they had all entered the church, Rev. Zackery walked up to Sheriff Harris. Both men had stern looks as they faced each other.

"Sheriff," Rev. Zackery said.

"Preacher," Sheriff Harris said.

"It's been a long time."

"Too, long," Sheriff Harris smiled. The two men hugged. When they parted, Sheriff Harris looked at Jason and Dave and nodded at them. They nodded back. "What happened Rev. Zackery?"

"I know you don't believe this stuff, but like I tried to tell you last year, there is a coven of witches up here right outside of Tipton," Rev. Zackery said raising up both hands. "They did this. They blew up my house and tried to blow up my church."

"Believe me, Zackery. I can believe just about anything now," the sheriff said. "Ran into one of them witches just this morning. What happened to the witches?"

"There were three of them, one male, and two females. They were trying to kill these people," Rev. Zackery said looking at Dave, Jason, and Pam. "The black guy over there killed the male witch in self-defense. The two female witches blew themselves up trying to blow up the church with us in it. I doubt if you will be able to find any body parts of those two." The two men walked closer to Dave, Jason, and Pam.

"So, we meet again," the sheriff said looking at Dave and Jason.

"Your deputy tried to kill me again, Sheriff," Jason said. "How did she get out of jail?"

Sheriff Harris was about to speak when he looked carefully at Pam. He suddenly pulled his pistol and aimed it at Pam. "Why don't you ask her? She put a spell on me."

"Hold on, Sheriff. That wasn't her. You must have met her twin sister," Rev. Zackery said grabbing the sheriff's arm. "This is Pam, Miss Mammie's god daughter. She didn't know it, but her twin sister, the witch you ran into, was trying to kill her. Anyway, her sister, the one who put a spell on you, she blew herself up."

"She's dead?" Sheriff Harris said relieved.

"Yes, sir. She is blown to pieces," Rev. Zackery said as the sheriff put away his gun.

"Okay. You do look different a little bit," Sheriff Harris said. "That's right. You were the one they thought was killed in the fire."

"Yeah, but she wasn't there, fortunately," Jason said.

"Sheriff," a deputy shouted as he ran from the back hallway. "There's a body on the side of the church!"

"He was the one who set my grandmother's house on fire," Jason said.

The sheriff looked at his deputy and spoke. "It's one of the preps. Rope it off and call CSI. Tell Neal to send a PM unit and a van." Then the sheriff turned back to Rev. Zackery. "I got all the information I need for now, but I'll need a statement from each one of you by the end of the week."

"Can we go ahead and take care of that now," Dave said. "I've got to get to a conference, Jason has to prepare for his grandmother's funeral, and Pam has to get back home."

"Sure, my deputy will take care of that. No need to inconvenience you any further," the sheriff said. "After that's done, can I take you anywhere, Zackery?"

"My brother's house is about ten miles up the highway from here. If you could take us up there, it would be greatly appreciated.

"Once the paramedics check y'all out, and I get my statements, we'll be on our way," Sheriff Harris said. "Are you sure the other one is dead?"

"Yes sir," Rev. Zackery said. "She won't be bothering you or anyone else, ever again."

Chapter 23
The Bridge

Early the next morning, Pam, Dave, Jason, and Rev. Zackery got into Rev. Zackery's brother's car and drove to the South River bridge. They all got out and walked to the middle of the bridge. Rev. Zackery had the safe with the crystal locked inside.

"Who wants to throw it in?" Rev. Zackery asked? He looked at Pam

"She hated me, and tried to kill me, but she was still my sister. I can't," Pam said. They all looked at Jason.

"She had my grandmother killed and she tried to kill me, but I've got to get rid of this hate I feel. I don't think I should do it," Jason said. They all looked at Dave.

"Don't look at me. I don't want to touch that thing," Dave said.

"I guess that just leaves me, Rev. Zackery said holding the safe over the rail. "Lord, deliver us from evil." He dropped the safe, the crystal, and Tamera. They all watched as the safe hit and vanished beneath the flowing waters.

"I'm so glad that's over," Pam said.

"That's right it's over, praise the Lord," Rev. Zackery said.

"Praise the Lord!" Dave yelled.

"We still have a funeral to prepare," Jason said sadly.

"No sir, not a funeral. It's a home-going celebration," said Rev. Zackery.

"Yeah your right Reverend. I believe the scripture says, no greater love than this, that a man would lay down his life for a friend. Gramma had that kind of love in her," Jason said as tears welled up in his eyes.

"She laid down her life for me," Pam said

"Anybody hungry besides me," Dave said.

He received a chorus of amens.

"You know Rev. Zackery I sure could use a plate of your grits and brain right about now," Dave said.

"I'm pretty sure my brother has some at his house. If so," Rev. Zackery said smiling from ear to ear, "grit and brains coming up."

THE END

Printed by Libri Plureos GmbH in Hamburg, Germany